CHORUS OF THE DEAD
By Tracy L. Ward

Willow Hill House

Ontario, Canada

Second Edition
ISBN-978-0-9958914-3-2
Copyright © 2012 by Tracy L. Ward

Cover Art Copyright © by Claudia McKinney
@ phatpuppyart.com
Cover Photo by Shutterstock.com

Edited by Lourdes Venard
CommaSense Editing LLC

Chapter Headings are linear excerpts from the poem
"The Bridge of Sighs"
by Thomas Hood (1789-1845)

All rights reserved. Except for use in any review, the reproduction or utilization of this work in whole or part in any form by any electronic, mechanical or other means, now known or hereafter invented, including xerography, photocopying, and recording, or in any information storage or retrieval system, is forbidden without written permission of the publisher,
Tracy L. Ward tracywardauthor@gmail.com
This is a work of fiction. Any names, characters, places and incidents are either the product of the author's imagination or are used fictiously, and any resemblance to actual persons, living or dead, business establishments, events or locales is entirely coincidental.

Dedicated to my husband, Daniel Ward, the bibliophile who has finally snagged himself an author for his collection.

The Marshall House Mysteries

CHORUS OF THE DEAD
DEAD SILENT
THE DEAD AMONG US
SWEET ASYLUM
PRAYERS FOR THE DYING
SHADOWS OF MADNESS

Chapter 1

*One more Unfortunate,
Weary of breath,
Rashly importunate,
Gone to her death!*

London, November 1867—Dr. Peter Ainsley desperately needed a stiff drink of something, anything to dampen this feeling of pity he had for the girl who lay dead on his examination table. Her body had been pulled from the Thames earlier that day. Scotland Yard had brought her to Ainsley, as they did with all of London's suspicious deaths. His workspace was overrun with bodies of the dead, nearly every examination surface was occupied, and many more waited in the adjoining room. He was slow and methodical, much to the dismay of his employers, who would rather see him quickly process the bodies and move on. No one cared about the poor and unfortunate, the children especially, who arrived there more often than most. London was rife with lowlifes and ne'er-do-wells; the morgue only represented a small fraction of the suffering that awaited them beyond the hospital's stone walls.

The girl before him possessed a classic beauty, a striking similarity with many ancient Greek statues, with a gently sloping jaw and high cheekbones. Her damp, needle-straight hair hung limp and motionless off the edge of the wooden table where she lay, the ends slightly matted together due to the churning of the muddy tide waters. She smelled like the putrid liquid of the Thames, made so by the vile filth and garbage thrown in by thousands of local residents looking to the current to wash it away. Her skin was nearly ash brown from the feces and urine tossed into the water by the bucketful. Ainsley did what he could to wash the grime away but much had already seeped into her pores causing permanent discolouration.

Her lips were blue and her skin waxy to the touch. Ainsley leaned over the body, carefully surveying her for any outward sign of what had brought her to the waters' edge. There was no bruising on her throat, no lacerations on her face or head. He lifted her limp arms and separated each finger so he could look at them better. There were no defensive wounds, no marks of struggle. Nothing that could justify her sudden loss of life.

Scalpel in hand, he cut a Y-shaped incision in her abdomen and then sawed through her rib cage to gauge the functions of her internal organs. His colleagues rarely had to go so far. Often it was enough for them to regard a wound on the head or neck to determine a cause of death. Ainsley was far more scrupulous and was determined to find out as much as he could about the moments prior to death.

He gingerly pulled each organ from her torso, separating them on the shelf behind him so he could weigh them later. By the time he was done, her corpse lay like one of Madam Tussauds's wax replicas of tortured criminals.

The sound of a distant door creaking open pulled Ainsley from his extreme focus. He saw Dr. Crawford heading toward him, weaving between sheet-covered bodies as he made his way to the examination table. Ainsley washed the girl's blood from his bare hands at a nearby sink. Dr. Crawford gave a quick glance to the girl on the table, her innards separated in glass jars on the opposite table. "From the Thames?" he asked, no doubt seeing the telltale signs with just a passing glance.

"She is. Haven't determined a cause—"

Crawford would not let him finish. "Suicide," he answered bluntly.

Ainsley gave an inquisitive look as he dried his hands on a towel. "I haven't examined the organs yet."

"No need," Crawford answered with a shrug. "A governess swore she saw this girl jumping from Waterloo Bridge. Her brother is outside the door." Crawford peered over his half-moon spectacles, as if daring the young upstart doctor to challenge his authority. "Now stitch her back up and let's get him in here to identify her. Then we can all go home." He gave a false benevolent smile and clasped a heavy hand on Ainsley's shoulder.

It was not the first time the supervising medical examiner overruled his findings. It seemed no matter how many accolades he received, no matter how many recommendations followed him from school, he still needed to prove himself worthy of his title of morgue surgeon.

Dr. Crawford left, without giving Ainsley another chance to impart any possible findings. The autopsy was finished in Crawford's eyes. Not that Ainsley wanted to make his job more strenuous, but his time in Edinburgh had taught him that nothing could be determined until all parts of the body had been examined. The process was precise and, Ainsley reasoned, the families deserved to know as much information as modern science could provide.

Ainsley stood over the body of the woman, resting his hands on the edge of the table as he looked over the corpse. Suicide would explain why no marks existed and why her lungs were full of fluid when he pulled them out. He had suspected she was a jumper, but why? Why would a young woman as beautiful as she take her life? She was young enough for marriage prospects. With her brother waiting just outside the door she obviously had a family who still cared about her. He glanced to the jars, and the bloody specimens they held. There had to be something, he thought, something that would help him decipher her death.

An hour later, having completed his thorough examination of her body, Ainsley slipped from the room. He had switched his blood-stained leather apron for a clean shirt and waistcoat and made sure his skin was clear of all evidence of the work he performed. The girl's brother was still waiting, perched on a rickety wooden chair placed against the wall in the hallway. There was a reception table with an empty chair next to him where a porter should have been stationed to wait with him. It was the porters who dealt with the grieving families, not the doctors. Ainsley hesitated, glancing to the empty chair, wondering what he could possibly say to alleviate the pain.

The brother had his face buried in the hollow of his

cap, crying, Ainsley thought. Sensing someone approaching he pulled the hat away and Ainsley's suspicion was confirmed. The man jumped to his feet as Ainsley approached.

"Doctor?" he asked, his voice shaking. "My sister Julia..." His voice trailed off as if he would cry openly with Ainsley standing right there in front of him.

Just then the porter returned, offering an apologetic smile. "This man will take you in to see her." Ainsley gestured to the young man who now stood behind him. "Then you can arrange to take her body to the church."

"No church will take her. She's is lost to us now."

Ainsley pulled a small script of paper from his pocket and leaned in on the reception table. He scribbled some words quickly on the paper. "Take her here," he said, giving the paper to the man in front of him. "I know the vicar there. He is a good man. He will see that she gets a Christian burial."

"Bless you, sir." The brother twisted his cap in his tightly gripped hands. His elation was short-lived. "I just don't understand," he said, raising his red-stained eyes to meet the doctor's. "Why would she do this? We are a God-fearing family. Why would she risk damnation?"

Ainsley gave the man a steady clasp on the shoulder as he walked closer. Leaning in so no others would hear, Ainsley whispered, "She was with child." He could feel the man's shoulders slump before he moved on. As he walked down the halls he closed his eyes and tried to ignore the sounds of the grown man openly weeping.

Exchanges like that were few and Ainsley liked it that way. He did not converse with families often. As a man of necropsy he was glad to keep his patients at arm's length, only focusing on the task, the body, the death, while trying to ignore the person that was once housed within. His training had been difficult indeed. While in school the cadavers sat for weeks on end awaiting further dissection, the cavernous openings in their stomachs becoming more and more slouched as time wore on, revealing each new organ as the aspiring doctors cut away. It had been hard for Ainsley to see those bodies sprawled out all around him and not view them as people. His well-bred upbringing had shielded him from all talk of death. The other student doctors bore the hard knocks of life better than he and treated the recently dead as playthings to be explored. One man, whose father was a butcher, explained his first dissection on a neighbourhood cat that had been killed by a passing cart. The muscles were still twitching, he said, when he cut her open in his father's backroom. That is when he knew he would be a surgeon one day, or so he told his classmates.

Ainsley had no such dark and dreary tale. He wanted to help people who were sick and dying. His first fascination was with cells, bacteria, and microscopic organisms, the newest faction of medical science. Then he gravitated toward diseases and a body's response to introductions of certain tonics, cures, and remedies. All of these scientific pursuits were acceptable for a man like Ainsley, a man from a noble house. He was the second son, after all, and fairly well-educated. Sitting in a study, pouring over medical manuals, and looking through a microscope were commendable pastimes. Becoming a surgeon, however, was completely unacceptable.

With daylight running out Ainsley hadn't expected anyone to remain at the hospital. But when he reached the office, the communal room where all other examiners hung their hats and processed reports, he found Dr. Crawford still within. He had his back to Ainsley and was slipping on his coat before turning to adjust his collar.

"Following instructions has never been your strong suit," Dr. Crawford said gruffly as he eyed the young doctor. Ainsley worked hard not to laugh at this very true remark. "You were to be done with her an hour ago."

Ainsley realized the severity in his boss's face and suddenly became sober to the fact that he was being reproached. "My apologies, sir," he answered sharply, "I only wanted—"

"You only wanted to waste more time! Do you think we have never-ending facilities here where we can house the dead indefinitely?" Crawford leaned on the desk, driving his white knuckles into the wood. "Our job is to work fast so that we may send the bodies home with their families."

"Are we not supposed to determine a cause of

death?"

Crawford looked as if he would tear Ainsley's head off and throw it in a fire. "How difficult is it to determine that the girl drowned, eh? She drowned four hours ago and no amount of dissection is going to bring her back, so don't waste your time! Don't waste *my* time!"

"I thought if I could give the family answers, if I could determine why she chose to commit suicide, then they could be at peace."

"She's a lowlife, that's why. A dim-witted girl, and I can point you to neighbourhoods all over London with thousands more. It is not our job to determine why. We must find out how, that is all!" Crawford rammed his fist on the top of the table to enunciate his point.

"Yes, sir," was all Ainsley could manage to reply. At this point he did not want to risk losing his position, which would surely prove to his father that he was not cut out for medicine. "I will follow your instructions, sir."

"Oh you damn well better," Crawford spat. His gaze trailed to his desk, settling on a folded letter. "I know what I will do with you." Crawford reached across the desk and snatched it up. "You're so fascinated by the details. I received a telegram from a former colleague of mine, Dr. Bennett. He is the physician in a small village to the north." Dr. Crawford paused for a moment, sucking in air as he peered at the telegram once more.

"It would appear he is in over his head and needs a doctor with more experience with diseases. Now that I think of it, you are a perfect fit." He scanned the telegram briefly before handing it over. "Two young girls, one dead, the other dying. Bennett is a physician, not a surgeon. He needs someone to examine the body, perform a dissection, and determine a cause of death." Crawford gave a forced cough. "That ought to keep you occupied for a while. Perhaps we could actually get some work done around here while you're gone."

Ainsley looked to the piece of paper that was thrust at him. Crawford brushed past him. His workday was done and he was likely eager to get home.

"One week, Dr. Ainsley," Dr. Crawford said at the door, "I am giving you one week, including travel time.

Determine the cause and get back here, ready to work. With winter coming we are sure to be busy." Crawford tipped his hat over his head and slammed the door behind him.

Chapter 2

Take her up tenderly,
Lift her with care;

Ainsley stepped out into the street to see the last thread of the November sun disappearing from the night sky. It was the hazy dusk before twilight that set the city in an eerie, almost translucent glow. The atmosphere on the streets was nearly frantic as people hurried to make their way home before dark, as if some unseen creature awaited them in the darkness of night. By the time Ainsley would arrive home, there would be few people about and most, at least in his family's neighbourhood, preferred to travel by the relative safety of an unassuming carriage.

The young doctor, however, refused to take a carriage, despite his mother's insistence that she would send one to the hospital at the end of his shift. He enjoyed his evening strolls home. He reassured her that her unease was a woman's perspective on the city, a dark and dangerous place once the gas streetlights were lit. As a man, he saw the city with a much brighter view at night and relished those half-hour jaunts home. In his mind, the walk was not nearly long enough.

The gaslights gave poor illumination compared to that of daylight and only served to create pools of darkness that were only somewhat lighter than the shadows beyond. Despite early promises, the new invention did little to cure the unease of London at night. Ainsley slipped on his gloves and pulled his coat in around his torso as he made the damp walk to Westminster Bridge. The bridge was swept with a harsh wind as he walked across. The damning cold only abated once he made it to the park grounds that surrounded Buckingham Palace. It was a lovely, near silent walk that allowed Ainsley the luxury of deep thought not permitted in the daytime bustle of city movements. His contemplation was only intermittently interrupted by single passing carriages with neither driver nor occupants paying him much heed. On foot, he was just a man making his way home, and not the second son of one of the wealthiest men in the Empire.

Not many people knew this about him. To most, he was just a bright young man who had been fortunate enough to have a benefactor pay for his schooling. But in truth, Ainsley wasn't his real name. He decided to use his mother's maiden name when applying to medical school and convinced his father he could be a surgeon and not have his profession affect the family negatively. In effect, he led a double life, and only a few people knew he was Peter Marshall, second son and heir to Lord Abraham Marshall. It was better that way. Ainsley could pursue a career in medicine and no one in London society knew his daily tasks consisted of more than what was befitting an independently wealthy gentleman. Assuming his mother's name gave him a freedom he had never thought possible.

His family had owned a house in Belgravia for a few decades, though he had spent most of his childhood at the country house with his mother and siblings. Their father preferred the city residence and they did not see him much. It was not an odd arrangement, certainly not to Daniel, himself, and Margaret, who grew up with things being so. But now, as they all stepped firmly into adulthood, their strange marital partnership became hard to ignore. It set the tone for the family, which was rife with division. Ainsley, who loathed any miniscule interaction with his overbearing father, preferred the company of their mother, while Daniel, the eldest, gravitated to the man who would pass him the family fortune. Margaret, bless her, remained in the middle, not letting her preference known—though Ainsley secretly believed she preferred their mother, who had been kinder and gentler to them as children when they were not being attended to by their full-time governesses.

It was when Ainsley accepted his post at St. Thomas Hospital that he knew he could not escape the city that winter as he had before, not as a professional man. He would be bound to his position and thus be forced to remain in his father's city house far longer than he desired.

Luckily, the old man remained disinterested and secluded in his study, rather than interfere with the daily workings of the house. Ainsley would not have to see him much.

The house looked almost dark from the street, the few lights inside doing little to illuminate the rooms. Thick curtains were drawn over the windows, giving Ainsley no indication of the mood of those inside.

The front door opened before he reached it, and the willing hand of the family butler, Billis, offered to take the young doctor's damp hat and coat.

"Good evening, Billis." Ainsley smiled as he handed the servant his hat, and then began pulling at his gloves.

"How was your day, young Peter? I trust you have been keeping busy," Billis asked, taking care to look Ainsley in the eyes.

"The hospital is a busy place, to be sure."

"Hospital? Are you ill, young master?" The servant suppressed a knowing smile. Lord Marshall forbade Ainsley from telling anyone his true occupation. He felt his son's aspirations to become a surgeon were crude and not befitting of a gentleman's house. Afraid of idle gossip reaching hired help in other houses on the street, the servants were not to know what it was Peter did all day. Billis was the only one who knew, though he could never openly admit as much.

Ainsley smiled at Billis's remark and was happy to play along. "No, not ill. I am the picture of health."

"Very good, young sir."

Billis accepted Ainsley's coat and bowed quickly before leaving the foyer.

Ainsley could hear chatter in the drawing room. Most likely, at that late hour, his family had finished eating and gathered there for further amusement. He could smell the pungent aroma of his brother's cigars and envisioned a brandy glass in his opposite hand. With an early morning ahead of him, Ainsley wanted to avoid the family if he could, namely his father, before making his journey to the train station. He had one foot on the staircase before Margaret came out from the drawing room.

"Peter!" She smiled at him openly. "I asked Cook to keep a plate warm for you."

Ainsley looked to the top of the stairs, longing for dry clothes, a warm fire in his room and that bottle of gin he kept hidden in his chest of drawers. "You are trying to avoid Father," she said. "You can't avoid him all winter."

"I have to catch a train in the morning. That is all."

"Train? Where are you going?"

"To Picklow, a small town in Norfolk."

"What on Earth are you going there for? Are there not enough dead people here for you to study?" In recent months, Margaret had shown a keen interest in Ainsley's work. She once begged Ainsley for a chance to see a dead body and, when given the opportunity, she lingered to watch him conduct a postmortem. She did not overt her eyes, or make a peep of protest. She watched with a curiosity that reminded him of his younger self. After that, Ainsley decided to remain mum when anyone in his class remarked that women did not have the stomach for surgery. Margaret could outperform any of those butchers' sons.

"The local physician needs a little assistance. I am sure you will fare well enough without me." He looked beyond her and strained to see who was in the withdrawing room before he heard the hearty laughter of his self-assured older brother, already boisterous with drink.

"Won't you eat before you retire?" she asked hopefully.

"I am not hungry," he said, making a motion to continue up the stairs.

"You sound just like mother," Margaret said, remaining at the bottom of the stairs, looking up at him.

After two steps, Ainsley turned and listened. In the least, his mother deserved to know where he was going. "Is Mother in the parlour?"

"She left for Tunbridge Wells this morning," Margaret answered with slightly downturned eyes.

"And you didn't go with her?" Ainsley asked. He had taken it for granted that Margaret would accompany their mother to the country estate, at least until she found a match. Otherwise, there would be no reason for her to remain in the dirty, polluted city throughout the winter.

Margaret hesitated and shook her head. "No," was

all she said, but Ainsley could tell there was more. He came back down the stairs and embraced Margaret with a tenderness no one else in the family received from him. "Did something happen while I was away?" he asked, his chin pressed into the top of her head as she clung to him.

"No," she answered in an unconvincing tone.

Ainsley forced her to release him and looked down at her face. He lifted her chin, forcing her to meet his gaze. "Margaret, you and I have been in this tumultuous family long enough to know that's not true. What is the matter? Did Father do something?"

Margaret remained silent for a moment, her eyes searching his face, as if he held the words she needed to say. "Nothing," she answered softly. "Honest."

Ainsley let out a breath and shrugged. He held no power with her and she could be just as stubborn as he. "All right then," he said, turning back to the stairs. "I have an early morning."

Chapter 3

*Fashion'd so slenderly
Young, and so fair!*

In the morning, Ainsley was summoned to his father's study. Begrudgingly, he left his spot at the breakfast table, throwing his napkin beside his plate before walking down the long hallway to the room where Lord Marshall spent most of his time.

"What is this I hear? You are planning a trip?" his father said when Ainsley was seated in a chair opposite the large oak desk. His father stood at the window. Dressed smartly in his hand-tailored shirt covered with a dark brown waistcoat, Lord Marshall was a commanding presence.

"Dr. Bennett requires some assistance," Ainsley attempted to explain. Defiantly, he glared at his father, determined to be quite unaffected by anything the old man might have to say. "My position demands it of me."

Lord Marshall looked as though he was contemplating the predicament set before him. Ainsley knew all too well how his father felt about his career choice and was under no illusions; he knew that his father meant to derail his efforts and keep him in London.

"I warned you not to get too attached to the scientific profession. Such a trade is beneath our house and would do great damage to the reputation of this family." Lord Marshall was not speaking to his son directly. He was looking out the window, like a self-assured cat soaking up the morning sunlight.

Ainsley was well aware of his father's opinions on the matter. A surgeon was a labourer, a tradesman, someone who could not avoid getting his hands dirty. It was just the sort of profession Ainsley longed for. Anything to stain his shirt and create callouses on his hands, the exact opposite of what he had been raised to become. "I am a grown man, Father. I have my own means of income now." Ainsley pursed his lips and shrugged. "I will do as I please."

"I will not abide by it," Lord Marshall said at last. He rounded the corner of his desk and took a seat. "I have supported your misguided adventures long enough. It is time you took your life seriously. You are the son of a Peer. It is high time you act like it."

"What profession would you have me perform, Father?" Ainsley asked. "Daniel has already taken place of bootlicker. You are the shrewd, cunning businessman. Between the two of you there is no room for me."

Lord Marshall gave a look of annoyance but let the remark slide. "I won't have you running off to the countryside at the behest of some two-bit doctor who cannot see to his own patients. Who is this Dr. Bennett?"

"He is a colleague and is in need of a surgeon. Is this because of Mother?" Ainsley shifted in his chair and crossed his leg. When he was younger, just sitting in the room intimidated him. But over the years his mother's rebellious nature seemed to have rubbed off on him and now he felt at ease. She was always a pillar of strength against their domineering father.

"What about your mother?" Lord Marshall asked, his face turning white as he spoke.

"Margaret told me she left," Ainsley explained. "Perhaps your anger has less to do with me than with her."

His father's face nearly turned to stone as Ainsley watched. The years had hardened Lord Marshall against any love or affection he may have once had for his wife. Ainsley's father had become even crueler since his wife began testing his patience. She baited him like a sleeping bear and was beginning to succeed at making him look like a fool in front of everyone. Lord Marshall once told his children she was ungrateful toward his goodwill and his passive nature would soon come to an end. He spoke openly of his discontent with her. Lord Marshall's anger toward his estranged wife was not a family secret, by any means.

"Hold your tongue, boy!" Lord Marshall pulled a ledger from the top drawer of his desk and slapped it on the desk in front of him. "Your mother is dead to me!"

Ainsley realized it must be clear to everyone that Lord Marshall truly had no command over the family anymore—his wife was gone without his permission, and his son threatened to leave as well. The defiant young doctor plucked a speck of lint from his pant leg and looked up to his father with a hint of challenge in his eye as he flicked it to the floor. "Is that a confession of guilt?" Ainsley asked.

Lord Marshall stood up abruptly and walked to Ainsley, lifting his hand in such a way as to slap his son. Ainsley immediately stood to his feet, fury clenched in the fists at his side. He was the same height and build as his father, slender with well-defined muscles. It had been years since his father had struck him and many things had changed since then. Ainsley would no longer accept his blows. He intended to return them.

With his jaw clenched, Ainsley met his father's eyes and refused to back down. "See you in a week, Father," Ainsley spat before turning to leave.

Within minutes, Ainsley had bid Billis to hail a carriage and called for his trunk to be brought down from his room. Standing on the pavement, he waited for his trunk to be stowed safely on board the carriage while ignoring the silhouette of his father in the window. Margaret was the only one who came out to the street to bid him farewell. Knowing their father was watching them Ainsley felt awkward and not as free to express how much he would miss her.

"How long do you plan to be away?" Margaret asked.

"Not long," Ainsley answered with a laugh. "If I am gone too long I will get fired. Wouldn't that just give Father more ammunition?"

Margaret's face fell at the mention of their father. Ainsley knew she must have heard the entire argument from the breakfast table. No doubt the whole house was aware of how at odds father and son had become.

"I shall not be long," Ainsley reiterated before slipping into the carriage. The carriage jerked to a start and Ainsley watched through the window as Margaret raised her arm to wave good-bye.

The train station was a flurry of activity but Ainsley saw none of it. His mind was awash with the words of his father playing over and over again in his head, like a poorly performed opera he had seen once that would not leave him for days. His one wish was to leave the city, leave the dust and debris, the stench and the busyness. He realized as soon as he was deposited in his cabin that this sojourn to the country was just what he needed.

Chapter 4

Look at her garments
Clinging like cerements;
Whilst the wave constantly
Drips from her clothing;

The train station in Picklow was little more than a long wooden platform with a small shed serving as a telegraph office at one side. As Ainsley stepped down from the steam engine, he saw some rail workers unloading mailbags, which they tossed carelessly toward the shed. The doctor was only one of four people who disembarked there; a handful of other passengers remained in their compartments bound for destinations farther along the line.

Ainsley eyed his trunk, which a porter had placed at his side, and wondered whom he should ask for directions to town. There was no village that he could see, just a mass of trees surrounding the station on all sides and only a thin bare strip in which the tracks were laid ahead of the engine. He did notice a lane, two parallel paths of dirt, made by the repetitive coming and going of carriages. The lane disappeared into the trees, one in a northerly direction, the other more to the south. His fellow disembarked passengers climbed into carriages and went one way or the other.

He approached the workers, who were sweaty with the heat from the locomotive's boiler and the nature of their laborious task. They wore kerchiefs around their throats, tied at the front just above their short collars. As Ainsley walked toward them the man closest to him removed his cap and wiped his glistening forehead with his forearm.

"Hello, sir," the worker said with a nod. "Good weather for this time of year, ain't it now?"

"Yes, it is. Would you mind telling me how far it is to Picklow from here?"

The man tilted his head in thought while his coworkers took the opportunity for a short break as well. They too wiped their foreheads and surveyed their progress. "Picklow is another four and a half miles to the north along that road there." The man pointed to one of the lanes. "I could take you there but I am not scheduled to leave for another two hours."

"That's all right. I enjoy a good walk," Ainsley answered with a smile.

"What about your trunk there? Can't walk with that. I can bring it to town on my way, if you'd like. Where are you to be staying?"

Ainsley hesitated for a moment. "Not sure at present."

"There's the village inn on the main street. Might want to check there. Though this time of year they are pretty full from travelers passing through."

"I am doing some work with Dr. Bennett, the physician. You could bring the trunk to his residence."

The man gave a half-smile, a smile of knowing. "Oh, that old dingbat," he said with a laugh. "You've got your work cut out for ya' if you're pairing up with him. My wife prefers Miss Dawson for her needs."

"Miss Dawson?"

"She's the midwife, a medicine woman, lives down yonder," he motioned down the south lane. "Many 'round here rely on her. Her tonics actually work. Dr. Bennett is not known for curing his patients, if you know what I mean."

Ainsley nodded but said nothing while his mind stored away this information. No wonder the old gentleman had contacted Dr. Crawford. Pressure from the village folk was mounting. If Dr. Bennett couldn't find out what was killing these girls, he'd quickly be replaced. In fact, Ainsley wondered, perhaps he already was.

"I'd be much obliged if you could take my trunk in with you this evening," Ainsley said, offering the man his hand to shake. "I will give you some sovereigns for your trouble."

The man shook his hand but refused the payment. "No trouble. Keep your money. We in these parts do what we can to help each other out." Ainsley saw the other men become restless. Their short break was over. Ainsley wondered if perhaps he had taken too much of this man's time.

"Have a good day, sir," Ainsley called over the piercing train whistle. He raised his hand in a gentlemanly wave and turned from the crew, who were back again making quick work of unloading their cargo.

~ ~

The path through the trees was just wide enough for a coach but no more. The autumn canopy overhead was thick, each branch intertwining with the others, creating a tightly woven ceiling of wood and brightly coloured leaves. The sound as they moved with the wind was loud, their hard, crusty surfaces scraping on the others around them, with the odd cracking of tree wood, as if protesting any movement from its natural position.

Ainsley walked briskly, eager to get out of the woods before dusk. He had been too hasty with his refusal of conveyance to the town. It was getting late in the day and the woods, he remembered, carried the blackness of night long before the towns and cities, which were illuminated by lantern light.

The train journey had been long and Ainsley was tired. He had thought the walk would be good for his stiff legs, but as he made his way through the woods all he wanted was a warm bed and a good night's sleep.

Ainsley reached the edge of town just as the last rays of sunlight slid behind the horizon. There were still people walking the streets and tending their chores as the sun dipped below the western facing buildings. He could see a pair of youths going from street lantern to street lantern, lighting the gas on fire, racing against the last moments of daylight.

"Excuse me, ma'am," Ainsley called out to a friendly looking woman who was sweeping her walkway. She paused her chore and met him at the gate that led up to her front door. "Would you know where Dr. Bennett resides?" he asked.

"Well now, he's just down that lane, third house on your right." She pointed beyond him to a side street a few yards off.

"Thank you." Ainsley tipped his hat to her and turned to continue his journey.

"Mind you be careful now," she said, "Mrs. Crane don't like solicitors just showing up on her doorstep."

Ainsley smiled. "I'll keep that in mind," he answered with a wave before turning down the lane.

 ❧ ☙

There was a carriage in front of the house with two properly dressed grooms waiting alongside the horses. They tipped their hat in acknowledgement to Ainsley as he approached. He made his way up the front walk to the door. A scruffy orange cat was curled up on a chair set to the right of the door. Before knocking, he held his hand out to her, which startled the feline. She hissed at him violently and swatted at his outstretched hand. It only took a moment for blood to appear at the wound she had caused. Ainsley snapped his hand away to inspect it and when he looked back the cat had fled. It was a minor wound, though it reminded him to be wary of all things, even those that appeared harmless.

He heard some noise on the other side of the door and realized he had not yet knocked.

"Blast woman!" he heard a man say. "Your constant fussing is making me late!" The door opened sharply and an older gentleman stepped out right into Ainsley, who was too slow to step away.

"And who the devil are you?" the man asked brashly. "Not a lawyer, I hope!" The rotund man laughed and turned to the matronly woman, who hovered at the door. She looked stern and ill-amused.

"No sir," Ainsley said, "I have been sent by Dr. Crawford. You dispatched a telegraph asking for someone capable of doing a dissection."

The woman gasped and raised her hand to her mouth.

"Postmortem! Goodness man, don't be so

disrespectful of the dead! We call them postmortems if there is a need to refer to them at all."

Chided, Ainsley agreed. "Yes, quite right. My apologies, ma'am." Ainsley was used to his work being secretive, though he was far freer with the terminology while among doctors like himself. He admitted it was a new science, and not one many people liked to hear referenced.

"Well, I hate to say it, but you came all this way for nothing. Mrs. Lloyd, in her infinite wisdom," Dr. Bennett sneered in sarcasm, "has decided it not necessary and she is refusing all my requests to have the child's body looked over."

Ainsley looked from the woman to Dr. Bennett, suspicion sweeping over his face. "She has another daughter ill, has she not?" he asked.

"Yes, though Mrs. Lloyd seems content to just let the poor girl die."

"That's preposterous!"

"Yes, I know." Dr. Bennett took his hat from the woman standing at the door. "Very well," he sighed, "you cannot travel back tonight. Might as well tag along. I am headed there now. Mrs. Crane," he turned to the woman, "prepare a guest room for this gentleman. We will return before long." The woman nodded and disappeared in to the house.

Ainsley followed Dr. Bennett to the carriage. A groomsman opened the door just as Bennett approached. Ainsley climbed in after him, taking a seat opposite him. It was a very fine coach with soft velvet benches and black curtains pulled back from the windows. A pair of black horses led the way with small lanterns dangling from either side of the coachman's bench. The two groomsmen climbed onto the front of the carriage and soon the carriage lurched into motion.

"This coach was sent from the Lloyd estate," Bennett said. "They are in the midst of the wake and I have yet to visit to pay my respects. You, young man, might just be the young blood I need."

Chapter 5

Take her up instantly,
Loving, not loathing.

"This should be a very interesting case for you, Dr. Ainsley," Bennett said. The two were jostled in their seats by the road's unforgiving roughness. "I'd be interested in getting your opinion on the matter." Bennett paused for a moment. "Has Dr. Crawford shared any of his knowledge about this case?"

"Only what was detailed in your letter," Ainsley answered. "A child is dead, her sister is gravely ill. I assume from the same affliction."

"Your assumption is correct, though perhaps you can validate that for me scientifically." Dr. Bennett took in a long breath and straightened his waistcoat as he shifted in his seat.

"I'd be happy to assist in any way I can," Ainsley said, aware that Dr. Bennett would surely inform Dr. Crawford about his performance while he was there.

Ainsley could see the hints of a smile on the old doctor's face. "Since you are already here, perhaps you can be of some use. I'd like for you to examine the body."

"You said Mrs. Lloyd refused consent for an autopsy?"

"Right, she did. We must make our observations discreetly, without giving away the nature or purpose of our enquiry." Bennett paused and shifted nervously in his seat. "The girl who passed away is Josephine Lloyd." Bennett paused for a moment and glanced out the window of the carriage. He gave a breath of despair as he ran his hand over his face. The man was weary, Ainsley thought, perhaps he grew more tired than Ainsley himself.

"What troubles you, Dr. Bennett?"

"There are three girls. Elizabeth, who is quite

matronly now, nearing twenty-five, has not shown any signs of disease... praise be to God." Bennett pressed his hands together, raising his gaze to the sky as if saying a little prayer of thanks.

Ainsley smiled slightly at this but said nothing. God had very little to do with the workings of science.

"The twenty-year-old Lillian is quite ill and has not left her room for weeks. I had feared she would be the first to pass away but I was quite wrong. Josephine, the youngest, is the one we bury in the morning. Her departure was quite unexpected."

"And the one who remains ill—"

"Lillian?"

"Yes, Lillian. How advanced is her condition?"

The old man pursed his lips in thought, letting out a deep breath of exhaustion. "I can regrettably say we may be attending her wake before long. Mrs. Lloyd will not allow her to attend Josephine's funeral. We must find the cause for this calamity, and we must find it soon or we will lose Lillian too."

Ainsley had seen many illnesses take out entire families, leaving no one immune. The suggestion seemed logical. "Have you ruled out consumption? Scarlet fever? Small pox?"

"Yes, I explored those options vigorously. I am perplexed. Their father, Mr. Lloyd, died not two months ago. Pneumonia, or so I thought at the time."

Ainsley leaned back in his seat, assured that he could find the root cause, though he was not so convinced he could save the woman who remained ill. "And such a diagnosis would explain this resurgence. The family is of sickly disposition. Do not carry this burden on your shoulders."

Bennett laughed at his young apprentice's words. "You are that experienced to comfort me thus?"

Ainsley smiled and leaned forward in his seat, despite the rocking motion of the carriage. "I know the facts as you present them to me. It would not be an entirely strange thing to see a family fall prey so easily. I saw such afflictions numerous times during my years in London. Entire families wiped out by a single sickness that you or I could stave off easily."

"How many of those sickly London families were of poor class and diet?" Bennett challenged. "I suspect a great deal of them. I could argue that the Lloyds are a family of great wealth, property and, in effect, good health. So why have three people fallen ill and succumbed so easily? I have a belief there is more here than meets the eye, Dr. Ainsley. There is something happening to this family."

"You have reason to suspect foul play?" Ainsley asked finally.

Bennett hesitated. "I have found nothing to substantiate my gut feeling..." the old man's voice trailed off.

"What would that 'gut feeling' be, Dr. Bennett?"

The old doctor gave a forced, uneasy smile and said, "Poison."

Chapter 6

Touch her not scornfully;
Think of her mournfully,
Gently and humanly;
Not of the stains of her,

The exterior of the house, illuminated both inside and out, seemed to mirror Ainsley's mood. Damp. Near frozen. It was an impressively large home with three stories and a labyrinth of balconies and landings. It must have been recently built, using a cornucopia of styles borrowed from architects of old. The mist that hung thick in the air made the limestone exterior appear to be sand, collapsible at any moment should anyone dare to touch it.

As Ainsley stepped from the carriage he noted the death wreath on the door, hastily created from laurel that must grow abundant somewhere on the vast property. The door stood slightly ajar, a gesture for mourners to come in, without ringing the bell. The noise would disturb the somber peace of the place, and perhaps would remind the dead that the living remained active while they had met their end.

Ainsley followed Bennett, who showed the way into the house. A housemaid met them in the foyer and took their coats. Bennett turned to the drawing room, where the young Josephine was laid out. Ainsley made a quick nod of thanks to the maid before remembering his flask. The maid turned away just as he called out. "Oh sorry, just a moment." He risked penetrating the calm quiet of the house but he was desperate. He reached into the inner pocket of his coat and pulled out a small silver flask. He would need that before long.

With the maid gone and his flask safely placed in the inner pocket at his breast, Ainsley stood at the threshold to the parlour. There were others there that night, lending support to the family and assisting in keeping watch over the body during the wake. He could see the small white casket held off the ground by two sturdy chairs strategically placed at the head and foot. Flowers were arranged in abundance around the corpse, staving off the distinctive smell of death he knew would be surrounding the body so long after her passing. From his position at the door, he could see no parts of the body save the tiny hands that were folded together on the girl's chest. He glanced around the room, wondering which of the ladies gathered there was Mrs. Lloyd.

Dr. Bennett led the way toward two women who were seated to one side of the room. The younger woman, with golden blonde hair and a slender physique not entirely hidden beneath a modest black frock and gloves, held the hand of another woman who was seated beside her weeping. The crying woman appeared to be slightly older, though the two of them looked so alike they could be sisters. Neither of the women spoke. They simply sat side by side, their gazes transfixed on nothing in particular, both looking in opposite directions.

"Mrs. Lloyd," Dr. Bennett began softly.

The older woman raised her gaze and then stood, recognizing the doctor. "Dr. Bennett, so good of you to attend."

Dr. Bennett grasped Mrs. Lloyd's hands in his own. "Allow me to introduce Dr. Ainsley. He's come all the way from London to assist me."

Mrs. Lloyd turned to Ainsley then, revealing a sullen face with stone cold features and a hardness he had never seen in a woman of her station. "Dr. Ainsley." She nodded in greeting and extended her hand.

Ainsley took her hand gently. "Mrs. Lloyd, I am deeply sorry for your loss."

She nodded.

The younger woman spoke then. "Mother, you should sit. Your health." She led her mother back to her seat, as if the woman was a hundred and could not seat herself.

"Elizabeth Lloyd," Dr. Bennett said to Ainsley very quietly. "The eldest girl."

Ainsley nodded as he watched Elizabeth escort her mother back to her seat. No wonder she was still unmarried. She bore the same sullen and bitter face as her mother but looked even more disagreeable, given her younger age. "Charming," Ainsley said in a whisper.

It was then that Ainsley noticed that a mirror in the hall was draped with black fabric, and the family portraits were overturned and lying faces down. It had become tradition to cover mirrors so that the spirit of the deceased could not find themselves trapped in them. Family portraits were covered or overturned to guard any others in the family from being called to the spirit world by the ghost of the person who had passed. These observances were simply superstition, he thought, devices to appease their obsession with the dead. The flowers that surrounded the body, on the other hand, were a practical addition. They masked the smell of decay.

The young doctor also noticed a sizable grand piano situated near a generous bay window, which would overlook the front lawns. Sheet music was folded neatly in leather folders, though the corners stuck out, revealing their identity. Books lined a nearby shelf, and a sizable framed portrait was draped in thick black cloth. A tiny pair of gloves was folded on top of the piano and a single lily was placed on top. A gesture, he thought, to say good-bye.

"Dr. Ainsley," Bennett said, approaching with a young, smartly dressed man who had just crossed the room and was walking toward them, "allow me to introduce you to Walter Lloyd Jr., the eldest of the Lloyd children. Mr. Lloyd, this is the young doctor who has come to assist me."

Ainsley shook the man's hand when it was offered and gave a forced smile. "I wish our meeting was under more amiable circumstances," he managed to say.

Walter looked solemn but his manner was all business. "Thank you," he answered. "I hardly see the point in bringing a doctor all the way from London for my sisters."

Remembering Dr. Bennett's concerns, Ainsley was careful not to give away the true reason for his attendance. "Merely a formality," Ainsley answered. "The university has an interest in studying all cases of sudden illnesses resulting in death. I would also like the opportunity to assist your other sister, who remains ill. If there is a way to help, I would like to do that." He gave a quick glance to Bennett, who nodded his approval.

The young head of the household gave a slight laugh. "Lillian is as stubborn as a mule and refuses tonics that will do her well. If she dies, it certainly is not for lack of trying to save her."

Walter was cold for saying such things though his demeanor reminded Ainsley of his own brother, Daniel, who also at times made similar disparaging comments. Perhaps it is the way with businessmen. "Well," Ainsley began, "I shall see what I can do."

"Indeed." Walter nodded, as if he agreed, but Ainsley could tell his mind was elsewhere.

"She will not stick to her room, you know," Walter offered. "She is constantly venturing down, so Mother tells me. She has threatened to put a lock on her door if Lillian does not stay in her bed." Walter shifted his gaze around the room. "Mother is expecting a throng tomorrow afternoon. She spares no expense and funerals are no exception, I assure you. You are both welcome anytime. Now if you'll excuse me, I have business matters to attend." Walter slid past the two doctors and retreated to the hall and a room further beyond.

Bennett leaned into Ainsley, pulling him closer to the hallway, and spoke in a hushed tone so no one else could hear. "The Lloyds own two woolen mills, one here in Picklow and the other further north. Since inheriting the business Walter has been seeing to both and spends very little time at the home."

Ainsley nodded, grateful for the information. His gaze returned to the room and he saw Elizabeth looking at him. He nodded but she did nothing and turned away sharply.

From all accounts, the family appeared normal enough, though there was something more that Ainsley could not put his finger on. The way they looked at him, as an outsider, unnerved him. Their eyes bore a chill that matched the weather outside. He turned to Bennett. "Have you known the family long?" he asked.

"Yes, I attended all of the births... except Miss Josephine, but by then there was a midwife in the area to assist Mrs. Lloyd." Bennett rocked back and forth on his feet, smiling slightly. He was obviously proud of his loyal service to the family.

Ainsley knew the doctor spoke of Miss Dawson, whom the labourer at the train station had referred to.

"All Lloyd children were strong, you say. Any infant deaths?" Ainsley asked.

"No. Though..." the doctor hesitated. "Martha has had a string of miscarriages, which resulted in large age gaps between the children. Those who made it to birth were of the healthiest constitution."

Ainsley spotted a tall woman entering the parlour slowly but deliberately. She passed both doctors and approached the casket, obscuring the body from view. A black mourning veil hid her face. Ainsley saw Mrs. Lloyd lift her gaze as she realized who was standing before the body of her daughter. The veiled woman's attention was focused on the casket before her until the grieving mother jumped from her seat and bounded for the woman in a rage. "You keep your hands away from my daughter, you witch!" Mrs. Lloyd cried as she grabbed for the woman.

Defensively, the woman raised her arm, as Mrs. Lloyd reached to strike her.

"Mrs. Lloyd!" Bennett and Ainsley rushed toward the pair. The veiled woman was able to shake Mrs. Lloyd from her body and stepped back quickly as Mrs. Lloyd lunged for her again. The veil was pulled from the woman's face and her hat fell to the floor. Bennett struggled to hold Mrs. Lloyd back while Ainsley used his body to protect the guest.

"You keep her away, Doctor!" Mrs. Lloyd called over his shoulder.

"Martha, please! Calm yourself. She is paying her respects," Dr. Bennett said sedately. Elizabeth appeared at her mother's side and rubbed her back as the doctor tried to calm her. The female mourner who had caused the stir turned back to the casket. Ainsley saw her pull a coin from her pocket, kissing it before placing it in the hands of the corpse.

"Don't let her do her magic on my child. You tell her to keep away!" Mrs. Lloyd struggled to be free of Bennett's arms. "She did it, Dr. Bennett! She killed my baby!" Martha screamed and charged again. She broke free from Bennett's grasp and struck the woman from behind.

Ainsley tried to stop her but he was too late. The woman stumbled and fell backward into the casket, knocking it to the floor, the body falling halfway out from the impact. The entire room of mourners gasped then quickly fell into a stunned silence. Ainsley glanced around and saw a small child huddled, terrified, beneath the piano. He did not know or recognize her but he knew she had seen the entire exchange and his heart fell at the thought.

"That will be all, Mrs. Lloyd," Ainsley bellowed, raising a pointed finger. "Calm yourself!" He turned, kneeling at the woman's side, and lifted her to her feet. He grabbed her hat from the floor and presented it to her. "Are you harmed?" he asked.

The woman shook her head and accepted her hat. She did not meet his eyes, though he could tell she had been crying for some time prior to arriving. Her face was red and ruddy.

"You don't understand, Dr. Ainsley," Elizabeth protested, as she pulled her crying mother from the scene, caressing her as she would a child. "That woman has been a curse to us."

"I am sure she has been no such thing," Ainsley yelled. "If you cannot allow this woman her right to—"

"She is a witch!" Mrs. Lloyd yelled.

Ainsley's face hardened instantly. "Madam! Remove yourself from this room or I will have you removed."

"You cannot demand me to leave. This is my own house!" Mrs. Lloyd yelled from her daughter's arms.

"No, it's my house." Everyone turned their attention to the door and saw Walter, a glass of whiskey in his hand. "I came to see what the trouble was. Mother, I think it is best if you retire for the evening."

"Walter!"

"Mother."

Mrs. Lloyd lowered her gaze, while Elizabeth escorted her from the room, neither one attempting to look at Walter as they passed. Once they were gone, other mourners began to gather and leave. Soon, Ainsley, Bennett, Walter, and the strange woman were the only ones left with the overturned corpse. The little girl remained huddled beneath the piano, looking at them all.

Bennett motioned toward the corpse, and Ainsley nodded. The two doctors, Bennett at the feet, Ainsley at the head, rolled the girl's body onto its back and lifted it back into the righted coffin.

Having handled cadavers often enough, the body was no difficulty for Ainsley, save a conscious effort to remain respectful. The skin, Ainsley noticed, had been treated with fragrant oils and powders to mask the smell of decay, a condition that made the mass slippery in his hands. The dead weight was heavy and unwieldy, which required both men to shift their own weight in response to the unpredictable movement of the corpse.

"My apologies, Miss Dawson," Walter said calmly, once Josephine's body was restored. Ainsley looked to the woman standing quietly next to him, the realization dawning that she was the midwife of which the villagers had spoken.

"No need to apologize, Mr. Lloyd," she said in a subdued voice.

"My mother is... overwrought." Walter glanced to the two doctors and nodded in thanks. "You are more than welcome to attend in the morning. If there is anything else you require please send word."

"Thank you, Walter. You are very kind."

"I will escort you to the door."

Ainsley watched the small girl slip from under the piano and follow behind Miss Dawson, who left the room without so much as a backward glance. He looked down to the corpse, readjusted her slightly opened eyelids to give the impression she was sleeping, and folded her arms gently on her chest.

Chapter 7

*All that remains of her
Now is pure womanly.*

The tired pair, Ainsley and Bennett, sat silently as the carriage conveyed them back to town. Ainsley shifted nervously in his seat, unable to reconcile the scene he had just witnessed and the basic facts he knew about the family. Never before had he seen such a public display from the higher classes. Even his own ill-functioning family knew to keep their squabbles behind closed doors and beyond prying eyes. There had to be more to this family and their relationship to Miss Dawson, something that made emotions run high and vanquish all sense of propriety.

Ainsley looked across the carriage. Bennett was staring at him inquisitively. Ainsley wondered if the old man could read his thoughts.

"I am trying to figure you out, Dr. Ainsley," Bennett confessed. "You are unlike many doctors in some respects."

"How so?"

"Your manner… it's quite refined."

"Shall I be disrespectful and ill-bred?" Ainsley answered with a laugh.

"You jest, Dr. Ainsley, but one would mistake you for a… well, to be blunt, a higher-ranking citizen than a doctor."

Ainsley forced a laugh but it came out fake. He could scarcely hide his identity forever. He knew he would one day be called to task for his deceitfulness, but for the time being he needed to hide his real name and position as long as he could.

"I would never presume to speak to Mrs. Lloyd in such a manner," Bennett confessed.

"Something had to be said. I could not let that poor woman be abused so abrasively."

Ainsley saw Dr. Bennett smile and betook it for doubt. Ainsley decided to shift the conversation to another subject.

"When did you first suspect Josephine was poisoned?" Ainsley let the words drop from his lips and watched closely for any reaction from Bennett. "What markings did you see?"

"I've been scarcely permitted to view the body."

"So why do you believe it is a case of poisoning?"

"From Lillian, herself." Dr. Bennett let out a deep breath. "I was given a letter written in her own hand. I never would have believed it myself had I not been..." his voice broke off. "Mr. Lloyd's death was very odd as well."

Ainsley leaned in closer. "You believe Mr. Lloyd was the first victim?"

"No, I believe he died of pneumonia. It was the reaction to his death that I thought suspicious. It was... as if there was a knowing between all the females in the house. No one was tearful, as you would expect." His face betrayed his unease, his mind drifting to a place he'd rather forget.

Ainsley shifted his gaze, peeking outside the carriage window to the blackness beyond. "Did you perform a postmortem on Mr. Lloyd?"

"No. Mrs. Lloyd would not allow me near the body. I had to resign myself that the true cause might never be found. Without access to the body how could I be sure?"

"Mrs. Lloyd denied you access? Just as she is doing so now. She may very well be behind all this," Ainsley pointed out.

"She was adamant that I should not touch his body lest his spirit be doomed to roam the earth for eternity."

"She said as much?" Ainsley asked with a laugh.

"Word for word," Bennett replied.

"A religious woman is she? Attends church?"

"Not in the twenty-odd years I have lived here. I had thought her melodramatic, though."

"Many women are," Ainsley added. The young doctor sat silently for a moment, with his hand to his chin and his mind twisting and turning over the facts in his head. He could scarcely help if he were not allowed to examine the body. "Tell me, Dr. Bennett, what would you like me to do? Mrs. Lloyd has refused to let us touch her dead child and there is hardly enough evidence for you to contact a magistrate who would force her. My expertise is in dissecting dead bodies but you have me in a situation where I cannot even touch the girl."

Bennett shrugged and gave a look of nonchalance as he leaned back into his carriage seat. "You are a young lad with experience. Are there no other ways?" he suggested.

None that Ainsley was aware. He had specific training. He could not diagnose a cause of death without at least a proper dissection.

"I am not a detective, Dr. Bennett. I am not trained in deciphering clues."

"Are you not?" Bennett asked. "I had thought all doctors were entrusted with as much. We examine physical evidence and determine appropriate causes. Whether it be a cause of illness or death. Your expertise is in determining a cause of death."

Ainsley did not try to hide his laugh. "I can only determine death when I can properly examine a body."

"Give me time," Bennett implored. "I just need a bit more time to convince Mrs. Lloyd."

Ainsley would have to agree to it. It was hardly the time of day to be heading back to London, and he was bone weary from travelling such a distance to get there.

"In the meantime," Bennett continued. "I have volunteered you to sit with the body in the morning prior to the funeral and internment."

Ainsley could not hide his shock. He had no close connection to the family to recommend him for such a service.

"You are startled? Are you not comfortable around dead bodies?"

Even in the dim light Ainsley could see the old man raise an eyebrow. "I can manage well enough. Though I am not sure I should be so entrusted, since I just met the Lloyds this evening."

"Everyone will be preparing for the funeral," Bennett offered. "Besides, could there be a better time to examine the body without anyone of the household around?"

Ainsley returned Bennett's knowing smile. The old man had some character in him, Ainsley decided. Devious fellow.

As the carriage rolled on toward the dimly lit town it was agreed that Ainsley would stay in Bennett's guest room until his job was concluded. No longer than a week, Ainsley repeated in his head. Crawford was expecting his return in six days' time. Easily accomplished, he told himself. The body would reveal all he needed to know. They always did.

Chapter 8

Make no deep scrutiny
Into her mutiny

Lady Bettiscombe's Millinery was the finest hat shop in all of London. It was the perfect place for a privileged young lady like Margaret Marshall to spend her exorbitant allowance on frivolous and pretty things. It was a place to indulge herself, forgetting the sordid affair the day before between Peter and their father.

"Good day, Miss Marshall!" Lady Bettiscombe smiled from the arrangement she was primping at the window. "I have some lovely peach ribbons for you. They just came yesterday."

"Sounds lovely." Margaret smiled, and pulled her gloves off one finger at a time while Lady Bettiscombe retreated to the back room.

Lady Bettiscombe had found herself in dire straits a few years prior, after the sudden death of her deeply indebted husband. Accustomed to a life of leisure, Lady Bettiscombe decided to use her talent for design, and her well-to-do connections, and opened a hat shop. She created the most elegant designs, at least in Margaret's estimation, and she soon won over many of the women who once counted her as an equal. Now it seemed no one cared for her past and many flocked to her tiny hat shop to plunder her creations, making Lady Bettiscombe a very rich woman in her own right.

Margaret spotted an arrangement toward the back of the store, a variety of green hats with ostrich plumes and sleek black and brown ribbons tied in extravagant bows. Green had become quite the fashion since textile mills discovered a way to make a true, vibrant green. Margaret ran her fingers over the smooth surface of the ribbon and smiled.

The door opened with a loud flourish of the bell that hung overhead. Two women, boisterously laughing, entered the shop, not seeing Margaret near the back behind some bolts of cloth and fabric.

"She is not the first one to tire of her husband!"

Margaret recognized the voice in an instant as Mrs. Delilah Robbins. She was a speculative woman, with a propensity to gossip wildly. "But the entire thing is quite scandalous. Leaving the city so abruptly, without so much as a word to anyone. Never thought I'd see the day," Delilah Robbins continued.

"Oh I saw it coming for years—" the other woman quipped, but was cut short when Lady Bettiscombe returned.

"Good day, ladies," she said. "What is this you say? What did you see coming for years?"

"Lady Marshall, of course. She's run away from home," Delilah said in that high-pitched tone Margaret recognized her by. She often used a singsong voice when she was excited to pass on her nuggets of titillating gossip.

Margaret clasped a hand over her mouth to muffle a gasp and then slipped further behind the cloth.

"I cannot say I believe it," she heard Lady Bettiscombe say. Her voice was soft and almost apologetic. No doubt she questioned whether to tell the women that Lady Marshall's daughter was hiding among the fabric.

"I can," Mrs. Robbins laughed. "Those two were ill-matched from the beginning. She's so headstrong and... unladylike in many respects. I am sorry to say it, ladies, but it does not surprise me in the least."

Margaret heard the voice of Mrs. Robbins coming closer and closer to her, and then imagined the woman standing practically on top of her as she crouched in the shadows. Margaret gripped her mouth tightly, struggling to remain silent in the midst of such accusations. She could not stifle the tears that spilled over her cheeks. To be talked about in such a way, her family's respectability coming into question, was horrifying to behold. She bit her lower lip hard and closed her eyes to stave off the tears.

"Many women leave the city for their health," Lady

Bettiscombe tried to explain.

"But do they take their lover with them?"

Margaret pounced from her secret spot. "I beg your pardon?" she growled, unable to control the anger. "Of all the spiteful, malicious rumours to perpetuate! I have never heard such mean-spirited gossip!" Margaret glanced to Lady Bettiscombe, aware of the scene she must be causing in her friend's shop. Seeing Lady Bettiscombe's face, Margaret's anger left her and she lowered her tone. "For your information, my mother has gone to our country house, *alone*, to help her lungs," she lied.

Margaret reached for the peach ribbons in Lady Bettiscombe's hands. "Thank you, Lady Bettiscombe. You may charge these to my family's account." Margaret forced a half smile, gave a slight curtsey more out of habit than respect, and left hastily.

ஓ ✍

A few blocks away she looked down to her hands and found the peach ribbons crumpled in her tight grasp. Propelled by fury, she had charged down the pavement, sidestepping couples walking arm in arm, and governesses with their small charges close at hand. She recognized no one and saw no haven from the gloom that engulfed her. The ribbons only exemplified how everything that was once gay had turned sour and unrecognizable.

It was hard to tell if she was angry that her mother possessed a lover, or angrier still that she had been caught. Margaret could hardly say she was shocked. She had known for a long while that her parents no longer harboured any passion for each other. Her mother had always been a wild card, refusing to play along in society, always living on the edge of respectability. She often said outlandish things, breaking standard conventions and protocols, and every so often allowed herself to become drunk in public. Her mother answered to no one, least of all her husband, and now she had created an even greater scandal than public drunkenness or committing a societal faux pas. Her mother's rash behaviour had finally caught up with the family and now they were paying the price for her heedlessness. Anyone who bore the name Marshall would be associated with her and the ill-bred choices she made.

Margaret intended to head straight for home, to write to Peter immediately, but as she walked that plan seemed horribly unsatisfying. If she possessed any source of strength at all, she'd demand her mother return to her husband in the city, where they could hopefully erase any thoughts of a lover from the whispers of the gossips.

But what if it were true?

Margaret stopped at a corner, unable to catch her breath. What if the rumour were true and not just the product of idle tongues?

She turned in place, placing a hand to her bosom as her breath quickened, the pace of pedestrians and carriages quickening along with it. The world around her became a streaked fog without distinguishable shapes. Closing her eyes momentarily she willed herself to calm. She pictured The Briar, her family's country home in Tunbridge Wells, where her mother was no doubt passing the time reading a long neglected volume or surveying a healthy pile of social invitations. Margaret smiled at the thought and opened her eyes, with a renewed sense of assurance. Her mother would never take a lover, she told herself. Such a disgrace was unthinkable. All Margaret needed to do was head to The Briar to prove it.

With Peter gone, however, the simple task seemed that much harder. Her father would never permit her to travel alone, but then again she doubted she would bother to tell her father of her intentions. She needed an escort, someone she could trust to take her from the city and see her properly deposited in Tunbridge Wells. Someone without connections to London society.

Pushed along by a rush of people, Margaret walked, contemplating her need to be free of the city when she saw him, Jonas Davies, a friend of Peter's whom he had met in medical school. Both doctors now, they kept close ties. Margaret had met him many times, though because of his profession he would never been seen as a proper companion, and now that she saw him, she knew he was the answer she sought.

"Jonas!"

A block ahead of her, he stepped down from a carriage and walked a few steps along the pavement before turning into a building. Margaret hurried along, hoping to catch him, and turned quickly into the front door where she had seen him disappear. Pushing past some men at the entrance, she craned her neck and watched him slip further away from her.

"Jonas!" she yelled again, but the noise in the dark room was too loud.

Someone stepped in front of her, smiling devilishly. "Pardon me," she said, and squeezed by. The room was so tight with people, men mostly. Margaret became entangled in the crowd and she was forced to weave between people just to keep pace with Jonas. Then she felt someone pull at her arm and she jerked it away. "Pardon me!" She gave a hard glare to the man who had touched her and when she turned back to Jonas she saw that he had turned and recognized her now.

"Jonas," she breathed. He was a tall man, taller than her brother Peter, though not by much, and wide in the shoulders. Where Peter had a lean, compact strength, Jonas was bulky and intimidating, not at all what you would expect a surgeon to be. He looked more like a prison warden or military captain. Despite this, he reminded her of Peter in every way and that was most likely why she was so desperate to reach him.

"Miss Marshall, what brings you here?" He licked his lips nervously and glanced around the room.

Margaret followed his gaze and for the first time noticed where she was. At first glance, it resembled a pub with a serving bar along one wall and men standing with drinks. There were a few tables at which the men gathered around them held playing cards, thick cigars perched in their fingers. Jonas himself had a lit cigar in one hand. It was only when a barmaid passed between her and Jonas, wearing a dangerously low-cut bodice revealing milk-white mounds, did Margaret realize the place she stood in was a gentleman's club with drink, gambling, and women at their disposal.

Margaret's eyes went straight to the floor. "Forgive

me." She turned quickly, dreading the long walk back to the street through the throng of men who had practically molested her as she walked in. She could sense Jonas closely behind her, which made her feel better. She felt his hand on her shoulder and his other arm around her motioning for those in front of them to move aside and let them through. Once out on the street and a sufficient distance away, Margaret turned to him, aware that her face had flushed a deep crimson. "It would appear my day is fraught with errors," she said.

Jonas smiled. "I doubt that."

"What is that pl—?" She shook her head quickly. "No, I don't care to know."

"It's the kind of place I had never expected to see you in." Jonas smiled, almost unapologetically. He slid his hands into his pockets and breathed heavily, as if glad the awkward encounter had finished. "Come, let me see you home." He raised his hand to summon a hansom and helped Margaret as she climbed in.

With the carriage rolling along toward Belgravia, Margaret waited, unable to look at him and yet very much aware of how much he was transfixed with her. "What kind of desperation could have brought you to me?" he asked after a long silence.

"I was not desperate!"

Jonas cocked an eyebrow. "Oh no? So you had intended to follow me straight into a gambling den?"

Margaret pressed her lips together and turned to look out the window. "I scarcely knew you were the type." This was not entirely true. She knew rumours abounded regarding his entertainment choices. He enjoyed a good drink, just like her brother Peter, but Jonas also liked to gamble. He had once arranged a betting pool when Peter had been scheduled to box the champion from a rival school. Margaret only heard of this after, of course, when both her brother and Jonas had fifty pounds in winnings to brag about. Had the outcome been different she doubted they would have been so bold to tell her about it.

She saw the look on Jonas' face and knew she couldn't continue with the charade and keep her dignity intact. "If you must know," she relented, "I need to travel to

Tunbridge Wells and I have no escort. I naturally thought of you."

"Naturally." A smile teased the corners of Jonas' lips. Margaret ignored him.

"It won't require more than a day in travel time. You could be back in your gambling den before this time tomorrow." She avoided his gaze but desperately wanted to see his reaction to her plan. From the corner of her view she saw his reluctance. "I will pay you for your time, of course."

After a moment of silence, the carriage stopped in front of Margaret's home. Jonas left the carriage first and offered a hand to Margaret from the pavement. Walking down the three steps to the ground, she looked him in the eye but could not decipher his thoughts.

"Very well," he said at last. "When do we leave?"

Chapter 9

Rash and undutiful:
Past all dishonour,

Josephine's body lay like the china doll Ainsley's sister, Margaret, had once received at Christmas. In its white box, the doll had been laid on a cushion of billowing white satin, a small pillow propping up her head as streams of long blonde curls cascaded down the sides of her pale face, her rose-coloured lips revealing the slightest of smiles. At length, Ainsley stared at Josephine, wishing he were simply looking through a doll maker's window and not at the corpse of a dead twelve-year-old girl.

School never prepared him for dealing with dead children. He doubted he would ever get used to it. That day she was slightly more blue, the lids of her eyes and curves of her lips especially. She had been lain out for four days, he suspected. The family would be grateful that she be interred that day. Any more delay and he figured she would hardly be presentable.

He circled the coffin, stepping closer to her head. With his hand clasped behind his back, he studied her face, neck, and any visible part of her that would tell him anything about her demise. He wanted desperately to perform an autopsy. That was the only way to know for sure. It bothered him that Mrs. Lloyd would not allow it.

Daringly, he leaned in closer to the body. Any fears or apprehension he felt about his task had vanished. He was not a man, but a doctor using the evidence and not emotion to determine the cause of death.

He lifted her hands, separating the fingers as he examined her. Her left hand and arm were clear of any marks but on the right arm he found a small scratch and slight bruising on her wrist. He turned the limp hand over and moved out of the light so he could see it better. It was faint, but visible. He studied it for a while before determining the mark could have been made prior to death, though he was not entirely certain.

He moved to her head then, the only other part of her body he could easily access. Regrettably, her mouth was sewn shut, preventing him from looking inside. He regarded the appearance of her skin around her neck and ears. There was a smell he recognized for a brief moment. The smell came to his awareness and was gone. He leaned closer, nearly putting his face to the girl's lips before he recognized what he was sensing, a hint of garlic.

"Is something wrong?"

Ainsley jumped, startled by the sudden sound. He whirled around and saw Elizabeth standing at the doorway to the parlour. "No," he said, glancing back to the body nervously. "Just admiring... admiring the work of the undertaker," he lied, while trying to mask his fright.

"A man of science would appreciate such details," Elizabeth answered plainly without missing a beat. Ainsley could tell she was well-versed at playing hostess. She would laugh at all the right places, smile demurely, and offer flattering comments whenever she could fit them into the conversation.

She looked tired, though. She was the first family member he had seen that morning. Outside, it remained dark, with dawn breaking beyond the trees. The house was quiet, save for the servants who allowed Ainsley in. He had not expected any of the family members to be up at such an early hour. Despite her obvious fatigue, she stood still, taking her place close enough to hold conversation yet far enough not to give the impression of familiarity. She must have scored high marks at finishing school, Ainsley guessed, seeing how calm she was in spite of the tragedy that embraced her family.

"Forgive me," Ainsley spoke quickly, realizing he was staring, "Such a tragic loss. I can only imagine your family's grief."

"Yes, I agree. You can only imagine."

Ainsley glanced over the room and saw the large piano and its prominent place in the parlour. "There's a musician in the family?"

Elizabeth glanced toward the instrument but she clearly had no attachment to it herself. "My sister Lillian is the pianist. Not I." Her tone was level, a trait that unnerved him. Either she was a great actress, able to shield her grief from the outside world, or she was hardly affected at all by the death of her sister. He remembered Bennett's remarks about Mr. Lloyd's death and how the women shared a look of knowing.

"My colleague, Dr. Bennett, says her health declined rapidly," Ainsley ventured. He figured she already despised him greatly. What would a few carefully chosen questions hurt?

"Do you define seven hours of agony as a rapid decline?"

"When did you send for a doctor?" Ainsley asked.

"Mother did not wish to send for the doctor straight away. She had us wait. Walter rode for Miss Dawson but by then it was too late. There was nothing she could do for her." Elizabeth glanced beyond Ainsley but decided to take a seat closer to the door. "We tried to make her comfortable."

"Dr. Bennett was not available?" Ainsley followed her lead and took a seat not too far away.

Elizabeth pressed her lips together tightly before speaking. "Mother no longer trusts him. He had been giving Lily tonics but they had not made any difference. We sent for Miss Dawson too late."

Ainsley nodded. "Your sister—" he began but was quickly cut off when the maid from the night before entered the room with a tray of tea. Elizabeth was startled by the girl's sudden appearance and quickly stood up. "Place them here, Mary," she said. "I told Cook to bring you some scones and tea," Elizabeth said to Ainsley. She gestured for the tray, which Mary placed on the side table. She was quite scrawny looking, almost too skinny to be able to maneuver such a weighted tray filled with plates of pastries, a teapot, cream, sugar, honey pot, and related china cups and saucers. Her dress hung loose from her extremely slender form and her sleeves were rolled up at the wrists. Her hair was pulled back in a neat bun, except for one tendril, which rebelled and slid forward into her face as she bent to pour the tea. She avoided looking at Elizabeth and Ainsley the entire time she was in the room.

"Thank you, Mary," Elizabeth said coolly. "Be sure to prepare a tray for Lillian."

Mary gave a slight curtsey and left quickly. Ainsley found himself watching her as she left, wondering if the waif was any older than Josephine.

"One of our newest girls," Elizabeth said, seeing Ainsley's interest. "She is still learning. Mother thinks it is our duty to take on inexperienced help to train them. She says sometimes experienced help come with their own independent ideas."

Ainsley brought his gaze back to Elizabeth, who had returned to her straight-backed, calm composure. She held an air of a woman completely in charge and, perhaps, she regarded him as yet another person beneath her who needed education and training to be admitted into her world.

"I must check on my sister now. She remains quite ill." She stood to leave and Ainsley rose.

"How does she fare?" he called, as Elizabeth turned away. She stopped at the door, looking over her shoulder.

Elizabeth did not answer immediately. "We thought she was on the mend. Now, we are not so sure."

"May I see her?"

Elizabeth's eyes grew wide at the notion. "Mother said I am to not let you venture out of this room. She does not trust you."

"The feeling is mutual then, for I do not trust her." Ainsley said, plainly looking at Elizabeth.

She looked aghast. "You cannot mean that!"

Ainsley raised an eyebrow. "Two people have died in this house and I am being denied the opportunity to save a third. You will allow me to treat Miss Lillian or you will find a magistrate on your doorstep by dinner time."

Chapter 10

Death has left on her
Only the beautiful

Ainsley peered from the hallway as Elizabeth opened the door to Lillian's chamber. He was not sure what to expect on the other side of the door. He imagined the middle daughter would be equally like Elizabeth and Josephine both. Blonde curls, pale skin, slight figure. His expectation was not far from reality.

Elizabeth walked into the room, allowing the housemaid, Mary, to enter before her. Mary approached the small bedside table and placed the morning's meal next to the patient. She looked to Elizabeth then, pausing a moment in case there were further directions. Elizabeth shook her head and motioned for the door with a slight tilt of her head. Mary slipped out, almost thankfully, and left the two sisters alone with the doctor.

Holding his hands neatly behind his back, Ainsley stood near the door. It was a rather large chamber room with one fairly impressive wood poster bed. There was a lone dressing table and wardrobe but that was all. No books, no toys, no adornments of any kind save for a delicate ivy pattern on the wallpaper and matching green drapes that framed two bright windows. Lillian was lying on her side in the middle of the bed, with her eyes fixated on something outside the window.

"How are you feeling today, sister?" Elizabeth asked, as she rounded the corner of Lillian's bed.

Lillian did not move from her reclined position. She clearly had no interest in the food that had been brought to her. She gave no indication that she was even aware that the doctor was there.

"You should eat before your food becomes cold,"

Elizabeth pressed, slipping into a bench placed at the window. "Lillian?"

"I am not eating," Lillian muttered, her voice muffled by the quilt on her bed. Her eyes shifted from the now obstructed view and she changed her focus to the intricate threads on her bedclothes. "I will not give you any more means by which to kill me."

"Lillian!" Elizabeth shot up from her seat and formed fists at her side. "How dare you suggest such a thing? I would never—"

"You wouldn't?"

"Come now, Lillian, you are simply overwrought." Elizabeth glanced to Ainsley then, clearly embarrassed by Lillian's behaviour. "This is Dr. Peter Ainsley," she started, gesturing to the door where he stood. "He's come from London to help."

Lillian grew more aware then, lifting her head from her pillow to look at the man in her room.

Ainsley watched the patient turn in her bed, her eyes darting from him to Elizabeth and back again.

Beneath white linens and a matching quilt lay a slight girl, young woman, actually. She looked solemn at first glance. Almost half-asleep and yet waiting for him. She was not the child he was expecting when he first arrived on the train. In fact, this girl was just as grown as her sister Elizabeth. She was blonde as well, but lacked the curls of both sisters. There was no mistaking the relation. Their faces gave their blood connection away.

From the bed, Lillian made no motion to invite him in further. Lillian was quite pale and sickly. Her head lay on the pillow, which was propped up against her headboard so that she may sit up.

"I wish to speak to the doctor alone," Lillian said at last.

"Mother would never allow it."

"Then it is a good thing that *Mother* is not here." The young woman spoke the word "mother" with utter contempt. Her mouth spat it out as if it hurt her to even think of it.

Elizabeth let out a breath, glancing to Ainsley and then back to Lillian. Ainsley could tell she was not pleased with the arrangement.

"Leave us," Lillian commanded.

"So be it," Elizabeth answered. "I will return within half an hour."

With the door closed after Elizabeth's departure, Ainsley remained at the foot of the bed. So seldom did he converse with his patients, it seemed odd to him and he was terribly out of practice.

"Good day, Lillian," Ainsley said.

"I saw you when you arrived yesterday." Lillian motioned toward the window and Ainsley could not help but look beyond the panes of glass. He smiled. She had a rather prominent view of the foregrounds of the house and the lane way that led visitors to and from the estate. "Why have you come?"

"I can help you."

Lillian snorted. "No one can help me," she answered with a teasing smile. Ainsley raised his eyebrow. He had never encountered a girl so refined yet distinctly defiant. "Mother would have something to say about that. She is very particular, you know. Has everyone on a very tight leash."

Ainsley could not help but smile. This description suited Mrs. Lloyd perfectly.

"You know her then," Lillian jested.

"We have met," he said, nodding.

"She does not respect doctors. She thinks that physicians are mostly quacks with little substance."

"She'll be glad to know I am a surgeon then. Not a physician."

Lillian gave a slight look of confusion matched with interest.

"Physicians traditionally heal using tonics, remedies, and pharmaceuticals. Surgeons, on the other hand, deal mainly with the inner workings of bodies and set about to heal patients using surgery and—"

"You cut open bodies," she said.

Ainsley hesitated. Normally, he would not converse with a lady on such a matter but Lillian looked genuinely intrigued by his profession. "In a manner of speaking, yes."

"What do you find?"

"All sorts of things. Certainly not a topic of discussion in the presence of a lady. An ill one at that."

Lillian seemed indifferent to his protest. "How many bodies have you...examined?" she asked.

He laughed nervously. "Enough to fill a graveyard," he answered. "All in the name of science, mind you."

Lillian smiled slightly. "Of course."

Ainsley took a seat at the very edge of the bench and sat rigidly while taking in all the information he could on this young woman on the verge of death. He knew that if she were to pass away in the night, he would be barred from examining her body as well. "You look pale," he said, meeting her gaze. She pulled her eyes away quickly.

"That's simply my face cream we brought home from Paris. The women there are divine with very few freckles." Lillian slid her hand over her cheek, smiling at the memory. "It's designed to make one quite pale."

"That is the fashion," Ainsley answered, recalling his own sister's plight for unblemished skin.

Lillian pulled herself up higher in her bed, clenching her teeth as she did so and then clutching her stomach as if moving brought on pain.

Ainsley stepped toward the bed. "I'm all right," Lillian said, putting her hand up. "Comes and goes."

"Stomach pains then? Any vomiting?"

Lillian nodded.

"Light-headed? Dizzy? Lethargic?"

"Yes on all accounts. I cannot keep any food down. My stomach churns and aches relentlessly."

Ainsley leaned in and reached his hand out to her face. Lillian flinched slightly as his hand came near. He stopped suddenly. "Oh, I am very sorry," he said quickly, pulling his hand away. "I am not used to dealing with patients who are awake. May I touch you?" he asked.

Lillian looked up to him and smiled. She nodded demurely and then braced herself for his touch. She closed her eyes and parted her lips slightly, taking in air, as Ainsley moved in closer.

Ainsley placed his hand over her forehead to check for fever. She felt somewhat cold and her skin had an odd texture to it. "Listless? Fatigued?" He pulled away to remove his jacket. He placed it on the window seat. He sat on the edge of the bed facing her and used both hands to reach out to her. "I am just going to feel around your neck."

She nodded and he reached behind her head, one hand on both sides and moved his fingers along her neck and the base of her hair. She moved to brush the loose hair from her shoulders when their hands touched.

"Sorry," she said, with a laugh, and pulled her hand away.

Ainsley could not help but smile. Their faces were inches apart but neither seemed to mind. As much as Ainsley wanted to remain professional, he could hardly concentrate with her eyes gazing up at him so intently. She certainly had adjusted to his touch rather quickly, it seemed.

Her muscles were very strong, he noted. Her hand had touched him with a strength he would not expect from a women who had spent weeks in bed. He could tell she was a tall girl, though naturally slender.

"Perhaps you should eat," he said, gesturing to the food on the table next to the bed.

"I do not eat what she brings me."

"What she brings you?" Ainsley slipped back and settled farther down the bed. "Why would it matter if she brings you the food?"

Lillian pulled her eyes away and began to study threads in her quilt again. "I get sicker when she brings me food. Yesterday, she seemed very upset to see I had not eaten."

"People who are ill need to keep their strength up. She is looking out for your well-being." Ainsley held up her chin so he could look into her eyes and examine the features of her face.

"She is poisoning me, I am sure of it."

Ainsley dropped his hand. "Poisoning you?" He remembered the letter she had sent to Dr. Bennett and would request to see it when he saw Bennett again.

"I became ill after Father. We were both terribly sick and then he died. I got better for a time and then Josephine fell ill and the pains came back." She bit her lower lip. "Elizabeth hates me, just like she hated Josie."

Ainsley let out a deep breath and stood up beside the bed. Was it possible for a woman to hold enough hatred to want to kill her younger siblings? Ainsley had seen babies in his examination room killed by their mothers, and he knew of fathers who beat their children in the city streets. Anything was possible. In his line of work, he knew there could be any number of possibilities. Even the wealthy were not immune. His own family troubles were proof of that.

He noticed two medicine bottles on a desk positioned against the wall. He reached down and picked one up to read the label. The first one, he recognized, was a tonic meant to settle the stomach. The next one targeted the bowels.

"Have you been taking your medicine?" Ainsley asked.

Lillian did not answer straight away. She sulked silently, most likely because Ainsley did not immediately agree with her assessment of the situation. Ainsley opened the bottles of tonic and breathed in their smells.

"Do you not believe me then?" she asked quietly.

"Too early to tell," he answered honestly. "I always try to gather facts before pointing fingers in any direction."

Lillian nodded, though her eyes gave a look of apprehension.

"I hear you are quite the pianist," Ainsley said with a smile.

"I was." Lillian's head dropped. "I have not played in months, though."

"You miss it, I can tell."

She looked up sharply, "How can you tell?"

Ainsley smiled and lifted a stack of sheet music from the desk and showed her his evidence.

"I can hear the notes in my head," she said, reaching for the sheets. Ainsley gave them to her. She glanced over them briefly before placing them beside her on the bed. "They remind me of Josie now." Lillian's face fell when she mentioned her sister. "I wonder if I will ever be able to play without expecting to hear her voice alongside me."

Hardly knowing what to say, Ainsley hesitated. It

was not often that he could converse with his patients, hear their life stories, and see their pain and sorrow. This new business of curing people contrasted boldly against his regular day-to-day procession of dead bodies. After a pause, he spoke, "I regret I never met her."

"You would have liked her. Everyone liked her." The morning was slowly becoming midday and Ainsley knew the funeral procession would begin soon. "You must be getting tired. I will leave you." He gathered his coat and made his way for the door. "Take your tonics as Dr. Bennett prescribed and I will check back... in a few days."

Chapter 11

*Still, for all slips of hers,
One of Eve's family—*

Ainsley was greeted at the bottom of the stairs by Dr. Bennett, who had come to the house for the funeral. While Ainsley had been with Lillian upstairs the house had woken and was now ablaze with activity. People, many more than could be comfortably contained, were filing into the foyer and parlour, many coming to pay their last respects before partaking in the funeral procession through town.

"How does our patient fare?" Dr. Bennett asked glumly.

"As good as to be expected. Severe gastric issues. Refuses to eat anything." Ainsley leaned into Dr. Bennett so no one else could hear. "A tad bit spoiled, in my humble opinion."

Bennett stifled a laugh. "Of course. She is a challenge, that one. All things considering, I think we can make some allowances for her behaviour, don't you?"

"I am not used to dealing with patients. Is it always this difficult?"

"And more," was Dr. Bennett's knowing reply. "Did you grab a cake?" Bennett held up a small black cloth package, wrapped neatly with a black satin bow. Ainsley recognized the favor as a funeral cake. A long-standing tradition dictated that a family in mourning provides the often-bland morsels for everyone who showed up at the funeral.

Just then, Mary, the young servant girl, appeared in a simple black frock with a deep basket nestled into the crook of her arm. With her free hand she handed Ainsley a wrapped cake. Ainsley caught her eyes for a moment as he thanked her but she looked away quickly, as if afraid to meet his gaze. Before he could say anything, she had moved on to the next person and continued to hand out the cakes.

"My ribbon is white," Ainsley said, showing the small parcel to Bennett. "What do you suppose that means?"

Bennett shrugged and Ainsley slipped the wrapped cake into his pocket.

With a tilt of his head, Bennett gestured toward the front door, and Ainsley nodded, feeling the need to break free from the tightly knit throng of people, more arriving each minute. He glanced into the parlour as they passed and saw a huddle of men, Walter included, gathered around Josephine's casket. Mrs. Lloyd stood nearby, a white handkerchief held to her nose as she directed the group. Elizabeth stood a few paces away, her hands folded in front of her, her gaze tight to the floor.

As if sensing his gaze she looked to him then, rising her head ever so slightly. Could it be, he wondered, as Lillian said. Could Elizabeth be poisoning her family one by one?

A moment passed and their mutual gaze was broken as the crowd swelled. Ainsley realized Dr. Bennett had made it to the fresh air of the outdoors and began maneuvering through the crowd to join him.

Once outside he noticed the entire length of the drive was awash with black carriages led by black horses, many of them stationed side by side to allow for more room along the procession route. Ainsley and Bennett stood watch just outside the door, surveying the high volume of people who had come to attend the funeral. The horse-led hearse was stationed directly in front of the steps, and two elegantly dressed coachmen stood at attention beside the open and waiting doors, ready to receive the body of little Josephine Lloyd. The team of six black horses, adorned with high black ostrich plumes on their bridles and silver-studded reins, pounded their hooves in anticipation, the activity around them causing them to become restless.

Ainsley could see women silently crying all around him, each finely dressed lady dabbing their eyes with lace handkerchiefs. Many of the accompanying men held folded black umbrellas in case the threatening grey clouds decided to open up. The sea of people gathered at the front of the house parted suddenly, as if almost on instinct, allowing the procession of six servants to carry the white and gold leaf-accented casket out of the front doors and down the few steps to the gravel laneway.

A loud gasp rose from the crowd and more than one person cried out as the pallbearers came forth. Stepping down the steps had caused the casket to tilt forward, revealing that the body was leaving the house head first. Bennett shook his head disapprovingly, and Ainsley glanced around to hear what people were saying as the casket was carried past.

"I don't understand," said a young man, who was standing next to him. "What is the matter?"

"Hush boy!" an older man, most likely his father, admonished.

Ainsley bent down, and lowered his voice. "It is tradition for bodies to leave the house feet first. If the body is removed head first it gives the soul a chance to look back on its life and refuse to rest in peace."

The boy nodded, his attention riveted on these macabre details, most likely finding it just as fascinating as Ainsley did.

"It is also said," Bennett interjected, "that the spirit will look back and beckon another to join him."

Instinctively, Ainsley looked up, knowing Lillian would be perched at her bedroom window in an effort to say good-bye to her sister. Sure enough, she was there, looking over the crowd with her fingers pressed up against the cold panes of glass. Ainsley could see she was crying freely, her lips trembling and body shaking as she stood there, watching, most likely wondering if she would be next.

When Ainsley looked back to the casket, the hearse doors were being closed and latched, signaling the start of the procession. Everyone scattered for their carriages en masse, aware that the hearse would only wait so long. As the people cleared the lane, the mist descended like a blanket and everything was quickly covered in a cold, unforgiving rain.

The hearse lurched into motion and led the way down the drive, proceeding slowly so the other carriages could follow behind. The train of carriages passed the manor gates, draped with mourning cloth, and began its journey through town before turning back to the small chapel on the outskirts.

Winding its way through the nearly empty streets of Picklow, the rather long and extravagant procession drew attention from everyone out that day. People murmured to each other as the hearse passed. Men removed their hats out of respect and children pointed and gawked at the spectacle of it all.

As the carriage rocked its way along, Bennett unwrapped his funeral cake and began to eat. Ainsley merely looked at his and set it aside. He'd have no interest unless it was laced with a bit of brandy.

"I am surprised Lady Lloyd allowed you to see her daughter," Bennett said after finishing his cake.

"I doubt the woman even knew I was there," Ainsley replied.

"What did you find out then?"

Ainsley shrugged. "I'm not quite sure. Elizabeth has followed her mother's lead and hates me."

Bennett nodded, as if none of this surprised him. "You are a doctor, son. You have little respectability among the noble classes. You are in a far worse position than I was. At least I am a physician. You, my friend, are a labourer."

Ainsley cocked a smile.

"Are you going to eat yours?" Bennett pointed to Ainsley's cake. Ainsley smiled and handed the old doctor his small portion.

The church was the largest building in Picklow and it dominated the landscape between Lloyd Manor and the village. Its stone exterior was nearly black with age and the web of stone walls marking the perimeter of the cemetery matched its dreary tone. Black smoke billowed from the church's chimney as parishioners filed in and took their seats in the pews.

After a somber service, not many stayed to view the internment. The misty cold kept most mourners away.

Ainsley and Bennett remained, taking a position alongside the family and the parish reverend, watching silently as the small casket was installed into the grave cut deep into the near frozen ground. It pained Ainsley to watch as the servants slowly lowered the ropes, Josephine's casket slipping further beneath the sod.

He allowed himself a bold glance at the few who ventured out to the graveside. Elizabeth closely guarded her mother, of course, who was crying loudly into a handkerchief. Walter stood a few paces away, vacantly staring like any dutiful brother would be expected, but showing little interest in the proceedings. A few servants, the butler and above-stairs staff mainly, stood just behind the family. A few curious onlookers from the village, oblivious to the cold and rain, gathered and watched the bereaved family say their last good-byes.

Their bereavement seemed subdued, muted even. Ainsley wondered if the reality of their shattered normalcy had hit them yet. He presumed it had not or else Mrs. Lloyd would surely have allowed him to examine the body to determine the root cause of her mounting misfortune, unless, Ainsley stammered in his mind, unless Martha herself was behind these illnesses.

His eyes grew wide involuntarily as he stared down the family, conjuring up possible reasons for Martha's desire to kill them all. His face hardened at the thought, the audacity of such betrayal. A self-sacrificing mother, tired of her lack of relevance in a world created for men, decides to take matters in her own hands. Plausible. He had certainly witnessed his own mother's struggle with the demands of the family and a domineering husband. The papers were rife with stories of female hysterics and all the manifestations they took. Suicide attempts, sexual affairs, sudden rampages, and divorce all fell under the umbrella of hysteria. Murder could be attributed to this phenomenon, he reasoned.

"Shady business, eh?" Bennett broke his train of thought.

"Entirely." Ainsley agreed.

A rain-sodden man, a gravedigger employed by the church, sliced into the mound of dirt with his spade and unceremoniously began filling in the hole that was Josephine's grave. Ainsley hesitated and moved forward as if he would halt the whole process. Josephine deserved justice. If she was poisoned it was his duty to find out how and ultimately by whom. If it was illness, he could save Lillian with one autopsy.

Ainsley could feel Bennett's eyes on him, and when he turned the old doctor's gaze burned into him, pleading with him not to make a scene. Ainsley ignored his silent pleas. Clearly, the old man was more interested in appeasing the family than finding out the truth.

Ainsley stepped forward, being careful not to fall into the six-foot deep hole, and approached Mrs. Lloyd just as she was turning toward her carriage. "Mrs. Lloyd, one moment, if I may?"

She turned, giving him her signature scowl. Evidently, she had not forgotten his brash treatment of her the night before. "What can I do for you, Doctor?" Her words came from her lips slowly, emphasizing doctor as if she doubted whether he was one.

"Please, if you love your daughter, I can help her. I can stop this man right now and it would give me a chance to examine the body."

"Are you suggesting I don't love my daughter?"

"Of course not." Ainsley hesitated. He looked to the grave, now even more filled in and then turned back to Mrs. Lloyd. "I can save your daughter. I can find the cause of Josephine's illness and I promise I will be nothing but respectful."

Mrs. Lloyd swallowed hard and shifted in place. Ainsley saw her lip quiver slightly as they stared at each other.

"I am a man of science, and we are on the brink of some amazing discoveries. Your youngest child need not die in vain. Let me help. I need to examine the body, properly. Lillian deserves this chance."

At the mention of Lillian's name, Mrs. Lloyd's scowl deepened and her eyes narrowed. "Dr. Ainsley, why do you presume yourself to know who should live and who should die?"

The question surprised Ainsley. He did not have an

answer right away.

"Can modern science save us all? Do all of us deserve to be saved?" Mrs. Lloyd raised an eyebrow and slipped her hand deep into her muff. "I have made my decision, and I am at peace with it. Now, excuse me, Doctor," She nodded and bent slightly in a curtsey before turning from him and walking to the carriage. Elizabeth remained briefly, looking at him.

"Elizabeth, think of Lillian."

Elizabeth turned sharply and retreated, joining her mother at the carriage door.

With a clenched jaw, Ainsley turned from the departing family and shoved his cold hands into his pocket. His flask was hidden deep within. Without care to any who watched him, Ainsley took some large gulps before replacing his flask in his pocket. He watched for many moments, lulled by the sound of the dirt being thrown on the casket, as Josephine's grave was slowly filled in.

The more Ainsley thought about it the more certain he was that Mrs. Lloyd was behind these misfortunes. She was so domineering and commanding in her house that there was no other who would be capable of pulling the wool over her eyes. She was either the murderous hand or she wasn't as domineering as she would have everyone believe. In Ainsley's mind she was murdering her family one by one, but he severely lacked the evidence to prove it.

"Come, Dr. Ainsley, the skies threaten rain." Dr. Bennett pulled Ainsley from the scene, just as the scattered droplets turned into a drenching rain.

Moments later, Ainsley and Bennett were climbing into their carriage. With his passengers aboard, the coachman commanded the horses to go forward, snapping the reins. Exhausted from the day, Ainsley and Bennett slipped deeper into their seats, both looking forward to an evening of rest.

The two doctors watched through the carriage window as their conveyance weaved through the rather large cemetery to the broad iron gates at the other end. In the distance, just outside the gates, Ainsley could see two darkened figures walking down a mud path leading away from the cemetery. He watched them as the carriage grew closer. It was a mother walking speedily, as a girl skipped along beside her, oblivious to the rain. As if feeling the young doctor's eyes on her, the woman stopped walking and turned to watch the carriage go by.

"Miss Dawson." Ainsley had not intended to say it aloud.

"What?" Bennett looked out the window. "Oh, yes. It was better that she stayed away. In the background."

Ainsley nodded, well aware of the doctor's need for peace. "Why do you suppose Mrs. Lloyd is displeased with Miss Dawson?"

"Oh the well-to-do are a strange breed. Us plebs have only to sit back while we fall in and out of favor at their whims. I doubt Miss Dawson did much to make them displeased." Dr. Bennett laughed. "Perhaps she looked at Mr. Lloyd for one second too long." Bennett let out a deep, exhaustive sigh. "I am hopeful Mrs. Crane will have some tea for us and perhaps something a trifle bit better than those funeral cakes."

Chapter 12

*Wipe those poor lips of hers
Oozing so clammily.*

The country house was not far and Margaret's long, nerve-wracking journey was almost at an end. She had visions of her father hunting her down and dragging her back to London. Every delay in their departure as they made their way south kept her on edge. Jonas had said little but his presence was enough to calm her erratic nerves.

"You've been unusually quiet, Mr. Davies," Margaret teased, as a way to keep her mind from the reason for her sudden trip to the country.

"Have I?" Jonas asked in a dismissive manner. He smiled when their eyes met. "Perhaps your company is all I need."

She slapped him playfully. "We should talk of something," Margaret said, with a raised eyebrow. "How is your work at the university? Is it all you expected?"

Jonas chuckled, almost nervously, and actively avoided her steady gaze.

"Peter told me you are well-suited there," Margaret pressed.

"Yes."

Margaret laughed but it faded quickly. "I do believe you are deceiving me," she said, "Very well." She adjusted her cape, pulling it in tighter around her shoulders. "I will keep my comments to the weather."

"Forgive me, Miss Marshall," Jonas said. "At one time I felt my work at the university suited me well."

"Is that no longer the case?" She gave a sly smile. "Have you found another place of employ?"

"No, not exactly." He avoided her gaze, his self-assured demeanor gone from his tone. Margaret's smile faded. "Why do you think I was free to escort you as I have? Would I not be expected at work in the morning?"

Margaret had not thought of that. She was so used to her family being free to come and go as they pleased, never limited by hours of work or demands of employers. She had not thought to ask if Jonas needed leave from work.

"You have not left your position, not for me?" She shook her head partly from disbelief, but partly from disapproval. "Jonas, how could you? Assisting a professor is a superior position...." Margaret's protest was short-lived when she saw the disparaging look on Jonas' face. "Oh. You did not resign."

"They terminated me last month."

"Last month! Jonas, why did you not say something? How have you been able to meet your obligations?" She did not mean to behave so familiar but she was shocked to find him in such circumstances while knowing where she had found him the day before.

Jonas returned to the arrogant demeanor she recognized. "I do not patronize gentlemen's clubs for the girls, Miss Marshall. I am well adept with a hand of cards."

"Jonas!" She could not say what disturbed her more, the fact that he admitted to playing cards for money or that he was so well-versed at the games that he was able to sustain himself. Margaret let out a deep breath. "Luck runs out," she said, after a long pause. "Peter will help you, when he gets back to London," she insisted. "I know he will."

"Your confidence reassures me." Jonas gave a half smile.

They sat in silence for some time, allowing the rocking of the carriage to lull them into a near sleep. The day was late with the last rays of sun creating a pink aura over the farmland in the distance. They had been either in a train or coach for most of the day and the November chill crawled beneath their skin. Margaret regretted not accepting the fur wrap the coachman had offered at the start of the journey.

She shuffled closer to Jonas, slipping her arm

under his and bracing herself against the rocking of the carriage by leaning into him. As the carriage rolled through the dark town the only building elaborately lit was the tavern. The others remained dark and dreary in the deadness of night.

"Once I see you installed at The Briar, I will seek a room in town," Jonas said, knowing the country home was not far from the village proper.

"You are my guest. I have invited you." She lowered her head to his shoulder. "It was so good of you to come," Margaret said. "Peter would have brought me, had he not been called away suddenly."

"What business does he have in the north?" Jonas asked.

"The hospital sent him. A girl died and her sister remains ill." Margaret pressed her lips together, imagining what it would be like to have such a tragedy hit their family. "Quite sad really."

"Indeed."

The Briar was a plain stone structure with little embellishment. Its windows were all perfectly aligned, one half of the house mirroring the opposite side, with a large door in the exact middle. The exterior was simple but the wealth of the owners was well known. The Marshalls had held the deed for over a hundred years and in recent years the summer home began to show its true age. Margaret remembered her mother's plans for improvement during the previous summers but her father had refused to fund them. He spent the majority of his time in the city and very rarely ventured from the sanctity of his townhouse or regular metropolitan haunts.

"He wishes me to leave here," Margaret remembered her mother saying at the time. "His plan is to drive me out and have me crawl back to the city. Well, roof or no roof, I am not living with that brute ever again!" Before then, Margaret had never heard her mother speak so harshly. Yet, it did not surprise her. Margaret knew from an early age that her mother had married the wrong man. She could never say why, of course. She just knew her parents were not well suited for each other and was thankful she rarely was in the same room with both of them together.

Perhaps that is where the rumours stemmed from. It was plain to everyone how ill-suited they were. It may all be just a misunderstanding, Margaret reasoned. She could hardly believe her mother was capable of having an affair. She was a beautiful woman but she was not the devious kind. She felt almost silly for dragging Jonas out of the city on such short notice. No doubt, she had overreacted, again, and would soon find out there was not an ounce of truth to what Delilah Robbins had said.

ᚕ ᚕ

Margaret would have been embarrassed to bring anyone else there, especially with the house being in such a state of disrepair, but Jonas was more like a brother and she trusted him far more than anyone who was embroiled in London society. Their arrival was not expected and no doubt the servants were nearly settled in bed.

"Did you send a telegram to your mother to expect us?" Jonas asked.

"There was no time," Margaret said apologetically. "Besides, why should I have to ask permission to visit my own family's house?"

The carriage driver stopped the horses at the foot of the steps that led to the front door. Jonas left the covered carriage first, pushing open the door and jumping the distance to the ground. He lowered the two steps for Margaret and then offered a hand to assist her down.

"Doesn't look like anyone is home, Miss," the driver called from his perch.

"Do not worry. I know someone is home."

Margaret and Jonas let themselves in, not expecting a servant to greet them. The coachman brought their small pieces of luggage up the steps and set them just inside the door. He left, with some sovereigns for his trouble, and was hopping into his carriage as Jonas closed the door slowly.

"There's a fire in the parlour," Margaret said, straining her neck to look down the hall and into a far-off room. "We should warm there and then I can show you to one of the guest rooms." Margaret slipped her cape from her shoulders and laid it gingerly on a nearby table for one of the servants to find in the morning. She smiled at Jonas in the dim light and grabbed his hand as an invite to follow her.

"Why do you suppose no one has come to greet us?" he asked.

"Everyone must be asleep," Margaret explained. "Father always said the servants at The Briar were far more lackadaisical about things."

The door to the parlour was left slightly ajar, and the blazing fire could be seen just beyond the opening. Margaret pushed the door in, intending to walk through straight to the elusive warmth when she saw a bundle move on the rug. It took a moment for her eyes to adjust to the dim light. Two people, a man and a woman, entangled on the rug without a stitch of clothing between them.

"What is going on here?" Margaret demanded, expecting to see one of the maids raise her head. She stepped further into the room but stopped when her eyes recognized the startled face of her mother, Lady Charlotte Marshall, looking up at her from under the naked man.

"Oh my God!" Margaret raised her hand to her face and tried to quickly retreat from the room. She collided with Jonas at the door and found herself melting into his arms as she cried.

"Did you see?" she asked from the folds of his shirt and jacket. "Did you see her?" she asked in desperation. She could feel Jonas's reassuring hands on her back as she clung to him.

"Yes, Margaret. I saw." He pulled her away from the door and huddled with her in the dark hallway until her uncontrollable sobs subsided.

Chapter 13

*Loop up her tresses
Escaped from the comb,
Her fair auburn tresses;
Whilst wonderment guesses
Where was her home?*

Mrs. Crane was indeed waiting for the two doctors when they returned to the house. She met them at the door, taking their soaking overcoats quicker than they could release their arms from them. "One could catch their death out in that rain!" she proclaimed, ushering them into the prepared parlour. She had a roaring fire in the hearth and tea with sandwiches waiting on a nearby table. "Really, Dr. Bennett, at your age you need to be more careful."

"At my age?" he exclaimed indignantly.

"Yes!" Mrs. Crane gave the elder doctor a defiant look. "I have no desire to be a nursemaid to an old goat like you."

Ainsley smiled at the exchange. Like an old married couple, they fought with loving vigor. A pairing as familiar to each other as salt and vinegar. Ainsley made himself comfortable in an awaiting chair and watched the insulted old goat do the same.

"Old goat indeed!" Bennett complained. "I have a mind to cut her wages if this abuse keeps up."

"You'll do no such thing," Mrs. Crane claimed knowingly. "Now get close to the fire, both of ye."

Not one to argue with the apparent matriarch, Ainsley did as he was told. It had been a dreary day but he hadn't noticed how cold he was until he edged toward the established fire. He felt his legs instantly become warm in front of him and instinctively he raised his palms to the embers.

"Pour yourselves some tea," Mrs. Crane called as

she walked by, motioning to the table set with teapot, and a service of tea for two. Some freshly baked biscuits also awaited them. Bennett poured tea for both and leaned in close to Ainsley as soon as Mrs. Crane left the room. "I will have some of whatever is in that flask of yours, if you please."

Ainsley raised his eyebrows at the old man but obliged. Together they spiked their tea and Ainsley had it safely deposited back in his breast pocket just as Mrs. Crane returned. Bennett smiled and winked at Ainsley before lifting the teacup to his lips.

Ainsley knew Bennett had seen him stealing some sips at Josephine's grave. He was normally more careful than that but, circumstances as they were, Ainsley felt he had no choice. With that encouragement from Dr. Bennett, Ainsley felt more at ease. He had made it a rule early on to hide his taste for brandy or whiskey, never knowing exactly who would make a fuss, especially with teetotalers on the rise. Bennett only spoke again after Mrs. Crane left the room.

"Don't let Mrs. Crane see you with that. She would have my hide if I drank openly in front of her."

"A teetotaler, is she?"

Bennett nodded. "Her husband, you see, never could hold his liquor. He died not long ago but she doesn't like to see anyone drinking. I haven't the heart to tell her it's my own house and I'll do as I please." Bennett bit into a jam-smeared biscuit. "She's the best housekeeper and cook I have ever had."

Ainsley nodded, sipped his spiked tea, and let the warmth of the fire seep into his chilled body. The heat slowly worked its way up his body as he sat staring at the flames of the fire. It did not surprise him that Bennett made peace with Mrs. Crane, never showing dominance, the same way he dealt with Mrs. Lloyd.

"How come you never thought to marry?" Ainsley asked, finally seeing an opportunity for one of his questions to be answered.

"Bah," Bennett huffed, shrugging his shoulders and sinking deeper into his chairs. "Never had a mind to. I was married to medicine, you see, during my youth, and I suppose as I got older I never thought anyone would have me." Bennett exhaled deeply. "What about you, Ainsley? Anyone catch your eye yet or are you destined to live your days like me?"

"Alone then?" Ainsley laughed despite of himself. "I would prefer the silence. Some peace and quiet when I came home." Ainsley recoiled at the thought of living as his mother and father did, in communal silence with only the muted tension between them. No such drudgery and pain would haunt him as it did his parents' marriage.

Bennett raised his teacup to his chin and let it hover there as if allowing the steam to warm him. When he spoke, vaporous wisps swirled in front of him, dancing between him and the rim of the china. "Peace and quiet is all well and good, but loneliness is like a prison. Once inside, it becomes harder to see yourself breaking free."

"I feel quite free, actually. Never in my life have I felt so free. Reminds me of my days in school when my father was not waiting for me in my room to scold me or reprimand me."

"But that, Dr. Ainsley, is what fathers are supposed to do."

Ainsley laughed. "You would not say that if you met my father. He strikes fear among children in the streets. He has a very commanding presence, not so unlike Mrs. Lloyd."

Bennett took a sip of his tea and placed the cup back on the saucer. "Ah, yes," Bennett hesitated, as if he didn't want to ask but knew the subject could not be avoided. "What do you make of it then?"

"It's quite possibly Mrs. Lloyd."

Bennett raised an eyebrow. "You are quite sure? So soon?"

"Those are crocodile tears if I ever saw them."

"Perhaps you are being a bit hasty," Bennett suggested.

"She is hiding something, Dr. Bennett. I would not trust that woman if my life depended on it." Ainsley sat back in his chair and crossed his legs.

Dr. Bennett leaned forward and looked intently at Ainsley. "'Tis not you're life I am worried about."

"Why do you suppose she is guarding the body so closely?" Ainsley asked. "Those two men she hired to watch the grave—does she expect them to be stationed there all night? There isn't likely many body snatchers in these parts."

"Well now," Bennett breathed somewhat laboriously, "we are not that far from London. For a while, the trade moved into the outskirts, since all the cemeteries in the city were under close watch. We have had a number of cases in these parts."

"You don't believe she is trying to keep us from the truth?"

"The truth?" Bennett's face gave way to realization. He paused for a moment, forcing a frown, while wrapping his chilled fingers around his teacup to warm them. "I have known the Lloyds for many years. She is a woman of impeccable character. Don't misunderstand me now, she is rough around the edges, but murdering her own child is unthinkable."

"And her husband?" Ainsley enquired.

Bennett shrugged. "That I cannot say. Their marriage was intense."

Ainsley gave him a quizzical look.

"Mr. Lloyd was a womanizer. There were four women that Mrs. Lloyd knew of. There may have been more. He was hardly home, traveling with the girls, for the mills and such, and when he was at the Manor things could grow physical." Bennett drew an audible breath again and pressed on. "I was summoned to the house one day. Mrs. Lloyd was concerned about her husband's... encounters. She was worried he had made her sick somehow. That it was a disease that caused her miscarriages."

"You said the miscarriages were the reasons for the large age gaps amongst the children."

Bennett nodded. "Four miscarriages. One after Walter was born. Two more after Lillian was born. The last one was two years ago, when she sent for me."

"What do you believe is the culprit?"

"Syphilis."

"So she was right?"

Bennett nodded again but could not meet his young

apprentice's eyes. "The old man brought it home years ago and she has been suffering all this time. It is a miracle those girls made it to term, let alone near adulthood." He sipped his tea. "Walter Sr. was a good man... with a wandering eye." In one smooth action, Bennett downed the last of his tea and replaced the teacup on the table with a slight thud. "If she killed the man, she has my blessing. But her own child, she could never stomach." Bennett rose and gave a fatherly pat to Ainsley's shoulder as he passed by on his way out of the parlour. Ainsley could hear him climb the stairs and assumed he had retired to his room.

❧ ☙

Ainsley remained reclined in his chair alone in the parlour, the warmth of the fire doing much to revive his near frozen appendages. The house had become quiet. The crackle of the fire and sounds of passing carriages out in the street beyond the window were the only sounds Ainsley could hear, and soon he was lulled into the first stage of sleep. The previous full day of travel, coupled with his very early start that morning, had finally caught up with him and he could not help himself.

A short time later, he was startled awake by Mrs. Crane, who had not realized he was asleep. "Dr. Ainsley," she said, "I can serve dinner to you in the dining room."

Bennett did not come down for supper that evening and Mrs. Crane excused the absence of Ainsley's host by saying the elder doctor was quite under the weather. "Serves him right," Mrs. Crane proclaimed, presenting a dish of lamb to Ainsley, who sat at one of the four seats at the modest table. A thin lace tablecloth hid the weathered wood beneath and the chair on which Ainsley sat rocked easily with the slightest movement.

"Gallivanting in this weather as if he were some young doctor. I keep reminding that man he's not as young as he once was." She sighed then, and wiped her hands on her apron.

"Won't you join me then, Mrs. Crane? I am not used to dining alone." Ainsley gestured for the seat opposite him.

Mrs. Crane paused for a moment, surveying the

table and its scarcity of diners. She must have felt sorry for him, the visiting doctor, alone at the table. For a moment, Ainsley thought she would decline; no doubt she was not used to eating with her employer or their guests. Ainsley was surprised when she agreed to join him. She left the room to retrieve her plate from the kitchen.

Ainsley waited until she was settled opposite him before taking a bite.

"You'll have to forgive me, Dr. Ainsley," she said with a hint of trepidation. "My table manners are quite rusty and I doubt a gentleman like yourself would appreciate my country manners."

"Not at all," Ainsley said in reply. "I am not so refined."

Mrs. Crane let a smile pass her lips and took a bite from her plate. After a time of no words passing between them Mrs. Crane finally spoke. "Your work is very interesting, Dr. Ainsley. How is it that you came to... to be a surgeon?"

Ainsley could tell she resisted the urge to refer to the bodies he dissected and the human cadavers he examined.

"A natural love of science is what led me to it," he explained.

Mrs. Crane smiled, as if relieved he did not reveal a more sinister reason.

"Your family must be very proud of you."

Ainsley tried to remain pleasant. "I am merely the second son, ma'am," he answered with a jovial smile, "of no importance, whatsoever." Mrs. Crane nodded but her inability to carry a conversation began to show.

"Have you been employed with Dr. Bennett for long?" Ainsley asked.

Mrs. Crane seemed startled by the question. "Oh well now, these last ten years or so. No wait, thirteen years." She gasped. "Has it truly been that long?" She looked at Ainsley with her eyes wide.

Ainsley smiled.

Nodding, she continued, "Yes. Thirteen years. I can tell you I was so glad to come work for a bachelor than some of those enormous houses. Now mind you, the pay is better there, yes sir, but this position has its own perks."

"You didn't work for the Lloyd family at any time, did you?"

Mrs. Crane paused, her fork positioned on her plate in mid motion. "That I did. For a short time, until my husband John begged me to find another employer. He never did like the Lloyds."

"And you?" Ainsley worked to create a lightness in his voice. "Did you like the Lloyds?"

Mrs. Crane hesitated. Her eyes shifted about the room and for a moment Ainsley thought she wouldn't confide in him. "No," she said at last. "Not at any time during the twenty months I worked there, but please don't say as much to anyone."

Ainsley's face fell into a conspiratorial grin, "Not a soul."

"I should hate to think if I ever needed another position that I ruined my chances by saying what ought not be said." She laughed nervously and Ainsley smiled in an attempt to ease her anxiety.

"I understand, Mrs. Crane."

The dining room fell nearly silent then, only the faint sound of cutlery hitting china broke the quiet.

"Miss Lillian, though," Mrs. Crane said suddenly, "she can play a fine tune. I enjoyed listening to her for hours while I turned the beds or polished the silver. Mr. Lloyd taught her, you know."

"Did he?" Ainsley asked.

"Yes. Lillian and he were nearly inseparable when he was home. For a while it seemed she was destined for stardom with those fingers. I think Mr. Lloyd would have liked that too."

"What happened?"

"I think Mrs. Lloyd didn't like the idea, you know, of a girl performing for…men and such." Mrs. Crane's voice dropped to a whisper and she shifted nervously in her creaking seat. "Performing is not a proper profession for a young lady of good repute. She is much better off where she is. God willing, she will find a good husband and put this entire tragedy behind her."

"Yes, God willing," Ainsley agreed, and if Mrs. Lloyd

was willing to accept his offer of help, he added silently to himself.

A few moments later their plates were empty. The housekeeper scoffed at Ainsley's offer to help clean up the kitchen and shooed him from the door when he tried to enter. "Go on with ye now," she laughed. "I'm sure you have enough on your hands with Josephine so recently dead and buried." She closed the door, barring his entry.

Ainsley slipped from the dining room and found his way to his lodgings on the second floor. He was only a temporary lodger, but a distinguished one, and Mrs. Crane had been careful to give the young doctor the best of the two guest rooms. It was the one at the back of the house, with windows looking out over the yard of mature elms and the lane that slipped behind the houses and into the fields beyond the village. The room itself was meager; a simple abode with four plaster walls, a post-beam ceiling and a wide plank floor. There was a bed, a desk, a chest of drawers but little else, save Ainsley's own trunk, neatly positioned at the foot of the bed.

The pristine condition of the room was a testament to Ainsley's preference to tread lightly. Since graduating school, he had apprenticed all over Kent and Norfolk, then performed a rather brief stint in Germany before gratefully accepting the permanent post with London's St. Thomas Hospital. His frequent travel allowed him to keep fewer attachments and, most importantly of all, gave him a myriad of excuses to avoid his father.

The house remained eerily quiet as dusk transformed into night. The ferociousness of the dark was staggering compared to the relative lightness of London, and Ainsley had yet to adjust. When he glanced out of the windows he was always shocked at the lack of light on the laneway or garden outside. In London, there was always a lamp, fire or some form of light illuminating the shadows, but in the country he found the absence of light very disconcerting. He had never noticed how much he relied on the light to ease the discomforting quiet but he missed being able to look beyond his window to the people, trees or carriages below, like he would have done in the city. His view was no more than dark motionless nothing. He could scarcely see beyond the windowpane.

Nonetheless, he forged on, burying his head in medical texts he commandeered from Bennett's study. Before he accused anyone of poisoning Lillian, he had to know for sure it was an intentional poisoning. He had a single lantern, and a small candle to light his textual journey. Both light sources couldn't provide much illumination but it would have to do. Ainsley sat at the writing desk by the window for many hours, flipping pages and pressing on. The reflection he made in the darkened window was a small comfort to his growing unease.

It was when the hairs on the back of his neck stood on end that he grew leery. He could feel a sensation, a bit like eyes staring at him from some unseen source. Instinctively he glanced out the window, squinting against the dim light to focus on what lay beyond the window. He did this many times before deciding to snuff the candles for a better view.

When he looked the second time, pressing his face to the glass, he saw nothing. Absolutely nothing. The moon was no match for the misty night sky, which dispersed and robbed the landscape of any light it could bring. Ainsley watched and waited but eventually he returned to his textbooks.

Chapter 14

Who was her father?
Who was her mother?

In the morning Ainsley was startled awake, having fallen asleep at his desk, texts and journals open beneath his arms. The candle had burned itself out, the wax once liquid, had slipped down the sides of its holder and spilled on the desktop before hardening on the surface. Realizing the hour, Ainsley snuffed the still-blazing lantern and closed the books, leaving them where they lay, before grabbing his coat.

He left the house without seeing anyone and began to retrace his steps through the woods toward the train station. He was not destined for a train but planned to visit Miss Dawson, whom he was told lived just beyond the station in a small cottage in a clearing.

The hour was early and much of the ground was covered in a silver dusting of frost that glistened in the orange morning sun. Ainsley could hear the gentle crunch of the frozen ground cover as he walked. It had only been a few days since he last walked this path but it was enough time for the majority of the leaves, once clinging to the branches above, to settle into a thick blanket on the ground.

The woods were much changed now, and only stark naked trees covered the landscape. The grey wrinkled trunks and branches more closely resembled hands and arms reaching for the heavens than mighty oak and ash trees, as they did in full foliage.

A horse and rider approached Ainsley at a relaxed canter and it took a moment before Ainsley realized it was Walter Lloyd who was mounted on the horse.

"Whoa!" Walter commanded, while pulling on the reins. The horse halted his steps with grace before letting out a soft whinny, which sent puffs of visible breath into the cold autumn air. "You are about rather early, Dr. Ainsley." Walter leaned on the horse's neck, clinging fast to the leather harness and reins in his gloved hands.

"I have come to the woods to think," Ainsley lied.

"Not many woods where you're from, I'd imagine," Walter offered with a laugh.

"That is true." Ainsley reached out and stroked the gelding's neck and mane. It had been a year since he last rode at his family's country estate.

"Do you ride?" Walter asked, seeing the doctor's yearnings.

"One of my mother's pet projects," Ainsley explained, stroking the horse's nose. The animal leaned into Ainsley momentarily, enjoying the attention before feeling the bit jerked in its mouth and reverting back to its intended purpose.

"If you have a wish to ride you are welcome to use a horse in our stables. Lord knows we have enough mounts to outfit the cavalry." Walter sat up in his saddle, pulling the reins in to maintain control of his horse. "Just ask Humphrey at the barn, he will see to you."

Ainsley smiled. "I would be grateful for the chance. Thank you."

Walter shrugged with nonchalance. Clearly, he was used to making offers and receiving gratitude.

"I apologize for my mother's treatment of you," Walter said. "She can be as stubborn as a mule."

Ainsley nodded. "Perhaps she just needs some convincing," he suggested. "Lillian would stand a far better chance."

Walter shrugged. "Perhaps. I will bring it up once more but I am warning you, Ainsley, do not hold your breath."

Ainsley chuckled.

"They are expecting me at the mill shortly."

Ainsley stepped away from the horse, giving them a wide berth to continue on their way. "Have a good day then."

Walter tilted his hat and kicked the sides of the horse, propelling it forward.

Resuming his walk Ainsley wondered which road or path led from the Lloyd manor house to this road near the train station. It seemed an unlikely route for a morning ride.

ಞ ಕಿ

Soon, Ainsley was walking past the train station, tipping his hat to the gentleman who ferried his trunk to Dr. Bennett's house, before heading down the south road that would take him to Miss Dawson's residence. He was not sure exactly which house would be hers but he knew, at least here in the country, he could find someone to point him in the right direction.

The young doctor walked for a time, thinking of all the information Dr. Bennett had shared with him the day before. Mrs. Lloyd certainly had enough motive to kill her husband if she were angered enough about his infidelity. With Walter Lloyd Jr. well into adulthood, she must have known if her husband died the family would maintain the lifestyle to which they had become accustomed. Killing her husband was revenge without changing anything else. It was the perfect murder.

Ainsley walked for quite a while before a small cottage came into view. Surrounded by a walled garden, with a weatherworn gate, the house looked like it belonged in the pages of a children's storybook. Ainsley imagined the garden was once overrun with sprawling plants and sweet flowers but, in the November cold the greenery had all withered and died away, leaving the gardens looking sparse and unkempt.

There was a girl in the garden, crouched down among the browned drooping stems, intently studying something in the fallen leaves. She was singing softly, her voice muffled by the brisk wind that swept through the clearing in the woods.

"Excuse me, would this be the Dawson house?" Ainsley asked from the road.

Upon hearing his voice, the girl sprang up from her place and ran for the forest of trees at the back of the house without saying a word. It did not matter. Her presence in the yard was enough to confirm that he was indeed at the right house.

His knock at the front door was answered swiftly. The woman he recognized from the wake and the funeral stood in front of him, dressed entirely in black as if still mourning. Her eyes were tainted with red and still held a glassy look like she had been crying. "I am not taking patients at present," she said softly. Her eyes avoided his and she looked down as she closed the door.

"I saw you yesterday at the cemetery," Ainsley said quickly, unsure if he should forcibly stop her from closing the door. "And I saw how Mrs. Lloyd treated you at the wake."

The door, which was slowly being closed, stopped and Miss Dawson peered out at him from the small space that remained.

"My name is Dr. Peter Ainsley. I'm a surgeon assisting Dr. Ben—"

"I remember now," she answered quietly. "Everyone talks in town when someone new comes near. Doctor or no doctor."

Ainsley smiled at this, agreeing with her observation. "I'm trying to figure out what killed Josephine Lloyd."

Miss Dawson nodded at the mention of the girl's name. With resignation she pulled the door open and stepped aside. Ainsley removed his hat as he walked past the threshold. The cottage was small but there was an astounding level of luxury found within. It was obvious to Ainsley that Miss Dawson took great care of her home tucked in the woods. She must receive quite a few patients here, Ainsley reasoned. Hanging above them from the beams were herbs and plants tied in bunches drying. A large shelf at the far end of the room was reminiscent of a general store and held various glass jars, some with liquids, others dry goods. Nothing was labeled.

Gesturing him toward the upholstered chesterfield, Miss Dawson chose a chair to the side. Ainsley waited for her to sit before taking his seat. Folding her hands on her lap, Miss Dawson swallowed nervously. "You should know I am no longer welcome at Lloyd Manor," she said plainly.

"She was quite angry. Mrs. Lloyd, I mean."

"That is her way," Miss Dawson smiled knowingly. "She is in mourning." Miss Dawson seemed willing enough to create excuses for Mrs. Lloyd's outlandish behaviour.

Ainsley gestured to her black attire, "As are you. You must have been close to the family."

She turned, partially hiding her face. When she looked back at him she was sniffing and blinking her wet eyes. "I was…" She paused then, before letting out a deep sigh of resignation, "I was there when Josephine was born."

"Were you there when she died as well?"

Miss Dawson hesitated, glancing up to see Ainsley intensely looking at her, eager to hear what transpired. "Last week Mrs. Lloyd contacted me and asked if I could help the girl. She was quite ill by the time I arrived." She pushed a loose strand of hair from her face. "I did the best I could. And yes, Dr. Ainsley, I was in the room when she died."

Ainsley nodded, seeing just how Mrs. Lloyd, in her grief, could come to believe Miss Dawson was responsible. "Was Mrs. Lloyd there as well?"

"No," Miss Dawson answered. "It was the early hours of morning. The house was asleep."

"Dr. Bennett?"

Miss Dawson laughed slightly then. "Surely you understand that Dr. Bennett and I don't generally see eye to eye on matters of medicine? I doubt he would abide by my presence."

"He tells me you are a medicine woman, a practitioner of the old ways."

"Yes, some call us much worse," she said. "I have delivered most of the babies here in this town in the last twelve years. I help the women with their courses, and can stitch up a wound without leaving a scar. I barter with my clients for services rendered, unlike Dr. Bennett. It took a while but some people don't seem to mind that I am a woman."

Ainsley nodded. He knew the stigma attached to the female gender, they were soft in mind and stomach apparently. Margaret would surely have something to say about that.

"I understand where this is going, Dr. Ainsley," Miss Dawson said with a deep exhale of breath. "The Lloyds would like to lay this tragedy at my doorstep. Soon everyone in the town will suspect me and refuse my services all on the say-so of one bereaved mother. I will be run out of town." Miss Dawson shrugged. "I did everything I could for that child, and more." She stood up then and walked to the window. Ainsley wondered if the woman could see her own daughter, who was about Josephine's age, playing in the garden. Miss Dawson stood there for some time, her eyes misting over and then she raised her hands to calm her quivering lips. She closed her eyes and turned abruptly then. "I am sorry I cannot do anymore for you."

Ainsley stood, yet still felt dissatisfied with what he had learned. "Do you know the Lloyds well? You have lived here long enough to judge their character. Perhaps you can help me decipher some family secrets so that I can find a motive or meaning to all of this?"

Miss Dawson's grief turned to amusement with Ainsley's suggestion. "Secrets?" she asked with a slight laugh. "Who doesn't carry secrets?" She looked out the window again. "I'm afraid I cannot help you, Doctor."

Chapter 15

Had she a sister?
Had she a brother?

The village was awake and in full speed when Ainsley returned. Three children ran past him, close enough to flip the tail of his jacket, as he made his way down the main thoroughfare of Picklow. Opening their shops for the day, vendors were displaying some wares just outside their doors. A barrel of brooms, bolts of fabric, and crates of apples began to line the streets as the early shoppers sauntered down the streets. Within a few minutes, he was turning off the main road and headed for Bennett's house.

Once inside, he found Mrs. Crane setting the breakfast table, wiping her hands on her apron as she appraised the meal she had prepared. "Oh, Dr. Ainsley, I was about to call up and enquire on you. Both you and Dr. Bennett have been in bed for much longer than is usual." It was then that she saw Ainsley's attire and realized he had just come in. "You have been up for some time, I see," she said, chuckling at her own mistake. "I shall go knock on Dr. Bennett's door." She rounded the table and made for the stairs. She was not gone for long before Ainsley heard her call out to him. "Dr. Ainsley!" Panic laced her words. "Come quick!"

When Ainsley came into Dr. Bennett's room, having run up the stairs, he was struck first by the smell that hit him full force. It was the smell of sick and bile, excrement and sweat. It was the smell of hospitals and morgues alike.

Ainsley saw his colleague twisted in the bed covers, unmoving as he lay on his side. "Dr. Bennett?" Ainsley asked as he approached. Mrs. Crane was sitting on the bed well enough away from Bennett's face, her hand touching the doctor's back as he lay still. Ainsley could see vomit slipping down the sides of the elder doctor's mouth, staining the white sheets beneath him. With Bennett's wide, glassy eyes fixed on him, Ainsley reached for Bennett's neck to feel for a pulse. "He's dead," Ainsley breathed. "Mrs.

Crane, he's dead."

Mrs. Crane's wailing startled Ainsley, who was not often so close to the scenes of death. In his shock, Ainsley closed his eyes and slid down into a wooden chair next to the bed. His body landed with a thud. For many moments he sat staring at the opposite wall, his head propped up by his hand, his elbow supported by the arm of the chair.

"This cannot be. This cannot be." Mrs. Crane's voice sounded like a far-off whisper to Ainsley, who was busy surveying the room and trying to piece together how Bennett had come to such an end. The white, porcelain chamber pot which sat next to Bennett's bed and directly beneath the elder doctor's head was overflowing with bile and vomit. The sweat- and excrement-stained bedclothes were twisted, no doubt as Bennett doubled over and fought off the bouts of sudden illness. His struggle must have been short, though not short enough for the pain he would have felt at the end.

Bennett's night shift was twisted as well and raised, revealing the man's feet, legs, and part of his buttocks. The sleeves were stained yellow with bile.

"What shall we do?" Mrs. Crane asked amidst sobs.

"Mrs. Crane," Ainsley began, finding his voice. "Fetch some warm water and new sheets. You and I shall restore him to dignity." Mrs. Crane left hastily and without another word.

Chapter 16

*Or was there a dearer one
Still, and a nearer one
Yet, than all other?*

The news of Dr. Bennett's passing swept through town. From pedestrian to street vendor, everyone was aghast. It was only a matter of time before the disbelief morphed into panic. If the infallible Dr. Bennett could fall prey to this unknown disease, then before long the entire town would be afflicted and they would all be looking to Peter Ainsley for answers.

Ainsley felt it best if he visited the Manor house to tell the Lloyds about the circumstances surrounding Dr. Bennett's death before any of the servants brought the news from the market that day. Recent circumstances being what they were, Ainsley doubted the already frail constitutions in the house would be prepared for the shock.

When he arrived he was shown into the parlour where Mrs. Lloyd and Elizabeth were seated. The room was much changed since the day before. The ornate mirrors had been replaced and freshly cleaned. The family portraits were unmasked, allowing the full splendor of the commissions to show. Ainsley could not help but let his eyes wander to a portrait of Lillian and Josephine that hung above the piano. Josephine was depicted in a long flowing cream dress. She had a thin blue ribbon tied at her waist, with some flowers attached to the ends. Lillian, who was much taller than her younger sister, wore a blue dress, the same shade as Josephine's ribbon. Both girls' hair was pulled back with a few curly tendrils cascading around their bare necks. A slight smile could be seen on Josephine's lips, but Lillian's face remained annoyed and ill-amused.

"Dr. Ainsley, won't you please come sit down?"

Mrs. Lloyd, still in her black dress of mourning, gestured to the sofa.

Ainsley nodded and took his place. "Thank you for agreeing to see me, Mrs. Lloyd."

"Seems we are never to be rid of you," Elizabeth said under her breath, keeping her eyes to her needlepoint. Ainsley could not decide if she had intentionally said it loud enough for him to hear. He chose to ignore the comment, as did Mrs. Lloyd. "You have noticed our change in decor. To be honest, I am glad it is over. I will still wear my mourning clothes but we must continue living."

Ainsley winced at her words. It did not seem right that he should be bringing them such news on the day after Josephine's funeral. For a moment, he thought to conceal the true reason for his visit but then he thought better of it. Surely they deserved to know.

"What is the matter, Dr. Ainsley?" Elizabeth asked slyly. "Does the subject of death revolt the necropsy doctor?" She almost laughed then. She was teasing him, though her tone denoted a more sinister motive. It occurred to him that what he was about to tell them would certainly give her more ammunition.

"There has been another death, I am afraid," he said at last.

The benevolent smiles quickly faded from the faces of the women. At last, having refused to acknowledge his presence long enough, Elizabeth lowered her handiwork and looked at him. "What do you mean? Who died?" she asked before her mother raised her hand to hush her.

"Elizabeth, please. Allow the man to speak."

Chided, Elizabeth titled her head and pursed her lips. Ainsley tried to ignore her stare but kept finding his gaze drawn back to her.

"I am sorry to tell you… Dr. Bennett died sometime last night."

Gasps filled the room, not only from in front of him but behind him as well. Ainsley turned to find the servant, Mary, who had been returning with a tray of tea. She looked as if the shock would dislodge the burdensome tray from her grasp. Ainsley rushed to her, taking the tray before the contents were scattered everywhere.

"Mary! Contain yourself. Now go ask Cook to give you something to busy you!" Mrs. Lloyd commanded over Ainsley's form as he placed the tray on the table between them. Mrs. Lloyd turned to Elizabeth then, "I certainly do not know why I keep that girl in my employ."

Ainsley took his seat before Mrs. Lloyd addressed him again. "Are you quite sure?" she asked, concern spreading over her face, her annoyance with Mary a distant memory. "Oh, of course you are," she said in answer of her own question, remembering his profession. Her face fell then, the realization hitting her. "I am sorry to hear it," she continued, giving a quick glance to Elizabeth beside her. "He was a good friend to our family."

Elizabeth nodded though Ainsley could not be sure if she performed this gesture out of genuine recollection or out of duty.

"I suspect Dr. Bennett has died from the same affliction as Josephine," Ainsley explained.

"Truly? You have reached this conclusion so soon?" Elizabeth asked suddenly, before being able to stop herself.

Ainsley nodded and was careful to keep his gaze straight and unwavering. Elizabeth's lack of sentiment was concerning. "Yes, I must perform a postmortem exam to be sure—"

Mrs. Lloyd gasped, but Elizabeth only gave a slight glance in her mother's direction. Mrs. Lloyd clutched her stomach then and, raising her other hand to her lips, gestured as if she would be sick. Ainsley saw Elizabeth sigh slightly at her mother's dramatics. It was obvious Elizabeth was made of sturdier stock than that of her mother. Perhaps it was her upbringing that made her behave more like the second eldest female of the house. "Do not speak of such things," Mrs. Lloyd warned.

"Mother hasn't the stomach for...well for most things, actually," Elizabeth whispered, knowing perfectly well her mother could hear.

"I am afraid I must, Mrs. Lloyd," Ainsley pressed, "I must implore you to revisit the matter of an examination of Josephine."

Another audible inhale came from Mrs. Lloyd's direction. She began fanning her face with her needlepoint hoop and slowly taking in concentrated breaths. "I cannot," she spat. "Such a vile act." Mrs. Lloyd sneered and wrinkled up her face at the notion.

"Is it not too late then?" Elizabeth asked. "There is still a means to determine a cause of death?"

"Absolutely," Ainsley replied. "Until there is but hair and bones scientists can gather much information from a corpse."

Mrs. Lloyd was sure to faint then. She flew back into the cushions behind her and abandoned her fanning altogether. Placing a hand to her forehead, she massaged her temples and closed her eyes.

Ainsley had forgotten himself, but more importantly, he forgotten his audience, two women who no doubt had never been called upon to hold such a conversation. For a moment he had thought he was talking to his sister Margaret, who would neither flinch nor coo at such a phrase. If Ainsley meant to be granted permission he must become better at presenting his case.

"I assure you, Mrs. Lloyd, I will proceed with the utmost respect and dignity," he explained. "If you hold any hope of saving your daughter Lillian—"

The young doctor was interrupted when Mary reappeared. "Excuse me, ma'am! It's Lillian, she's taken a turn."

Elizabeth rose instantly but Mrs. Lloyd remained seated, assured that her eldest daughter would see to it. Ainsley stood as well and reached for Elizabeth's arm before she was able to brush by him. "May I be of assistance?" he asked.

Elizabeth hesitated. She did not move or jerk her arm away and she met his gaze squarely, as if searching his face for sincerity before finally relenting. She did it because she must, Ainsley realized. No other accredited doctor was available and it was in that moment she realized it. "Come with me then."

Chapter 17

*Alas! for the rarity
Of Christian charity*

As Ainsley, Elizabeth, and Mary reached the second-floor landing, Elizabeth held her hand out to Mary, as if expecting something to be placed in it. "The key, Mary," she commanded. The servant swiftly obliged and placed the black iron key into her mistress's hand and Elizabeth quickly used it to unlock the door to Lillian's room. Ainsley stood puzzled for a moment. The room had not been locked before. He wondered why the family chose to lock the sick girl in her room.

Upon entering the room, they were struck by a pungent, putrid smell, reminiscent of the one that had surrounded Dr. Bennett's own deathbed. Lillian was writhing in her bed, the quilt and sheets twisted around her as she moaned in agony. Clutching her stomach, she rolled to the side of the bed, throwing up in the chamber pot.

Elizabeth stood back, content to watch her sister in pain from a distance, while Ainsley charged for the bedside. Sitting behind her, Ainsley pulled Lillian's copious blonde tresses, matted and frizzy from too many days in bed, and finding a clip at her bedside, fastened them behind her head. Lillian leaned back then, allowing her head and shoulders to rest on his legs. Her eyes were but slits of the bright blue oceans that gazed up at him inquisitively the day before.

"Mary, take her pot and bring a fresh one. We need water and some rags if you have them," Ainsley ordered. Mary was away from the room instantly while Elizabeth only came close enough to lean on the bedpost at the foot of Lillian's bed.

Ainsley felt for and counted Lillian's pulse all the

while, feeling Lillian's strength seeping from her body. "Her heart is weak," Ainsley said. "Has she eaten anything today?" he asked turning around sharply to look at Elizabeth.

Elizabeth shrugged. "The servants bring her food but I can't say whether she eats it."

Ainsley looked around the room. "Where is her service tray? Her dishes? What was she served?"

"I'd have to ask Cook," Elizabeth answered in near panic. Ainsley could not decide if she was concerned for her sister or if she felt she would be blamed. "I can't rightly say. She'd been on a strict diet of beef tea, though she has not had an attack of late, so perhaps we have become a bit lax."

Mary returned with a fresh chamber pot, while another servant arrived with towels and jugs of both warm and cold water.

Ainsley spent the next hour at Lillian's bedside, administering a cold compress and assisting her during her bouts of vomiting. With each passing episode, Lillian grew more and more weak. Ainsley found himself in utter agony, watching her life slowly slip away from him, but he knew of nothing he could do to save her. As a surgeon, he didn't know about treating illnesses, only the details of what caused them. What he performed while caring for Lillian was merely a replay of what he had seen his mother do when his siblings were sick. He knew, even as a child, that there was no miracle potion or tonic that cured him of whatever ailed him. He knew it was simply her presence that gave him strength enough to recover, and that was precisely what he intended to give Lillian.

After nearly two hours, the bouts seemed to have completely passed and Lillian's heartbeat became a little bit stronger. Her head lay on her pillow now, no longer cradled in Ainsley's arms, though he remained close at her side. When her sickness left her and she could open her eyes she looked up at him as he leaned over her. She raised her hand to his face and smiled. "I knew you'd come," she whispered, before being lulled into a restful and deserved sleep.

After giving the maids instructions on how to help Lillian should her illness return, Ainsley washed his hands in the basin next to the bed. He was weary though relieved to see her on the mend. While drying his hands he noticed the two bottles of tonic from the day before. Lillian must have taken some of these, he thought, eyeing the liquids inside each container. Something must have caused her recurrence. He slipped the bottles into his jacket pocket and turned to leave.

He found the stairs to the kitchen behind the main staircase at the back of the house and boldly walked down the narrow passage. Once over the threshold the room opened up into a sizable kitchen with red brick floors and well-worn wood countertops running along both walls. The room was dark, the only natural light seeping in through a pair of small windows installed along one of the stone walls. The kitchen remained cool and slightly damp, despite the hot fire blazing in the hearth on the opposite wall.

A blackened cook stove, with a large steaming pot placed on top and a copper kettle besides, was at the very back of the room. Sprigs of herbs were hung from rafters, drying, while defined streams of diluted sunlight beamed in from the slim windows over the cupboards.

Ainsley could smell cheese curing in a not so far off room and the familiar scent of homemade ale. He smiled at the domesticity of it all. He had to remind himself that even though the family was of a higher standard than most, their roots ran deep in country traditions. In these pastoral towns, manor houses would still partake in the coming and going of the seasons, something nearly forgotten among the wealthier families of London.

There were five servants in the main part of the kitchen, preparing vegetables and dough. One rather large woman lingered near the hearth, pouring hot liquid from the black kettle into a pot set upon an iron spider. "Lizzy, those potatoes need to be cut finer than that!" she commanded from her position at the end of the table. She must be Cook.

She took notice of him then, standing at the door to the kitchen with his jacket thrown over his arm and the sleeves of his dress shirt rolled to above his elbows. "Ye be the doctor, eh?" she called out from across the room.

"That I am."

"How is she?" the girl named Lizzy asked. "Is she recovered?" Her voice was laced with genuine concern.

"For the time being." A collective sigh went around the room and some of the servants raised a hand to their chests in gratitude.

"It is very nerve-wracking to us to think one day someone will come down those stairs and tell us she has passed, as was done when Josephine died," Cook explained. "Back to work, girls. Only thing that can save this family is food." She clapped her hands and Ainsley watched as the gang doubled their pace. "Come in, Doctor. I will fetch you a spot of tea."

Ainsley carefully made his way across the room to Cook. He saw a small room to one side and peered in. The walls were lined with shelves, each one lined with an array of various crocks and jars. Below the shelves were barrels of squash and pumpkins and apples, and pears in baskets on the floor. "The pantry?" he asked, cocking his head to indicate the room.

Cook beamed with pride. "Yes," she smiled. "Most of it was grown here on these grounds. We had a good year..." her voice trailed off as her face fell, "garden-wise, I mean."

"Of course," he said, while continuing to look around. He caught a glimpse of a pot simmering on the stove. "Is that apple butter?" he asked leaning in to take in the aroma.

"It's Lizzy's here," Cook said, nodding to the girl cutting potatoes.

Lizzy beamed but did not stop her task. "'Tis my grandmother's recipe," she said.

"Smells like what my mother used to make," Ainsley said with a smile, trying to hide his lie. His mother was never permitted near the kitchen.

"You can have some," Cook said, obviously proud of the productivity of her kitchen. "Meg, cut some bread for the starving doctor." Cook looked back at him then, giving him a long once over. "You look like you could use a good meal."

Ainsley was famished. His work with Lillian had drained much of his energy. However, he had no wish to join Josephine and Dr. Bennett in the village cemetery. If these deaths were a case of poisoning, it could have very well been one of these ladies who administered the fatal doses.

"I wanted to ask about Lillian's meals."

Cook eyed him suspiciously. "What is wrong with her meals?"

"She never eats them anyway," Mary said from behind the cook. Cook turned, raising her wooden spoon as if she would strike the girl. Mary flinched, and gave a look of relief when the blow did not come.

"Off with ye!"

Mary quickly backed away to the other side of the single long table that dominated the center of the kitchen.

Cook turned to Ainsley. "These young'uns have a lot to learn about speaking when spoken to. These mill towns spoil all these girls. Gets ideas into their head." Cook sighed as she poured water from the large copper kettle into a dainty white china teapot. "It's getting harder and harder finding decent help with d'em mills promising higher wages." Cook poured some tea into a small china teacup and presented it with the saucer to Ainsley. "Here. A restorative." She smiled.

Ainsley accepted the cup and saucer. He had seen her make the tea with his own eyes, and unless the water was laced with some poisonous substance, Ainsley felt he was safe to drink it. Then Cook prepared her own from the same pot and Ainsley knew it was safe to drink.

When he glanced around the room, he saw that the butcher's block working table was now empty and cleaned and all of the kitchen girls had left. Two mismatched chairs, with chipped and peeling white wash, had been pulled from the other room and set on either side of the table closest to the fire. "Take a seat, Doctor. You must be tired from caring for your patient."

Ainsley took a seat opposite Cook and she placed a small plate of gingersnaps between them. He waited until she took one before he took a bite out of his.

"So old Dr. Bennett passed away, did he?"

Ainsley couldn't hide his surprise. "News travels fast."

"Aye, it does." Cook took a sip of her tea. "I am

worried about you."

"About me?"

"The Lloyds are a strange bunch. Weren't worth much before Mr. Lloyd inherited those mills. He was a dabbler. A flighty sort with little drive for anything other than women and music." Cook whistled.

Ainsley raised his eyes, "I heard he was a talented piano player."

Cook shrugged, and waved a dismissive hand. "I don't know much about talent. He could play a might bit better than I, I can tell ye that. Lillian was just like him, flighty yet serious about that piano. And he was hard on her. Rapped her knuckles until they bled some days." Cook shook her head and took another cookie from the plate between them and pushed the plate toward Ainsley.

Ainsley happily took another biscuit but shook his head in disgust. "That's barbaric."

"Aye. No matter who those girls performed for, Queen Victoria herself, it t'were never good enough for 'im... and then he died. When Lillian fell ill she stopped playing."

"She plays in her head," Ainsley confessed. He held his teacup in both hands to warm them.

"Does she now?" Cook laughed. "I'd give anything to hear that piano start up again. We'd 'ear those girls and their sweet songs all day long while slaving away down 'ere. T'was like working beneath a dance hall or opera house."

"How did Mrs. Lloyd feel about her daughter's career on the stage?"

"Oh, she hated the idea. I overheard her say, more than once, that no daughter of hers would have such a vile calling. Expected her daughters to marry well, she did."

"Why do you suppose Mr. Lloyd wished for the girls to perform?" Ainsley asked.

"For the money, of course. He's run through his inheritance and the mills leave little enough to keep this manor running. The servants 'ave ears, you know. We hear things. The Lloyds are on the verge of losing it all." Cook sighed. "Mrs. Lloyd would never say as much. So prideful she is, Miss Lloyd as well. Neither one of them wants to let on."

Just then the door to the kitchen opened and both

Ainsley and Cook turned to see Elizabeth enter the room. "Oh, I thought you had gone home, Dr. Ainsley."

Ainsley stood up and tucked his chair back under the table. "Do you mean London, or Picklow?"

Elizabeth smiled slightly. "Either one."

Ainsley could hear Cook clicking her tongue quietly at the manner in which Elizabeth was speaking to him. He felt a reassuring pat from Cook's hand on his shoulder as she walked behind him.

"I see Cook has offered you something to eat." Elizabeth walked the perimeter of the butcher block table, careful to keep her hands clasped in front of her. She stopped directly in front of him. "You must not believe Lillian's accusations that we are poisoning her." In an eloquent show, Elizabeth reached for a cookie and bit into it. "We have no murderers here."

Ainsley's eyes remained locked on hers, "That remains to be seen."

She narrowed her eyes at him. "Is the patient quite well now?" she asked.

"Lillian is sleeping peacefully. I have assigned Mary to watch over her."

"Mary has her own duties. You should not presume to give orders to my family's servants." Elizabeth walked past him, running her fingers along the butcher block as she rounded the corner. She stopped on the other side of the table. "Perhaps that is more evidence of your spotty upbringing."

Ainsley had to work hard to bite his tongue. As much as he wanted to reveal that he was, in fact, born of a much higher rank than her, he knew he could not do so without risking his entire career. "My responsibility is to the patient. Lillian should not be left alone at this time. If her condition deteriorates again, summon me."

Elizabeth raised her eyebrows. "Is there anything else, *Doctor*?"

"I'd like to revisit the matter of Josephine with Mrs. Lloyd before I leave."

"Mother has refused your request," Elizabeth answered bluntly.

"I must protest," Ainsley answered, without

thought. "Lillian's chance for survival rests in my ability to determine a cause."

"Then you shall have to determine the cause through other means." Elizabeth did not flinch. She remained composed and staunchly indifferent to Ainsley's plea. "My mother is not keen on having her dead child's body butchered—" Elizabeth stopped short, perhaps realizing her insult.

"I do not butcher bodies," Ainsley answered coolly, wondering if anything he said made any difference to her.

"The mere thought of it is revolting" Elizabeth continued, ignoring him. "I cannot say I blame Mother for her decision. I doubt I would say differently if it were my own child."

"You say this knowing full well it could save your sister's life."

Elizabeth shrugged. "Perhaps I believe in your abilities, your resourcefulness."

Ainsley straightened his stance, pulling his shoulders back, not in a gesture of intimidation, but more out of exasperation. "Tell her I am disappointed to hear it," he said, bowing slightly, signaling his departure, and turned. He was nearly at the stairwell that would take him to ground level when Elizabeth spoke up, raising her voice slightly so he could hear her.

"Dr. Ainsley, are you so used to examining dead bodies to determine a cause of death that it has not occurred to you that there are other means by which to find the answers you seek?"

Ainsley turned at the sound of her voice. "Other means?" he asked cocking his head to one side.

Elizabeth nodded smugly. "There is far more to learn from those still living than those who have departed."

He did not wish to tell her he had been investigating the death since the moment he stepped off the train. He played his cards close to his chest and he was not going to be tricked into giving information to one of his prime suspects.

"I look to the bodies of the victims, Miss Lloyd, because dead people never lie."

Chapter 18

Under the sun!
O, it was pitiful!

    Margaret had never dreaded a morning so much. She lay in bed for quite a while, watching the sun's light become brighter and brighter until she was unable to deny the arrival of the day. She dressed soberly, all the while dreading the next meeting she would have with her mother. The topic could not be avoided. Margaret would have to confront her, demand an explanation, if one were to be had. If anything, Margaret hoped getting caught would halt her mother's illicit affair, and perhaps it could go a long way to repairing the family's reputation.

    The main floor of the house was quiet and for a moment Margaret thought she had been left alone in it until she heard her mother's unmistakably sweet laugh. Margaret found Lady Charlotte Marshall sitting opposite Jonas at the family's large dining room table. A modest spread of breakfast was on the table between them, but Margaret could tell they had already eaten and their dishes had been cleared.

    "Margaret dear!"

    Margaret cringed at her mother's attempt to appear docile.

    "We were just about to come find you. I was worried when you had not come down. Are you feeling well, my dear?" Lady Marshall smiled as she lifted her teacup daintily to her lips.

    Margaret looked to Jonas with wide eyes. How could she pretend nothing had happened? Jonas forced a slight smile but shifted uncomfortably in his seat.

    "She looks well enough, doesn't she, Jonas?" Lady Marshall asked.

"She looks splendidly well," he replied.

"Come, Margaret, sit with me, my dear." Lady Marshall patted the padded seat next to her. "Jamieson, fetch a plate for Margaret." One of the few remaining servants at The Briar, Jamieson bowed slightly and left the room.

Margaret slowly walked to her mother's side of the table while exchanging glances with Jonas. She slipped into the seat that her mother had indicated. Lady Marshall handed Margaret a napkin, which Margaret unfolded and laid over her lap.

"I am afraid the food is a bit cold. We had not expected you to be such a late riser." Lady Marshall laughed. "But I suppose your journey has been a tiring one." Lady Marshall moved all of the serving trays so they sat in front of Margaret. "Next time, however, I'd like a bit more notice."

Of course, Margaret thought, more notice to hide away your lover.

"So I can properly prepare your room," Lady Marshall continued.

Margaret could hardly believe what she was hearing. Was her mother behaving this way because Jonas was sitting across from them, or did she truly believe Margaret would have forgotten, or worse, forgiven her so quickly.

"Mother!" The room fell into a strained silence and Lady Marshall stopped her fidgeting with the serving utensils and trays of breakfast food. Margaret's voice was louder than she intended but no one could mistake her frustration. "I saw you!"

Lady Marshall stared at Margaret for a long while and Margaret actually thought her mother would drop the charade and confess to being unfaithful. Jamieson returned and quietly placed a plate in front of Margaret.

Lady Marshall finally spoke. "Saw what, dear?"

"I saw you and that man in the parlour—" Margaret closed her eyes, willing herself to forget the sordid scene. She could not finish her sentence without recalling everything in vivid detail.

Lady Marshall smiled demurely, giving Jonas an

apologetic look. "Margaret dear, you must have been dreaming. I was in my room when you both arrived, sound asleep."

Margaret shook her head. "I know what I saw."

"Have some ham dear, and perhaps we should order you some soothing tea. You must be overtired from your sudden journey."

Margaret's jaw clenched involuntarily and she could feel every muscle in her body tightening. Her mother meant to ignore the entire incident. Perhaps she thought her daughter would never betray her secrets. Margaret knew if she did so no member of their family would be immune to the scandal and fallout.

"Jonas was telling me Peter has been sent to the north," Lady Marshall said with a smile to their guest. "He is a mother's pride and joy. I couldn't be any more proud of him if he was personal surgeon to the queen."

Margaret clenched her fists, and stood suddenly, depositing her napkin in a crumpled heap on her untouched plate. "You should be ashamed of yourself!" Margaret hissed.

Lady Marshall looked as if she could laugh at Margaret's ill-timed outburst. "Really Margaret," she said, glancing to Jonas, obviously concerned about his impression of her, "What can possibly be wrong now?"

"You think I won't tell Father? You think I won't run back to London and let him know what you have been up to here."

Lady Marshall's self-assured smirk did not leave her face. "You think your Father does not already know?" she asked, raising an eyebrow.

Margaret could feel her heart beating rapidly beneath her tightly pulled corset. She struggled to keep her breathing steady but knew she had to leave the room soon or else all the dishes would find themselves broken on the floor beside her.

Lady Marshall turned from Margaret and reclaimed her lighthearted, singsong tone. "If you feel you need to return to London so soon after arriving then that is your choice, Margaret dear." Lady Marshall looked up to her daughter, the earlier challenge in her eyes gone, replaced by the demure and sweet mother Margaret remembered from her youth. "This is your home and you will always be welcome here."

Margaret left the room, feeling her eyes well up with tears as she reached the main hallway. She held to the handrail, took two steps, and felt a hand on hers. She looked over to see Jonas. "She's denying it all," she said, allowing the tears to stream openly down her cheeks.

"I know," he said calmly.

"I don't care if Father knows. It's not right. It's shameful." She raised her hand to wipe a tear from her cheek. "I can't stand to be here a moment longer."

Jonas nodded but did not move his hand from hers. "Tell me what to do, and I will do it," he said quietly. "Tell me where you want to go, and I will take you."

Margaret felt drawn to him. Despite her distress, she felt calm with him near and wanted to be nearer still. She searched his face and leaned into the bannister, placing her face inches from his. Any closer and her eyelashes would brush his cheek. She thought he would kiss her, and wanted him to, desperately.

"Jamieson!" Margaret saw her mother saunter into the hallway. She stopped when she saw Margaret and Jonas huddled close together at the bottom of the stairs. Instantly, Margaret stepped back from Jonas and pulled her hand away. "Oh. My apologies dear, did not mean to interrupt." Lady Marshall gave Margaret a self-satisfied smirk as she passed them. "I suppose I should discourage such impropriety." She smiled forcibly and patted Margaret's wet cheek with the palm of her hand before retreating to another room.

Margaret narrowed her gaze as she watched her mother walk away. Her eyes met Jonas's but she dared not move any closer. "I have to go see Peter."

Chapter 19

Near a whole city full,
Home she had none.

Ainsley stood at Bennett's body, his arms folded over his chest, postponing the inevitable. He would have to cut open his new acquaintance, dare he say friend, and it was a dissection he'd rather have avoided. He had to undress Bennett himself, not willing to subject Mrs. Crane to any further discomfort. She seemed to be taking Bennett's death very badly and since helping Ainsley clean up the original scene, she had refused to cross the room's threshold, or even look at the body.

Not moments before Ainsley had disrobed Bennett, removing his night shift and socks, and performed the cumbersome task of washing him. Had Ainsley been in his own morgue he could have performed these tasks with greater ease. Using a pitcher of warm water, a basin and various cloths and sponges, Ainsley gingerly bathed Bennett one final time. He took greater care with his colleague's body than he would have were it a perfect stranger. The duties he performed were no longer just the business of medicine, they had become quite personal.

With Bennett covered, Ainsley procrastinated. With his arms crossed and his eyes fixated on the body in front of him, the young doctor hesitated. For a moment, he wondered if he could do it, if he could actually cut open a person he knew, a person he was just speaking with the day before.

He needed a drink and tried to ignore the urge to pull his flask out of the pocket of his jacket, which had been laid aside in the other room. Ainsley bit into his thumbnail.

There was a knock on the door and Mrs. Crane appeared in the hall. "There is a young miss—" she stopped short and looked away sharply, her eyes having grazed the image of the newly deceased doctor on Ainsley's makeshift examination table. Though Bennett was covered by a white sheet, the image was obviously too much for her. She turned her body, crossing her arms over her stomach, and forcibly looked to the ground. She started again, more determined, "There is a young miss seeking the doctor. I had not the heart to turn her away."

Ainsley met Mrs. Crane in the hall, careful to close the door behind him. "Is she ill?"

"No, she says her brother is in a bad way."

Ainsley nodded and quickly made his way down the stairs. The girl, so skinny and malnourished, looked as if she could slip out of her pinafore without the slightest movement. She stood at the door to Bennett's house, her face fraught with worry. She twisted her fingers in front of her, bending them back and forth from anxiousness. "Are you the doctor?" she asked at once.

"I am a doctor, yes," Ainsley replied.

"Willy's hot as a fire poker and we've tried everything but he ain't gettin' no better."

Ainsley nodded. "Where do you live child?"

"Tallow Lane."

Armed with Bennett's doctor's bag Ainsley followed the girl, who he learned was named Callie, to Tallow Lane on the opposite side of town. As Ainsley hurried along, he noticed the houses became closer and closer together and their state of repair became less and less affluent. Turning from the main road onto Tallow Lane, Ainsley found himself staring into the dirty faces of malnourished children playing in the cobblestone streets. They wore no shoes and their clothes were so threadbare he wondered how none of them froze to death in the late season cold. Little girls with tangled hair and mud-smeared hands looked up from water pumps, their faces solemn and resigned. Little boys, no more than three years old, played with pebbles and sticks but quickly cleared the way as his ominous form approached. All of the small, broken faces looked at him as he passed but avoided his gaze, giving him a wide berth where he walked.

Ainsley was accustomed to such scenes. As a child, he often helped his mother in her efforts to comfort the depraved, ill, and penniless. The slums of London were far more crowded and smelled of urine and filth in a far more putrid way. This street, though clearly left for the unfortunate of this town, was a far cry from the poverty-stricken streets of London.

Ainsley watched Callie run to a blue door near the end of the lane, its rich colour a stark contrast to the mulled and chipped colours of the other doors he had passed. She slipped in before him and Ainsley could hear her yelling to her mother that she had brought the doctor.

The door was left ajar and when he rounded the doorframe he saw the smallest of rooms, where a scarceness of furniture left it looking stark and forbidden. He would not have believed that anyone lived there had he not seen a roaring fire in the hearth and four strings of drying clothes positioned in front of it.

The house was but a few rooms; each corner of this main one was filled with tiny fear-laced faces looking up at him, their eyes wide. Men were not a welcome sight, it would seem, not in these homes. Ainsley counted five children, not including the girl whom he had met earlier. Ainsley now saw that Callie was the oldest. A child lay, with his back to Ainsley, in front of the fire, swaddled in thin, dingy blankets, his head barely supported by the thinnest of pillows.

And then Ainsley looked to the mother, standing with another child on her hip, and a wooden spoon in her hand. Cally stood in front of her as she scolded the child. "We ain't got no money for no doctor!" the woman yelled, oblivious to the cry that erupted from the child on her hip.

"Ma'am, I'd like to help, if I may." Ainsley spoke up if only to spare Callie any further admonishment.

The mother let out a deep-rooted exhale of breath and pinched her lips together, shaking her head as she did so. "Be off with ye, sir," she called, cocking her chin toward the door and the street beyond. "We haven't the money and I don't have a mind to be beholden to no one."

"I charge no fee, not this day. In sovereigns or service. May I see the child?" Ainsley gestured toward the boy in front of the fire, who hadn't stirred during the entire exchange.

The woman eyed him suspiciously, resolute in standing in his way. "The only doctor I know is Bennett. You ain't look like him."

"I am staying with Dr. Bennett. Your daughter told me her brother has a fever."

The woman pressed her lips together and reluctantly nodded.

A boy, toddler more aptly, lay half asleep with his legs bent toward his stomach and arms crossed over his stomach. Ainsley knelt beside him and began peeling away the many layers of warmth he assumed the mother had applied earlier. So close to the fire Ainsley could feel the radiant warmth penetrating his clothes and he too began to feel ill with the heat of it.

As he revealed the boy, Ainsley saw his cheeks were burning bright red and yet the child was shivering as if cold. The other children gathered around him though none closer than arm's length.

"His name is William," Callie said over his shoulder.

"Hello, William," Ainsley said. The boy moaned, and began to speak, though nothing seemed coherent. The boy was struck with delirium.

Scarlet fever. Ainsley's heart sank as the realization hit him. "How long has he suffered?" he asked, hoping the mother did not pick up the panic in his voice.

"Three days." She spoke as if she did not want to admit her child was sick, as she possessed no money to see him well.

Ainsley's shoulders slumped. Most cases of scarlet fever turned fatal within the third or fourth day. The boy had little hope of survival so late into the onset his illness.

"Is there another room, preferably one with a window?"

The mother nodded. Ainsley gathered William in his arms and followed the woman into a room behind the main one. In it was a single bed, and a mass of blankets on the floor. Ainsley lowered the boy onto the bed, and pulled a single cover over him. He was still muttering incoherently as Ainsley walked to the window to open it.

"The chill?" the mother called in protest from the door.

"The fresh air is what this child needs." Ainsley turned to Callie, who had followed him in. "Fetch my bag. And some water."

Callie nodded and scurried away. She returned with the bag and left for the water. Ainsley opened it at the foot of the bed and began rooting through in search of a known remedy for scarlet fever. As he looked, he was not sure exactly what he sought. He had a vague memory of a treatment option, but all his years dealing with the dead left him ill-prepared for saving the living. If the boy died, Ainsley could scarcely forgive himself.

Ainsley found the carbonate of ammonia, distinctly remembering a dose of two grains for children.

"What's that?" the mother asked, peering in through the door.

Ainsley did not look to her. He placed some into the cup of water that Callie brought him. "It's carbonate of ammonia. It's been known to alleviate the symptoms. Do you have brandy or wine in the house?"

The mother looked at him with wide eyes.

"Just a tiny amount."

He saw Callie look to her mother and then the woman nodded suddenly and Callie scurried away.

"My husband drank. He left half a bottle when he left six months ago," the woman explained sheepishly. "We were hiding it from him, in case he came back."

Ainsley gave the woman a sorrowful look. "I am sorry for your troubles, ma'am," he said softly.

"No trouble. 'Tis better with him gone."

Ainsley pulled William to a sitting position, propping some pillows behind him to keep him from sliding back. Callie returned and placed the small bottle of brandy in Ainsley's hand. Ainsley took the spoon from the cup of water and measured a tiny bit of brandy into it. Carefully, Ainsley slipped the measured brandy into the boy's mouth.

"He needs to drink a cup of water with this every hour, more if he will take it. Give him some brandy every so often and let him rest as much as possible."

The mother nodded.

"Keep the other children away as best you can."

She nodded again as Callie looked on from the foot of the bed.

"And for heaven's sake keep the room cool, or he will never make it."

He administered the carbonate of ammonia and brandy slowly, throughout the course of the next hour, before William slipped away into a less fitful sleep. The boy's mother came and went, dividing her time between her sick boy and the rest of her brood, but Callie stayed at Ainsley's side, cooed softly for her brother to drink and accept the medicine the doctor offered him. When Ainsley finally allowed the boy to sleep his mother walked into the room. Ainsley stood, the burden of saving the child weighing heavily on his shoulders.

"Let him sleep," Ainsley said to the sedate mother. She was clearly in shock with it all and that was driving her actions. "Take this," he handed her the bottle of remedy, "And remember what I said. Summon me if he gets worse throughout the night."

Ainsley left with little hope of the child's recovery. Most likely the boy would die. The fever was far too advanced for his rudimentary experience to make any noticeable difference. House calls, the desperate begging from mothers of sick children, where so little difference could be made as a practicing physician, were what deterred him from becoming one. He was far better at examining dead bodies than he was at comforting the sick. He was a stellar surgeon to patients out cold from chloroform or, better still, already dead and awaiting burial. He could not comfort that mother, could not lie to her face and say he would cure her child any more than he could claim to be physician to the Queen.

As Ainsley stumbled back toward town, exhausted, he wondered if Bennett would have done better for the boy. The seasoned physician, who knew the town and its inhabitants, could have better prescribed a method of treatment, more so than Ainsley, who was lacking in this regard. Cocky and arrogant when he first arrived, Ainsley felt his confidence wane, so much so that he began to doubt his ability to save even Lillian, the girl languishing on death's door.

These thoughts haunted Ainsley as he made his way back through town. He scarcely knew where he was, though it did not matter. The day was late and there was little else he could do. His energy spent between two severely ill patients, and his ego deflated, he headed to the one place he knew he could find solace. The pub.

Chapter 20

*Sisterly, brotherly,
Fatherly, motherly*

His walk to the tavern would be a long one but he welcomed the silence and darkness as he made his way to the centre of town. The moon was shrouded in a mist that diffused its soft light and illuminated the trees to his left and right. There was a warm spray of fog all around him that clung onto his exposed face and hands as he walked.

He thought of Lillian as he walked. He hoped she slept soundly, allowing her body to fight off whatever demons threatened to steal her life. She had felt so helpless in his arms, so dependent upon the help he gave her. No one had ever needed him for something so basic, and yet she clung to him in the hopes that he would save her. His entire career was built on the assistance he could give after death. Lillian needed him in life, and despite Ainsley's attempts to remain professional, he started to feel attached in a way he thought he never could with his patients.

He held his flask in his hands, noticing it was nearly empty of its contents. He'd need a lot more than a few mouthfuls to get him to forget her arms around him and the feeling of her breath on his face. He smiled at the thought. Yes, he was going to need a whole lot more.

A snapped twig to his right jarred him from his daydream and he halted his step. He had been walking along the fence of the cemetery, where the lighted street lamps did not permeate.

"Hello?" he called out into the darkness. He squinted. "Is someone following me?" he asked in what even he knew was a feeble effort. It was only a twig, he told himself, resuming his walk, only now at a slightly quicker pace.

He emptied his flask, hoping the drink would dampen his heightened awareness, and slipped it back into his inner pocket. He was not afraid. He had boxed with the boys in school, far away from his father's critical eye, where he could indulge himself and his male whims. It was the not knowing, the creeping darkness, that unnerved him. The fact that he could not see his opponent unsettled him.

The cloud above moved on and suddenly he could see that he truly was alone in the darkness. He tried to laugh at his folly, but his amusement was short-lived. He had the distinct impression that he was being watched while in Picklow, though he knew not from where, by whom, or by what.

The tavern appeared like a beacon, a lighthouse in the misty night. The fog gave way to rain by the time Ainsley reached the main road and the pellets of searing cold pricked his face and neck. He flipped up his collar and hunched over to brace himself but the rain was unrelenting. When he reached the tavern doors, he was soaked to the skin. He struggled hard to peel the outer layers of clothing from his person and found comfort in the throng of people in the pub and the blazing fire in the hearth.

The tavern was the Inn, the dining hall converted after dinner into a place filled with music, merriment, and drinks. The room was alive with labourers, just come from work. Mill workers, Ainsley noticed, most likely the very workers who were employed under the late Walter Lloyd and now his son. The gathering was boisterous, the music loud.

Ainsley slipped into one of the empty chairs at a round table next to a window and glanced around the room. There was a giant stone fireplace, the focal point of the room, with a roaring fire radiating heat. There were a few other round tables like the one where he sat positioned around the outside of the room. In the centre of the room, two long pine tables ran parallel to each other, each flanked with benches, three to each side of the table. This is where the majority of revelers sat, mugs of ale in their fists, their cheeks already red with drink.

"Ain't seen ye before," a voice called to him. He

pulled his attention away from the others in the room and focused on a middle-aged woman in front of him. She stood over him with her arm bent and a round tray perched between her shoulder and hand, her free hand placed squarely on her hip. She looked like a woman no one would want to mess with, not in her husband's inn. "What'll ya 'ave?"

Ainsley pulled out his flask. "Can you fill this up with some whiskey and bring me some gin?"

She smiled out of one side of her mouth and gave him a wink.

She returned shortly and soon one drink became another, and then another. Ainsley drank with little care to his health or reputation. With each gulp and slap of an empty mug on the wooden table, his concerns for the boy and Lillian grew dull and muted until finally his recollection of the day's events slipped from his consciousness. His face grew warm and his thoughts vanished as the music played on and the gathered people grew more boisterous. The dancing commenced not long into the night and Ainsley found himself drawn to nearly every girl willing to hike up her skirts and slip her arm into his.

The evening became a haze of drink and dancing without the slightest concern for the world beyond. Ainsley was far more interested in continuing this euphoria than he was in facing the injustices of the world. The drink helped him forget about his father, the expectations of Dr. Crawford, and most importantly the death of his colleague, Dr. Bennett.

With the moon high in the night sky, Ainsley staggered back to Dr. Bennett's house. He walked through the dark streets of Picklow without a care in the world, nor any concern for his safety. Had he been sober, or even slightly less inebriated, his walk home would have been far less enjoyable.

※ ※

Ainsley woke with the chamber pot at his side, within it the contents of his stomach. The sunlight, blindingly bright, streamed in from his east-facing window, drenching him in a warmth that only made him want to hurl once more. His head throbbed with tight, reoccurring pulses that became even more heightened when he opened his eyes. Trying to get away from the pain, Ainsley pulled away and fell from the bed. He landed on the hard floor with a thud, smashing his elbow on the dresser and spilling the chamber pot as he recoiled in pain.

He would have laughed had the entire situation, the headache, the fall, and the vomit, not been completely his own doing. This performance, and many variations of it, had played out many times since college. The drink dulled his senses and, on certain occasions, the women completed his circle of self-loathing.

He must have fallen asleep again, sprawled out on the floor, because the next time he opened his eyes he was staring into the face of Jonas.

"What a disturbing sight," Jonas said as he stood over Ainsley. "That's one way to die."

Ainsley pulled the bed covers from the bed and used them to cover his naked body while watching his friend circle the bed. Jonas slipped into the desk chair, and glanced over the medical texts Ainsley had left out a few nights before. "Some light reading?" he said, flipping over one of the books to have a look at its cover. He pursed his lips before returning the book to its original position.

Ainsley stood up, buttoning his pants, and looked at Jonas seated casually in his chair, hands folded on his lap, and a smug look spreading across his face. Ainsley shook his head and continued to get dressed. "Never thought I'd see you here."

"I'm full of surprises. Mrs. Crane let me in. She encouraged me to wake you. It's midday and you, my friend, look like you have had better mornings. Wild night?" Jonas asked, taking out a cigarette and holding it in his lips. "You haven't changed much."

"There is no woman here," Ainsley answered, spreading out his arms to reinforce his point.

"Today," Jonas answered. "But that's because you aren't a total rogue and this isn't really your house."

"Did you come here to chide me? So far from London?" Ainsley answered, allowing his annoyance to show.

"No, actually," Jonas answered matter-of-factly. "Thought life would be dull for you. Thought perhaps you needed a little diversion." Jonas glanced around the ramshackle room. The bedclothes were twisted and bunched. Yesterday's clothes were scattered over the plank wood floors as if thrown, first the shirt, then the trousers. "Never knew such a sleepy town presented such...formidable entertainment."

"Nothing worse than the life you lead," Ainsley pointed out.

"You have always had a way with the ladies. Wish I could be so damned lucky." Jonas lit a match and drew from the flame at the end of his cigarette.

"Not luck, skill." Ainsley pulled on a clean shirt and began buttoning it from the bottom up. The shirt was loose around his slender middle and his bare chest, and his stomach muscles clenched as he buttoned, though his physique was not what his friend remembered. In school, Ainlsey was known for his physical and mental ability but now it seemed one had slipped while the other flourished.

Jonas allowed a smirk to spread across his face as he pulled the cigarette from his lips. "Old age is making you soft, I see." A halo of smoke blew out from his lips and rose into the air around him.

Ainsley nearly smiled. Jonas was the only person from whom he would accept this treatment. They boxed together while in school, never against each other. That would have been too much like beating up a brother you actually liked. Jonas had introduced him to rugby and they ran whenever the need for freedom arose. Perhaps he was becoming a bit soft, as his friend stated, though not as soft as some, Ainsley reminded himself.

Jonas quickly changed the subject. "So tell me, *Doctor*, what brings you so far north? Can't imagine this place is better than your father's house."

Ainsley raised an eyebrow. "But it is. That house is a tomb and I was rotting away in it. Dr. Bennett's letter could not have come at a better time." Ainsley tucked his shirt into his trousers and adjusted his collar in the mirror on top of the bureau.

"You're sister seems to agree. She practically begged me to escort her up here." Jonas took another drag of his cigarette and watched Ainsley closely as he spoke. "Two days' journey with the beautiful Margaret, not a bad arrangement, if you ask me."

"She's here?" Ainsley quickly gave his mangled hair some attention and eyed the stubble appearing on his chin and jawline. He'd have to shave but he knew his sister wouldn't care.

"We arrived late last night. Established ourselves at the Inn."

"You must do a better job of getting straight to the point," Ainsley pronounced as he slipped out the door.

❧ ☙

He found Margaret in the kitchen with Mrs. Crane. Both women wore shabby aprons with kitchen stains of yesterday smeared into the fibers. Mrs. Crane's apron suited her like a daily uniform worn by servants and tradesmen. Margaret, on the other hand, looked out of place in her taffeta dress with ribbon trims and a shabby apron splashed over her front. Her hands were wrist deep in flour and dough as she leaned over a wooden pastry board.

Ainsley could see Mrs. Crane was enjoying her new pupil's presence, but Margaret looked immensely uncomfortable with the task assigned to her.

"Now deary, just move your hands like kneading bread."

"Kneading bread?" Margaret laughed nervously. "Mrs. Crane, I have never kneaded bread in my life."

Mrs. Crane's singsong tone halted abruptly at the revelation. The woman, who no doubt has spent the majority of her life in the kitchen, was speechless. She glanced to the lumpy dough in front of them. "Tis no wonder you ain't snagged a husband yet." Mrs. Crane grabbed for the dough and began kneading furiously to smooth out the lumps and work the remaining flour into it.

"Don't be so hard on her, Mrs. Crane," Ainsley called out from the behind the door frame, finally allowing his presence to be known. "Our father never allowed her to step foot in our kitchen at home."

Margaret smiled when she saw her brother. "Good morning, Peter."

Ainsley walked over to his little sister, who was not so little anymore, and embraced her. When he left London, he was so desperate to get away. He had never thought he would miss the remarkably easy companionship of his sister. When she pulled away, she quickly apologized for getting flour over his clothes. "I'm a mess." It was then she caught sight of his growing facial whiskers, unkempt hair, and noticed an unmistakable smell of gin surrounding him. Margaret frowned. "You don't look too good yourself." She touched the side of his face and scratched his budding whiskers with her fingers. "Do they not have barbers here in Picklow?"

"Wash your hands then," Mrs. Crane called out from behind them. She had already molded the dough into bread tins and was placing a cloth over them to let them rise. Once Margaret had washed her flour-coated hands, Ainsley pulled her away, leaving Mrs. Crane to finish her morning duties.

"I would have died in there had you not come to rescue me," Margaret confessed to him as they walked to the parlour. "Either that or I would have killed myself in that batter. I cannot understand how women can do that work all day long and not be driven absolutely batty."

Ainsley chuckled. "Some women like it. Mother does."

"Yes, but that is only because she doesn't have to. She can enter and exit the kitchen as much as she likes and dinner will still be on the table later." The tone of the conversation turned less jovial, and became more pained. Speaking of their mother and father dampened their happy reunion.

"Father never liked it but Mother never did listen to him much anyway." Ainsley smiled at the memory of his headstrong mother, and realized how much his sister was like her.

"He absolutely forbade me from going anywhere near that room of the house. And I listened. Unlike another offspring of his I know."

The pair took a seat in two wingback chairs facing each other.

"How is Father?" Ainsley dared to ask. "I am surprised he gave you permission to come."

Margaret avoided his gaze and bit her lower lip.

"Father knows you're here, does he not?"

"I wasn't travelling alone. Jonas escorted me," Margaret confessed.

"And why was Jonas going to Tunbridge Wells?"

Margaret spoke after a moment of hesitation. "Because I begged him to."

A look of revelation spread over Ainsley's face. "Oh," he said with a smile. "I understand."

"Oh, Peter, it's not like that. I needed to get out of that house. Father has been absolutely dreadful. He's worse since you left. He is vexed with Mother."

"He is always vexed with Mother."

Margaret shook her head. "You should not have left, Peter."

Ainsley sighed and slid back into the chair. "How could I stay? My position at the hospital takes priority. I cannot risk my career for the sake of my tumultuous family."

"There are rumours of divorce. I do not think I can stand another minute under the scrutiny."

"Is this why you came to see me? To get away from the tittle-tattle of London society?" Ainsley laughed at this, aware of the many rumours circulated at his family's expense. If a scandal did not occur naturally, society was more than willing to conjure up a false one.

"Not exactly."

"You will have to steel yourself, Margaret. One day we will all find ourselves on the wrong side of the society pages but it is not the end of the world."

"Then why does it feel like it?" Margaret asked. For a moment, Ainsley thought she might cry.

"But a divorce, Peter. How can they get a divorce?"

Ainsley could not hide his amusement. The thought of such a turn of events seemed laughable. That his Mother and Father could suffer for so long, making pretenses and playing the part of marital bliss, knowing full well they despised each other insufferably, only to risk a scandal by way of divorce was highly unlikely. They made each other miserable, but if there was one thing Ainsley had learned in recent years it was that his parents would rather suffer silently than meet such an end.

"I doubt it, Margaret. Mother will live in Tunbridge Wells and Father will remain in London, as he always has. They will not risk a divorce. Now, please, no more of this. I have far more pressing concerns this morning."

"The girl?"

"Young woman, actually. She is your age, if she is a day. I was with her all yesterday." Ainsley allowed his gaze to wander as the image of the helpless Lillian came to mind. She had clung to him in her darkest moment and relied on him to save her. He wanted so much to live up to her expectations. "Her agony pains me."

"Is she in that much pain?"

"And more," Ainsley confessed. "She's teetering in this world and the next and..." his voice trailed off, "...and she is depending on me to save her."

"And you can, you will," Margaret exclaimed without a hint of doubt.

Ainsley forced a smile but avoided her gaze.

Jonas entered the room, disrupting their conversation. Margaret quickly pushed her tears away and forced a smile.

"Where is Dr. Bennett?" Jonas asked. "I should very much like to make his acquaintance."

Chapter 21

*Feelings had changed:
Love, by harsh evidence,*

The threesome, Ainsley, Jonas, and Margaret, stood around Bennett's body, which was draped in a thin white sheet as he was entirely naked beneath. His skin had taken on a dark, tinged appearance since the last time Ainsley had seen him, though it was not entirely unexpected since the old doctor still had not been treated and prepared for burial. Jonas and Margaret stood in disbelief, while Ainsley's face bore a pained look of defeat.

"Will you assist me, Jonas?" Ainsley asked. "I have no other whom I trust with such a task."

For the first time since they had entered the room, Margaret pulled her eyes from the corpse and raised an eyebrow.

"For pity's sake, Margaret! Do not look at me so."

Sucking in a deep breath, Margaret turned as if to leave the room. "Do not concern yourself with me. I am just another adornment in the room."

Ainsley let out a breath and shook his head in disbelief. "Margaret, please."

Margaret turned to face him. "You know as well as I that I shall not be able to do anything worthwhile in my life, at least not while people are watching. Let me help you." She reached out her hands and clutched the bedpost with the tight grip of a determined woman.

Ainsley knew his sister's prospects for a satisfying life were limited. She was expected to marry well, bring forth strong heirs and then slip into the background as their mother had been expected to do. He began to feel grateful for the opportunity to follow his interests, even if it meant a career based on deception.

Ainsley gave a glance to Jonas, who merely

shrugged. "Very well," Ainsley answered resignedly. "I will remind you, however, I have no patience for squeamishness."

Their work started when Jonas pulled back the sheet, revealing the withered, ashen skin of the town's only doctor. Ainsley stood to one side, Jonas on the other. Margaret had positioned herself nearby with a small array of medical tools in front of her, which Ainsley had brought from London. The curtains had been pulled back as far as possible and Jonas had fetched as many candles and lamps as could be found to illuminate the room even more.

With the first cut, a long thin line down the centre of Bennett's torso, Ainsley was transported back to his days at school when Jonas and he were often paired together to dissect a cadaver brought to them earlier in the day. The instructor would stand behind them, sometimes on the risers of the operating theatre to get a better view of the shaky, uncertain cuts of the would-be doctors. The entire class, eager to watch fellow students butcher the corpse and, in effect, butcher any chances of receiving a passable grade, would surround the pair being graded, often commenting and correcting procedure under their breaths to the person standing beside them. Ainsley and Jonas's peers were never there to encourage them, nor did it seem likely that they wished to learn from them. The reality was that Ainsley and Jonas were the best surgeons the school had seen in a dog's age and everyone, even the instructors, was eager to watch them fail.

"Just like old times," Jonas said in a hushed voice. "Never thought we'd be paired up like this again."

Ainsley gave a feeble smile, his attention fixated on the delicacy of the task. He pulled away for a moment, stretching out his back, which was threatening to become sore by day's end. The bed, even with a hard board secured beneath the body, was a far cry from a real examining table. "How's work at the university? Do you miss working with real people?" Ainsley pulled back Bennett's skin from his rib cage and kneeled in closer to examine the late doctor's lower organs. "You should see about a transfer."

Jonas shook his head. "The laboratory suits me," he explained. Ainsley saw him give a sideways glance to

Margaret before continuing. "Besides, Dr. McPhearson's daughter has taken a liking to me." Jonas puffed out his chest and allowed an arrogant smirk to spread over his face.

"Is she the young woman with the red hair?" Ainsley asked, turning from the corpse and grabbing the small saw that was part of his arsenal of tools.

"The very same."

Ainsley smiled. She was a lovely young lady, though it pained Ainsley to admit that she had spent more time talking to him at the college's garden party than she had with Jonas. "She's very fetching. You should ask her —"

"Ahem!" Both men turned to Margaret, who had been standing beside them, trying to concentrate on the procedure. "Gentlemen, please!" Her tone was more of a command than a plea for compliance.

Chagrined, both doctors turned back to their subject, abandoning the topic of the lovely daughter with red hair. "My apologies," Jonas answered quickly, giving a slight bow out of respect.

Ainsley did not bother to offer an apology; his focus was already on Bennett's internal organs. "Do not apologize. My sister said she wishes to learn the ins and outs of dissection. She needs to learn that such banter is part and parcel." Ainsley shot her a look of challenge. If the girl wished to be in the presence of doctors while they worked she must learn her place among them.

"Oh, please," Margaret answered with a laugh, "as if the state of Jonas's love affairs are of any concern to me." Margaret hitched up her skirt slightly as she rounded the bed to gain a better view. "You may do better to keep any chatter to the topic at hand." She approached the body, looking at the organs that were revealed. "May I remove the organs?" she asked, her hand outstretched, palm facing the ceiling, asking for the scalpel.

With a quick glance to Jonas, who failed miserably at hiding his amusement, Ainsley relinquished his tool and watched helplessly as his sister positioned it above the cavity he just opened. Unable to avoid it, Margaret pulled out the intestines with all the grace of a young mother trying to change her screaming baby's first nappy. Seeing her struggle with the cumbersome organ, Jonas reached out his hand and helped pull them out before placing them on the table behind him and Ainsley.

With his arms folded over his chest, Ainsley waited for his sister to ask for help, almost daring her to admit the task was too much. She worked slowly, he noticed, much slower than he would have and it took every ounce of self-control he could muster to keep himself from grabbing for the knife and taking over.

"That's the stomach," he offered, rather instinctively, as Margaret pulled the organ out with her bare and bloody hands.

"I know," she answered concertedly, lifting her gaze to meet her brother's, making sure he saw her annoyance.

Jonas took the stomach from her, and then the liver, placing them beside the mound of intestine she had already extracted.

"I am most interested in the contents of the stomach," Ainsley said, turning his back to Margaret and honing in on the stomach.

"Poisoned, you said?" Jonas asked. "Like the girl."

"I can't be sure." Ainsley lifted the stomach and held it up to the light streaming in through the window. "He died so suddenly. I didn't have the faintest clue he was even ill." Ainsley lowered the stomach back into place and turned to watch Margaret, his disdain for her slower pace vanishing as he relished in the plight for truth. "It could be unrelated but it seems odd that he would die right after Josephine's funeral." He looked over Dr. Bennett's body. "If it is poison, why did it take him so easily while Lillian fights it off?" Ainsley exhaled and turned to Jonas. "To tell the truth, I am not sure how to treat her, nor do I wish her to keep taking the tonics Bennett prescribed." Ainsley gestured to his desk across the hall where he had placed the vials he confiscated from Lillian's bedside table.

After washing his hands in a nearby basin, Jonas left the room briefly, returning a moment later with the vials in his hands. "Shall I process them for you?" he asked, looking over the adhered labels with academic interest.

Ainsley nodded, turning his attention slightly to Margaret, who offered him a pair of kidneys with outstretched hands, blood oozing down her lily-white wrists. It was the image of his own sister, engaged in such a scene, that prompted his visceral reaction. He raised his relatively clean arm to his mouth, in case he were to lose the contents of his stomach.

A glimmer of annoyance spread over Margaret's face. "Peter, you are acting like a novice," she said, thrusting the kidneys toward him. "Now here, take these before they slip through my fingers."

Chapter 22

Thrown from its eminence;
Even God's providence
Seeming estranged.

Later that afternoon Ainsley left Margaret and Jonas to examine the internal organs while he paid a house call to Tallow Lane. He had avoided thinking about it all day but it seemed to creep into his consciousness and his sense of urgency grew. The child's fever had either broken, that is if his mother followed Ainsley's instructions, or the illness had claimed the life of the boy and nothing more could be done. He had learned the family's name was Halliday, and were considered to be one of the poorest families in the village.

The lane where the family lived was deserted despite the unusual warmth of the day. He reached the house and knocked on the bold blue door. A small child let him in but said nothing, nor did his blank, unsure stare give any indication of the events the previous night.

The room was dark but the mood found within was light. Callie turned when she saw Ainsley enter the room and smiled broadly as she gestured to William. He was now sitting upright, cradled somewhat in his mother's arms. His eyes were wide, still somewhat hollow from days of illness, but they showed he was very much alive and on the mend. Ainsley sank to his knees in front of the mother and child, his face blank, his mind not registering the sight. He reached out a hand to feel the child's forehead and found it only slightly warm to the touch and not feverish as it had been the day before.

"When did his fever break?" he asked in astonishment.

"Last night," Mrs. Halliday replied. "I did not believe

in the medicine you gave us but Callie here kept bringing it." She beamed at her daughter. A lighthearted laughter broke out among the mother and her children, who gleefully acknowledged that William was going to be okay. Like a burst of sunshine through swiftly moving clouds, the room became bright and triumphant.

Ainsley checked the boy's pulse, and listened to his breathing. He held the child's hand for a moment and felt that it too was responding stronger than the day before.

"I wanted to fetch you," Callie explained, accepting her smallest sibling, a baby, into her arms. She cradled it while her mother sat with William. "Mother said you were very busy."

"That I am." Ainsley let the boy's hand slip from his. He turned to the other children and proceeded to give them all a quick physical examination. "But not so busy that I couldn't call upon a family in need of my help."

The family was malnourished; the dark circles under the children's eyes were hardly from lack of sleep. Their movements were slow, lethargic, as if each motion took too much strength to perform. Callie, the eldest girl, seemed able to bypass these feelings, the insatiable hunger, the dulled sense of life. The others weren't so fortunate. They wore torn and tattered clothes, which would have done little to stave off the penetrating damp and cold. He could feel the bones of their bodies as he gently positioned them closer to the light of the window so he could see them better.

"Mother says you look after the Lloyd family," Callie said. Mrs. Halliday's eyes widened, startled that her daughter would broach the subject with the doctor. Callie did not notice and continued, "You are going to cure Miss Lillian."

Ainsley paused at the mention of Lillian's name before forcing himself to focus on the small child before him. "I hope so," he answered, not wanting to portray any notion of wavering confidence. "She is a very sick young lady." He gently pulled the boy's lower eyelid down and squinted as he looked into his eyes.

"She was always very nice to me."

Ainsley could not help but give the girl a quizzical

look. Callie would not have had much contact with someone so above her age and class. "Mother used to work in that house, you know—" Callie's words were cut short when Mrs. Halliday clicked her tongue and motioned for the girl to hush.

Ainsley stopped his exam and looked to the mother. "Is that true?" he asked, knowing already that Callie spoke the truth.

Mrs. Halliday avoided his eyes and pressed her lips together. He saw Callie's eyes dart to the floor, her face bearing a look of shame at mentioning something she shouldn't have.

"Mrs. Halliday?"

The woman finally looked him in the eye, nodded, and then slid the boy from her lap. She positioned him on a cushion, drawing a thin blanket over his legs and torso before motioning for Ainsley to follow her outside into the main room. Once out of earshot of the children she spoke in muted tones, glancing at the windows around them as if ensuring they were unoccupied and closed. "'Tis not something I wanted you to know," she started. "If William died, and you suspected it was that same illness Josephine had I didn't want you to"—she pulled her shawl higher onto her shoulders—"cut him open."

Ainsley stiffened at the suggestion. His position carried a stigma he was not able to shake. "Not even if it meant Lillian could live?"

Mrs. Halliday swallowed hard. "Mr. Lloyd had many women and no one was surprised he came to an early end. When Miss Josephine died— people in the village believe it's God's penance for sinful behaviour. Forgive me for saying this, but if Lillian dies, the guilt is on that family, not mine."

Ainsley concentrated hard not to betray the information he already knew. In his mind Josephine was an innocent, and did not deserve the wrath of any god. "You see these tragedies as justice for sinful behaviour?" The notion was absurd. A man of science knew diseases and illnesses occurred because of viruses and bacteria, but the new discoveries of science were nothing compared to a millennia of superstition.

129

Mrs. Halliday seemed uncomfortable with his line of questioning so Ainsley softened his tone. "Mrs. Halliday, if there is anything you can tell me about that family, I would appreciate it greatly."

The woman swallowed hard. "I was the one who laid out the dead. I saw the bodies."

Ainsley's shock was only tempered by his need for details. He had wanted to examine the bodies. He desperately wanted to exhume them and dissect them. It was the only way he would know without a doubt what was killing Lillian. It pained him greatly that the best source of information about the bodies was that of a lay-person, a washer woman who wouldn't know a heart from a spleen.

Ainsley tried not to sound desperate as he began his questioning. "Did you see any marks on the skin, any injuries or cuts?"

Mrs. Halliday shook her head slowly. "No, not one."

"Was there anything different, anything that stood out? Smells, colours, that sort of thing?"

"No. She was sick for less than three days and was gone from this world before anyone knew what pained her. 'Tis not natural to die in such agony. We heard the girl wailing but no one dared fetch a doctor without the mistress' say-so."

Sadness came over Ainsley at the thought of it. Josephine had been twelve years old, innocent of the sins of her father, deserving nothing but to grow into adulthood. And then he remembered Lillian, writhing in pain in his arms while the rest of the family avoided contact with her. "They let her die in agony?"

Mrs. Halliday nodded. "It was most strange. All that money and none for a doctor. We begged Cook to intervene, and she wanted to, but I was the one who ended up begging Mrs. Lloyd to send for Miss Dawson. The witch could do nothing and I was sacked two days ago for my compassion."

"They fired you for begging to bring a doctor?"

"The mistress didn't say as much but I knew I spoke out of turn. Mrs. Lloyd hates servants who don't know their place." Mrs. Halliday smiled awkwardly and avoided Ainsley's gaze. "I am better off now. I work at one of the mills and make a better wage with better hours. Callie comes with me while my neighbour watches the wee ones. We are better off."

"And what about Mr. Lloyd, did you lay out him as well?" Ainsley asked.

She nodded. "Yes, did my best. He was fond of drink, he was. I saw the way he bawled at the girls. He pampered them, Josephine especially, but he was harsh. A tyrant, like me own husband. I told myself, I'd never be with a man like that again. Seeing the way Mr. Lloyd spoke to those girls, 'twas not right. He got worse when things went bad at the mill."

"When was that?"

"A year ago, perhaps more. That's when he started grooming Lillian for the stage. It was unpleasant to think of that young woman performing. That girl could not be happy with her lot. Figured my own young 'uns got a better life than those Lloyd girls. At least they don't got a father around to hit them no more."

"Did he strike her then?" Ainsley asked, feeling a twinge of anger spark within him. He did not want to think of anyone laying a malevolent hand on Lillian.

Mrs. Halliday looked at him, as if unable to say the words aloud. For a moment, Ainsley thought she wouldn't say anything and then she spoke. "One Christmas I was helping in the kitchen for a large party. It was late, and all the guests gone home. Cook and I were in the scullery when we heard some 'un shouting. She told me 'never you mind the master. Ain't no grand house in England without a hollering bloke.' We heard a woman's voice too but couldn't make out who it was. We's tried to ignore it but he raged like that for near an hour. I had it in mind to leave quietly by the back door but then we heard a crash and a scream. Cook ran out of the kitchen and I followed. The piano was covered in broken glass and Miss Lillian was crying on the sofa. She had her hands to her face." Mrs. Halliday showed Ainsley with her own weathered hands how her face was covered. "Mr. Lloyd wouldn't let anyone near them. He rushed us out of the room and I was sent on my way with an extra few sovereigns in my pocket for my trouble. I am certainly glad I don't need to accept their blood money anymore."

∽ ∾

  Ainsley left the house on Tallow Lane, offering to come back should any of the other children fall ill within the next few days. He knew his time in Picklow was running out but he had to offer some hope. Dr. Crawford would summon him back soon, and if Ainsley expected to retain his position he would have to return to London when ordered. He had already been there four days but felt he had made little progress in this mystery.

  Mr. Lloyd was a womanizer with syphilis who in turn infected his wife. He drank to excess and placed Lillian under a great amount of pressure to perform. Ainsley surmised the royalties she would have made were to most likely be used to offset the cost of Mr. Lloyd's many vices. With this information it seemed possible anyone could possess enough motive to kill him. Dr. Bennett himself had suggested Mrs. Martha Lloyd, and given his blessing if she had. It seemed unlikely though that she would pluck up the courage after years of docility. The fact that her husband was away from the home the majority of the time would give her enough of a reprieve from his domineering ways and, if she were an intelligent woman, she must have known his lifestyle would do him in soon enough. Whether it be his body or some mistress's husband, she must have known his death was most likely to be his own doing. Perhaps her patience grew thin and she decided to speed up his decline?

  She had far less motive to murder one of her own children, however.

  Either Walter Jr. or Elizabeth could be to blame. Walter seemed very at home in his father's shoes, running the mills, playing at being head of the house. Walter showed little remorse and even less affection for the women who comprised his immediate family. He appeared aloof and unaffected, a reality that concerned Ainsley greatly since he himself had good relations with both his sister and his mother. Such disregard for the women he was responsible for could provide reason to want to kill them, slowly, one by one. Walter could have killed his father, easily poisoned his brandy or some such thing in order to gain complete control of the mills, the family estate, and fortune. Walter could very well be doing away with the weaker sisters to save himself the expense of having to provide for them. It was a plausible motive, certainly not unheard of.

Elizabeth as well seemed quite capable of possessing enough envy and hatred to take it out on her more exalted sisters. She was obviously jealous of Lillian's success. The younger girls were so well-travelled in comparison. Everyone who Ainsley spoke to about Lillian and Josephine seemed so enamored by them. Elizabeth, on the other hand, was more of a matriarch than a sibling. Ainsley imagined that after many years of being overlooked in favour of the two younger Lloyd females, Elizabeth could have become very enraged. If she were the murderess, it could also explain the utter contempt she had for Ainsley and his attempts at digging up the truth. She was high on his list from the very beginning and she seemed a likely candidate.

Ainsley had been walking so slowly, his mind reeling with all the evidence before him, that he had not made it far from Tallow Lane. He had hardly noticed the decrepit townhouses and laundry lines strewn alleyways as he made his way out of the neighbourhood. His attention was brought back suddenly when Miss Dawson rounded the corner ahead of him and walked straight for him. The walkway was narrow and Ainsley stepped aside, tipping his hat as she came closer.

"Good day to you, Miss Dawson. You are far from home." Ainsley motioned to the deep basket nestled in the crook of her arm. "Provisions for a birthing mother?"

Miss Dawson smiled shyly. "I am paying a visit to the Hallidays. Their boy is ill," she said with a slightly apologetic tone.

Ainsley could not help but smile. "You will find that is no longer the case. The boy is quite changed. His fever broke in the night."

Miss Dawson's face fell, her disappointment apparent. "I had not heard. I brought some tea leaves and a remedy I know for drawing the fever to the feet."

Ainsley smiled. "I am sure it can do no harm."

She glared at him now. "Like you, I am a practitioner of medicine. Do we ever intend harm?" Her chin lowered and her gaze betrayed her annoyance.

"Forgive me," Ainsley said quickly. "I only meant that your visit should proceed should you still wish to call on the family." He gestured to the basket again, pointing to a loaf of bread nestled between the other contents. "There are items in your basket of which the family is in true need."

Miss Dawson dropped her eyes. "I do what I can."

"And you are to be commended for it," Ainsley said seriously.

"I had heard about Dr. Bennett and the news deeply saddened me," Miss Dawson said in earnest. "We are very fortunate that you are here in the interim."

"I am afraid I am not to stay here that long, Miss Dawson," Ainsley answered. "Just to see that Lillian is restored to health, then I must away to London."

Ainsley saw Miss Dawson draw in a deep breath as she glanced down the alley toward her intended route. She was still in black, the pains of mourning still borne on her face. She lingered in front of him, her eyes darting from him to the stone walls that surrounded him. She behaved as if she had something further to say yet lacked the words to commit herself to that action. Unable to justify his presence, Ainsley finally spoke. "Are you well, Miss Dawson?"

The medicine woman shook her head quickly in protest but then halted her actions when her eyes met his. "Have you made any progress in your investigations?" she paused momentarily. "I am only asking out of concern for the girl, and her family, of course."

Finally understanding, Ainsley nodded. "Of course. A friend of mine has recently arrived in town and my sister as well, actually. They are proving to be tremendous help."

"I am glad to hear it."

Miss Dawson avoided his gaze and it was then that Ainsley realized how self-conscious she was when he was around. She was obviously a quiet woman, used to living on her own, though she must be strong during certain times, if only for her patients.

Without saying anything else, she gave a slight curtsey and continued on past him and down the alley.

Ainsley watched for a moment; the characteristic sway of her skirts as she moved along was mesmerizing. She was a lovely woman, he suddenly realized, if a bit docile. He began to wonder how it was she had not yet married. With a figure and face as nice as hers, he gathered she should have had a throng of suitors at one time.

Ainsley caught himself staring after her and pulled his gaze away. When he was first told of the midwife who lived south of town, he had envisioned a weatherworn old woman with a slew of cats and sparse house. Miss Dawson was young, perhaps in her late twenties, and lived fairly comfortably in her small cottage in the woods. When he visited there it was quite apparent that she wanted for nothing. The woman was a mystery in her own right.

Before turning and making his way back to Bennett's house, he looked to her once more, and noticed her daughter walking dutifully beside her. It was only when he had walked a few paces onward that he became confused and stopped. He had not noticed the girl when Miss Dawson was right in front of him. He glanced again over his shoulder but the pair had turned a corner and were no longer in sight. Had he imagined her there, expecting to see the girl so he did? Or had he simply overlooked her presence while focusing his attention on Miss Dawson and her brimming basket of medicinal concoctions? There was scarcely enough room for him to move from the woman's path. How had a child gone unnoticed in such a small space?

Chapter 23

*Where the lamps quiver
So far in the river,*

Seated at a table at the Inn, Margaret saw Peter through the window, walking down the street with his hands in his pockets at a leisurely pace. He looked rather contented, which gave Margaret reason to hope that the child had recovered. With little regard for anyone in the Inn's dining hall or on the street, she promptly pulled back the lace curtain and shouted out of the opened window beside her. "Peter!" she called as she thrust her gloved hand out the open window. "Peter!" She waved at him expressively and only relaxed when she was sure she had attracted his attention.

Out of the corner of her eye she saw Jonas, who witnessed the entire exchange, merely lift his teacup to his lips for a drink. "Oh really, Jonas, like you weren't ready to flag him down yourself." Content that Peter had seen them and was making his way to the tavern, Margaret returned her attention to the spread of delectables in front of her. "Are you not excited to tell him what we have discovered?" she asked, plucking a cucumber sandwich from the tray between them and placing it on her plate.

"I think you are excited enough for both of us. There is no need for more jubilation." A smirk spread across his face as he spoke. Margaret pursed her lips and narrowed her eyes at him. He was a jolly fellow, with an amiable wit, something that Margaret found very attractive in a man, though she'd never admit as much out loud.

Ainsley was at her side then, leaning in to plant a kiss on her cheek before turning to Jonas and offering a hand to shake.

"The boy is well then?" Margaret asked. "Don't think I didn't notice that look of satisfaction on your face. Sit."

She gestured to an empty chair between her and Jonas.

Ainsley obeyed. Jonas poured some tea into Ainsley's cup while Margaret lifted a plate of biscuits and offered him some.

"They are quite good," Jonas offered.

"No," Ainsley replied with a slight motion of his hand. "Tea is enough."

Margaret gave a quick glance to Jonas. It was a look of concern but lacked a note of surprise. Ainsley was not known for his willingness to eat when his mind was on other things.

"Peter Marshall, you ought to eat something. Mrs. Mabel, the innkeeper's wife, has gone to quite an effort to produce this fine meal for us," Margaret spoke with a smile, as Mabel passed, "and you really should learn to humour me, dear brother." She slipped a scone onto his plate. "Now eat," she commanded, with all the love of a doting mother.

Ainsley obliged and began to eat with them.

"We certainly have some news for you, do we not, Jonas?"

Jonas nodded and leaned in on the table, aware of the busy room and not wanting anyone else to hear their conversation. "Traces of arsenic."

"Arsenic." Ainsley repeated.

"Yes, in the stomach," Margaret qualified. She smiled wryly, satisfied.

She saw Jonas give her a look of challenge. She knew he had been preparing with glee to relay his findings and she was now stealing his moment. Relaxing his face, he turned to Ainsley and continued, "Nine grains, in the contents of the stomach. Along with a myriad of other food sources. Hard to tell which was infected."

"What had he eaten, Peter?" Margaret asked. "Do you think it could be Mrs. Crane? Please tell me it is not Mrs. Crane, she is quite the dear."

"I hardly think Mrs. Crane would conspire to murder her own employer," Jonas answered before Ainsley had a chance to say anything. "That would hardly be efficient."

"Efficiency be damned! When a woman is scorned she can perform atrocious deeds, can she not, Peter?"

Ainsley shrugged but was given no air to offer an opinion.

"Correct me if I am wrong, gentlemen, but women nowadays are going to great lengths to have their opinions heard. Not that I would condone such an act, of course, but if we are to be ignored in society than what precious few choices are we left with?"

"Oh, please do not turn this into another diatribe. My head has yet to fully recover from the last one you offered me on the train." Jonas rubbed his right temple with his index and middle fingers.

Margaret huffed at his insult but turned her attention to Ainsley, who had leaned back in his chair, nursing his tea. "Peter, it has to be Mrs. Crane, she is the only one with access to Dr. Bennett's food."

After setting down his teacup, Ainsley pressed his finger to his lips and stared out the window aimlessly. "Highly unlikely," he answered after a length. "There is a far greater likelihood that someone at the Manor house meant for him to be killed or at least sickened so he could no longer assist me."

Jonas raised an eyebrow in Margaret's direction, indicating his pleasure at besting her. Her expression was less than amused.

"The funeral cakes," Ainsley blurted out without warning. "It must have been the funeral cake we received at the house. He fell ill shortly after we returned from the funeral."

"Who gave you the funeral cakes then?" Jonas asked.

"The servant, Mary, gave me mine, but Dr. Bennett already had one in his hand."

"Someone must have presented it to him. The mother, or sister perhaps. You said yourself that these women were impeding your progress. Mrs. Lloyd especially," Margaret offered. She looked across the table at Ainsley, who seemed even more relaxed than Jonas. She saw Ainsley raise his hand to his chin and lean into the arm of his wooden chair, his face somber and pensive. He seemed able to block out all the sounds around him as he contemplated what he had just learned.

"You can't just go around accusing innocent women of murder," Jonas said. "Someone poisoned Dr. Bennett, yes, but it could be very bad if you point your finger at the wrong person. The Lloyds could ruin you if you slander their family in anyway. They are very powerful in these parts, from what I gather."

Margaret snorted. Mother had already ruined them. No further need to worry.

"So, what would you suggest he do? They have killed one doctor, what's to stop them from killing another... doctor?" Margaret gave her brother a sideways glance and swallowed nervously.

"I have no proof, not enough in any case to say it is one or the other—"

"Perhaps it is both," Jonas suggested.

"True," Ainsley conceded. His fingers fidgeted with the silverware and then spun his teacup around on the saucer. Margaret knew he was contemplating his next move. She knew his methodical mind, his penchant for minute details. He was a scientist at his core and she knew he'd be approaching this problem just as his would a dead body, step by step, detail by tiny detail. "Peter, what are you going to do?"

Margaret could see him push his tongue to the inside of his cheek before speaking. "I am going to speak with Walter at Picklow Mills."

Chapter 24

*With many a light
From window and casement,
From garret to basement,
She stood, with amazement,
Houseless by night.*

The mill yard was an enclosed structure, with only a pair of wooden doors allowing access to the courtyard. Ainsley slipped through the one door that was propped open and was surprised to find a high amount of activity for a relatively small space. Men and women alike went about their duties with little regard to the stranger who had entered their midst. Ainsley dodged a moving cart, presumably loaded with bundles of cotton, as it drove past him toward a large platform where men waited to unload the newly arrived cargo. It was on this platform that he saw Walter, perhaps his only ally, his arms folded over his chest as he spoke with a bulky man, whom Ainsley assumed was the foreman in charge. When the man nodded and walked away, Walter's attention turned to scan the yard.

"Dr. Ainsley?"

Ainsley proceeded up the stairs at the side of the platform.

"Never thought I'd see you here, not in a dog's age." The men clasped hands in greeting. Walter looked genuinely happy to see Ainsley, who thought perhaps Mr. Lloyd felt more at his ease at the mill and less encumbered than when at the Manor. "Nothing has happened with my sister, has it?"

For the briefest of moments, Ainsley thought he saw a smile pushing at the sides of Walter's mouth as he spoke. Perhaps his initial gut feeling, that Walter would help him, was very wrong. "No, nothing like that. I was wondering if I may speak to you." Ainsley glanced around the courtyard at the workers, some whom he recognized from Josephine's funeral. "Alone, if possible."

"Yes, yes, of course."

Walter ushered Ainsley into the mill, where the droning noise of the mechanics deafened every other sound. The large room in front of them was alive with machines and people alike. There was no telling what duties each of the contraptions performed but Ainsley was impressed by the immensity of the operation. Children were stationed next to each machine; half-starved little bodies, dutifully waiting for their next instruction. There was so much to see yet Ainsley was not given a moment to take it all in.

Walter gestured to a flight of metal stairs that scaled the wall of the large room, at the top of which Ainsley could see a heavy wooden door with a window. Ainsley followed Walter into the office, indicated by a large desk and grouping of chairs on the opposite side. When Walter closed the door, the sound of the mill was muted and Ainsley was glad he would not have to speak above such clatter.

Ainsley waited while Walter slid behind his desk, gesturing for Ainsley to take a seat opposite him. Once seated, Ainsley noticed a sizable painted portrait of Walter Sr. prominently displayed above the room's fireplace and mantel. He looked like such a distinguished man, proud to have risen to such heights. In the picture, his hand clutched his jacket with a white knuckle grasp, as if he was clinging to his power and wealth, defying anyone to challenge him for it. Even in a picture, the man commanded attention and established a presence that even Ainsley could not explain.

Seeing the direction of Ainsley's gaze, Walter chuckled and reached for his crystal brandy decanter. Setting two glasses between them, Walter poured enough to fill them halfway. "My father," Walter said with an air of disdain, "his eyes follow me everywhere." Walter placed one of the glasses in front of Ainsley and took the other for himself. "I have plans to take it down, move it into the mill to remind everyone how much worse it could be." Walter laughed gregariously at his own spiteful joke and tipped his glass into his mouth with vigour.

Ainsley merely eyed his glass, turning it in his

hands and watching the liquid swirl toward the sides. The cause of Dr. Bennett's death remained present in his mind and, as much as he wanted a drink, needed a drink, he knew he must refrain. No one in the Lloyd family was to be trusted. That mistake cost Dr. Bennett his life.

Walter did not seem to notice Ainsley's decision not to drink. He slid into the back of his chair so he could cross one leg over the other. To Ainsley the heir looked quite at home in his new surroundings, relaxed, in charge. A man not to be reckoned with.

"That chair suits you," Ainsley said at last, unable to hide his amusement.

"It should. It was I who has been occupying it these past six months while he"—Walter gestured to the painting with his hand—"paraded Lily around like a trained circus bear." Walter's face turned downward, his amused tone giving away to a more serious one. "And look where that got her." He took another large mouthful of brandy and let it sit in his mouth a moment before swallowing.

"Perhaps he was training you, preparing you for the family business," Ainsley offered, not entirely believing his own explanation.

"Bah," Walter scoffed at the suggestion. "He was just running away from his responsibilities. My sisters were a convenient excuse, nothing more."

"Sisters?" Ainsley gave him a bemused look.

Walter nodded. "Josephine was to sing while Lillian played. They were to be his way out of debt." Walter's face twisted in anger and it was then that Ainsley realized the glass Walter held was probably not the first drink he'd had that day. "Trust me, Dr. Ainsley. The books he left me are a mess." Walter exhaled suddenly, and raked his hand through his hair. "It wouldn't be so bad if he hadn't spent so much of our money on his mistresses."

Ainsley hadn't expected Walter to speak of it so plainly. He was well aware of Mr. Lloyd's philandering ways and so too, it seemed, was his only son. Walter must have seen his surprise.

"He told me. He told me about them all. I know where each and every one of them are. He said I was to assist them if he should die. He did. Made me promise him on his deathbed. The bugger. I mean, what was I to do? He's my father. He's dying. I did what I had to do. What would you have done?" Walter pointed a finger at Ainsley, who pursed his lips and shrugged.

"I'd have probably told the man to see to his own affairs."

Walter's laughter filled the office. "I have no doubt you would have," he answered with a smile. "I, on the other hand, am less discerning. My father commands and I listen." The brandy glass found his lips again and he finished it off before reaching for the decanter for a refill.

"Your father took many lovers then?"

"Oh yes, quite a few. He had one or two of his favourites, of course. One even in this village, if you can believe it. Mother knew, of course. For how many years, I do not know. But she knew and it made her hard, very hard. That woman at the house is not the mother I knew growing up. After Josephine was born everything changed." His voice grew quiet when he spoke about Josephine. "Everything changed."

"One thing I don't understand," Ainsley began, "Did Lillian want the career he promised her?"

Walter shrugged. "That girl was just a pawn. We were all pawns in his game. Bet he never saw it coming." He sneered at his father, as if daring the deceased man to see him then in his chair, running his company. "I bet he thought he'd live to one hundred, the old goat!" He raised his glass then, as if toasting his father, and downed the entire contents.

Just then the door opened and Walter started, turning to the door with wide eyes, his scowl giving way to a slight smile as he recognized who stood there.

Ainsley watched as Mrs. Lloyd crossed the room briskly. An annoyed look came over her face when she saw the nearly empty decanter. She did not notice Ainsley at first. "You should be ashamed of yourself, Walter," she admonished, "with the mill in full production." She had an air of superiority, full command over all and sundry and, apparently, this part of her nature extended to her fully grown son as well.

"Just a trifle," Walter answered, dismissing her

admonishment with a shrug.

She picked up the decanter, surveying the remaining contents with disgust, the light from the window slipping past the cut crystal markings and dancing on the walls around the room.

"Besides, Mother," he said, gesturing toward Ainsley, "'Tis not like I am drinking alone."

Martha's face fell flat, like a wave of tidewater draining from an inlet, the look of recognition dawning on her. "Dr. Ainsley," she said, her happy tone unable to hide her discomfort. She placed the decanter back down on Walter's desk. "I had not realized you were about today, what with Dr. Bennett so newly deceased. I should think there is much that needs to be done."

"Lillian still remains in danger. I regret there is nothing that can be done for the doctor." He reminded himself to trust no one, least of all the woman he suspected above everyone else. "I trust Miss Lillian is better since I left her yesterday?"

"Somewhat," Mrs. Lloyd answered, giving a sideways glance to Walter. Her stance, however, did not waiver. She held her hands in front of her, fingers interlaced and clenched to show bare white knuckles. She stared at Ainsley for some time, not moving. Ainsley would not have admitted it, but he felt a cold sensation rising from the base of his back before feeling the hairs on the back of his neck rise up. Her stare was a warning. A challenge.

"We will assist in any way we can, am I right, Mother?" Walter interrupted, finishing one last mouthful from his glass.

"Of course," she answered softy.

Walter reached for the decanter, only to have Mrs. Lloyd snatch it away. She moved toward the fireplace and poured the remaining liquid into the unlit ashes. "Such a waste," she said as she watched the alcohol splash into the fireplace. Ainsley could not tell if she meant the alcohol or the drunken son sitting in the chair her husband once occupied.

Walter either ignored her comment or did not hear it. He gestured to Ainsley's half-full glass. "You haven't drunk anything."

"Oh, no," Ainsley fumbled, "I am afraid my sister has me on a very short leash."

Walter raised his eyebrows. "Your sister?"

"She just arrived in town, on the train," he explained, looking to Mrs. Lloyd as she returned the empty decanter to the side table. "I doubt she would like it very much if I indulged before dinner."

Mrs. Lloyd gave a disapproving look to her son, who had shown too much interest in the doctor's sibling. She turned to Ainsley, "Perhaps you should bring her to the Manor for tea before you return to London. We are not ready to entertain formally, so soon after the funeral, but it would be nice to meet her before you go."

"I won't be leaving until I see Lillian restored to good health. It appears she is in need of an ally."

He saw Mrs. Lloyd's upper lip twitch. She let out a long, drawn-out breath. "I must warn you, Dr. Ainsley, my daughter often finds herself easily attached."

"In what way, Mrs. Lloyd?"

"In every way. She is unlike my other children entirely. She is willful, disobedient, and often in her own world. You will understand if I am... protective." Mrs. Lloyd leaned into the edge of her son's desk and squared her shoulders to Ainsley.

"You lock her in her room to protect her?" Ainsley could not hide his displeasure at the thought. What sort of mother locks her child away?

Mrs. Lloyd did not blink at his remark. She stared at him solemnly. "My ways are unorthodox but you must trust me when I say there are necessary."

"I do not understand how allowing her to die protects her?"

"There is far more at play here, Dr. Ainsley, than I think you realize."

"Enlighten me." Ainsley felt like he was in his father's study, challenging his authority and questioning everything with the greatest sense of indignation. Ainsley realized he despised respect based on virtue of seniority. He'd rather die than let this woman cause Lillian further suffering.

Mrs. Lloyd shook her head and Ainsley saw the

slightest of smiles. "It is not a tale for me to tell. Perhaps another day when this sordid affair is behind us."

"You mean when Lillian is dead."

The woman shrugged. "If that is the will of God."

"Or the will of a murderer?" Ainsley challenged.

Mrs. Lloyd laughed openly. "You have spent far too much time in your London morgue."

Walter gave an amused look that only Ainsley could see, as Mrs. Lloyd turned and walked away from him toward the door. Opening it, she stood at the door, one hand holding it open, the other placed on her hip. She waited, her eyes not moving from Ainsley. She meant for him to leave.

Ainsley hesitated, dissatisfied with the lack of information he was able to gather. There was nothing more Ainsley could do, especially with Mrs. Lloyd present. Conceding, Ainsley rose to his feet, spying a self-satisfied grin on Mrs. Lloyd's lips as he walked toward her.

"We will receive you and your sister at the manor tomorrow afternoon," she said, in her well-groomed tone.

Ainsley stepped through the door, watching Mrs. Lloyd's hand on the doorknob as he walked past. When he was in the hallway she closed it slightly, keeping her eye on her clearly inebriated son before turning to Ainsley.

"You will speak to no one of this." She raised her hand, pointed a finger at him in warning. "Not a word of my son to a single soul."

Ainsley nodded and watched as she closed the door completely, leaving Ainsley by himself on the landing at the top of the stairs. He could hear their voices through the door, though he could not be sure what they were saying. The tone, however, was unmistakable, angry, and reprimanding. Ainsley remained to listen, practically pressing his ear to the door, but there was nothing he could decipher.

Mrs. Lloyd had scoffed at his suggestion of a murderer, though she did not outright deny the possibility. She spoke far less candidly than Miss Dawson or even Elizabeth Lloyd had, which only served to heighten Ainsley's suspicion of her. Despite her admonishments, he could tell she was floundering, wondering what would become of the family and their fortune should her only son neglect the business in favour of the drink. She was a strong woman, Ainsley realized, much stronger than he cared to give her credit for. Strong enough to commit murder perhaps?

Chapter 25

The bleak wind of March
Made her tremble and shiver;

The manor house remained somber, possessing a look that marked it as nearly uninhabited. The windows were dark and closed off by heavy drapery. In the dim November afternoon no light pierced the dull, gray exterior. The stone which was used to erect its walls looked like frozen blocks etched from the north tundra. It could be said that a dark cloud, a curse, had befallen the family who lived there and Ainsley saw a glimpse of this foreboding as he made his way up to the building's front steps. Ainsley did not believe in curses. No one, not even the rich and powerful, were immune to the tragedies of life.

The maid showed little emotion, neither pleasure or pain, when she answered the door and escorted Ainsley inside.

"Is Miss Lillian in her room?" Ainsley asked, allowing the maid to take his coat.

"She is sleeping, sir," she answered demurely. "But Miss Elizabeth is preparing to bring food to her presently." She pointed over her shoulder, leading his gaze down the hall to the kitchen.

With a great sense of liberty, Ainsley slipped through the door behind the main staircase and descended into the kitchen.

Elizabeth stood at the table in the center of the room placing a steaming bowl of dark soup on a tray while the young Mary stood next to her rolling out pastry dough. Cook stood at the stove placing a large roaster into the scullery. She raked some coals into a Dutch oven and placed an unbaked pie inside before closing the lid and placing more glowing coals and embers on top.

"Tea, please!" Elizabeth called over the busy hum of

the kitchen. She wiped her hands on her apron and turned to see Ainsley at the doorway. Startled, her expression turned sour when she saw him. The servant who had brought him in quickly made a curtsey and retreated from the room. Elizabeth placed a hand on one hip. "Another inquisition?" she asked.

"I have come to see Lillian."

"You can't. She has been resting. I don't want anything to disturb her. Least of all you." Elizabeth reached behind her waist and released her apron. Her words were short and gruff. Her movement about the room matched her tone. Ainsley wondered if the young woman, accustomed to servants and finery, often helped in the kitchen, for she seemed quite at home among them. "She has been acting rather strangely since you left yesterday," Elizabeth explained. As she moved around the kitchen she kept one eye on Ainsley, who remained by the door.

Elizabeth's gaze met his and she halted her movement. Her cheeks were freckled, Ainsley noted, the marks of a girl who once loved the outdoors. For a moment, he could see her as a child, not so different from Josephine, prancing the halls behind him in crinoline and kid boots, begging to go outside. Now she was older, less daring, and looking more and more like her mother every day. *This was it,* Ainsley thought, *the age when silly girls become serious women and never look back.* He decided to examine his sister the next time he saw her; perhaps she would possess that look as well.

"Is she better or worse?" Ainsley asked. He waited for a reply, expecting something curt.

She tore her gaze from him. "Difficult to say." Her manner softened as she spoke. She hung her apron on a hook beside him and paused. "She has not asked me to play for her. That in itself is rather odd."

"The piano, you mean?"

"Yes. She often likes to hear me play although I couldn't tell you why. I have about as much talent with the ivory as this here tabletop." She rapped the top of the table with her knuckle and let out a slight laugh. "She misses playing, I can tell. You'd think she'd try harder to get better if she really wanted to play again."

Ainsley sighed. "You cannot blame a patient for their illness."

Elizabeth knitted her brow and gave a wry smile. "She has a sick heart. That is all. She mourns for our father and now Josephine. She is my sister and I love her but... she hasn't the strongest constitution."

"What's on the menu today?" Ainsley asked, moving closer to the prepared tray for better inspection.

"Beef broth and tea." Cook replied sternly, appearing beside Elizabeth. She placed a small teapot on the tray beside a clean cup and saucer. "Go on now, Mary," she prodded the young pastry chef. "Take off your apron and help Miss Lloyd take this to her sister now." Mary moved swiftly, untying her apron strings.

A middle bell rang above the door. All four of them stopped and looked up at the ominous sign.

"Hurry now, child!" The woman cried. "She is awake!"

"Come now, Mary," Elizabeth said with a wry smile. "Let us see her mood this day."

Mary gave a nod of anticipation and the robust woman, the head cook, simply rolled her eyes.

Mary slipped her grip around the handles of the tray and followed Elizabeth out the door. Ainsley watched for a moment before turning to Cook. A wave of relief spread over her face.

"Not easily satisfied, is she then?" Ainsley asked.

"You could say that again. That child has been ruined. All that work on the stage, touring around Europe, performing and such. It's no wonder she has turned slightly sour."

"Perhaps it was all the attention."

"Well now, that is what I have said, many a time. She had a sweet disposition before her father gave her the notion that she was above everyone else. It seemed every time she practiced Miss Lillian become worse and worse. Lord, I ain't never seen such a sour child." Cook returned to the stove and lifted a lid on the pot. She stirred it once before coming back to the table to finish the pie Mary had been forced to leave in such a hurry. "Ain't no good prescribing her tonics and such. She refuses to take 'em.

She's been caught more 'an once pouring 'em bottles in the flower vases."

Ainsley raised an eyebrow.

"Yes," the cook continued, "it's like she's punishing herself. Making herself suffer as her father and sister suffered. I'd say she's asking to die, if you ask me."

"Do you remember when Mr. Lloyd fell ill?" Ainsley asked, leaning on the counter ledge while the cook worked on the pie dough.

"Yes, sir. They just came back from a trip to... can't recall where. He fell ill on the train, Miss Lillian said. Lingered on for a week and that quack could do nothing for 'em. I told Mrs. Lloyd she needed someone else, someone young like yourself who don't resort to bleeding and blistering a poor man when he's ill."

"Do you remember what ailed him? What were his symptoms?"

"The chamber maid was run ragged. Chamber pot after chamber pot. Coming out at both ends. I was shocked the old man had so much in 'im." A nervous chuckle escaped her lips before she tightened them. "I shouldn't be making light of the dead," she said as way of an apology. "We could tell he was wasting away."

"Did anyone stay with him? A nurse, perhaps?"

The cook shook her head as she lifted the rolled out dough onto another pie plate. "They all took their turn watching over him, 'cept for Master Lloyd, who saw to the mills while his father was away."

Ainsley nodded. "Were Josephine and Lillian in contact with him?"

"We all were at some point." She shrugged. "I suppose Miss Lillian and Josie caught whatever done him in. It is only a matter of time before Lillian is called away too." The woman broke down. She bunched her eyes together in an effort to squelch the tears, but to no avail. She turned, and raised her apron to her eyes.

Ainsley struggled to keep her focused. "When he ate did his condition worsen?"

"He did not eat much of anything."

"Who brought his food?" His questions came fast and almost frantic.

"Usually a handmaid though Mrs. Lloyd and Miss Lloyd approved everything that left this kitchen for him."

"Did Mrs. Lloyd or Miss Lloyd serve him most?"

"Well, Mrs. Lloyd didn't like seeing her husband in such a way, she'd often ask Miss Elizabeth to see to it..." Her voice trailed off. "What are you saying, Doctor?"

Ainsley was not given the chance to answer. Outside of the door behind him a noise sprung up. He could hear loud wailing and another voice cursing as they descended the kitchen stairs. Mary charged through the door first, her hair and clothes soggy. She was crying into her sodden dress and shielded her face from Ainlsey's concerned stare.

"That sister of mine can fetch her own food!" Elizabeth yelled as she walked through the door. "Mary needs some new clothes."

"What happened?" Cook asked, trying to sooth the tears of the young maid.

"She tossed the bowl of soup at Mary! She accused us all of trying to poison her and says she will not consume another bite." Elizabeth fell hopeless into a chair and slipped her fingers through her hair. It was then that she remembered Ainsley was in the room watching this entire exchange. "You did this to her. You filled her head with the nonsense of poisoning."

"She feels targeted," Ainsley explained. "She said as much to me."

Elizabeth shook her head in annoyance and turned to Cook. "She said someone poisoned Josephine and she was not going to be next." Elizabeth rubbed her face in exasperation. "She's been saying that for a week now, though she has never acted like this. She raised the bowl right off the tray, didn't she Mary? And hurled the dish, soup and all, at both of us!"

"Lord help us!" Cook said.

Elizabeth turned to the cook, her expression channeling that of her mother. "Remember your place!" she snapped.

This was a side of Elizabeth that Ainsley had never seen. Upon the reprimand, Cook escorted Mary from the room.

"Perhaps I should talk to her now," Ainsley offered.

Elizabeth shrugged, resigned to her inability to improve the situation. She slipped the key to Lillian's bedroom in Ainsley's hand but refused to look him in the eye as she did so.

Ainsley left her there, alone in the kitchen, and climbed the stairs to Lillian's room.

The room was silent when he entered and he found Lillian sitting at her window, crying. She turned to him as he walked in and smiled while wiping her tear-stained cheeks. "I know what you must think of me," she said, so softly Ainsley almost didn't hear.

Ainsley slipped past the shattered pieces of porcelain that remained on her rug, the remnants of the soup that were not dripping from Mary's dress oozed into the wood floors beneath. "I think you are scared," Ainsley answered, taking a seat opposite her on the edge of the bed.

Lillian hesitated, as if unwilling to admit that she was indeed scared. She smiled suddenly. "I am feeling so much better," she said as brightly as she could muster. "But I am terribly hungry."

Ainsley nodded. He reached out to tuck a rogue tendril of hair behind her ear. The dark circles under her eyes highlighted how tired she was. She looked as though she hadn't slept in weeks, and perhaps she hadn't.

"I have an idea," he said at long last. "I'll be back in one moment." He left the room briefly and when he returned he handed Lillian her housecoat, which she put on without question. As soon as she was decent Ainsley slipped his arms around her and scooped her up. Instinctively Lillian clung to his neck and shoulders as he carried her down the hall. Ainsley ignored the feelings of warmth between their close bodies and carefully concentrated on the stairs in front of him. Easily he carried her body around the staircase and past the door to the dining room, where the three healthy Lloyd family members dined in abject silence. Only the muted sounds of silverware touching china came from the room.

Ainsley felt Lillian's grip tighten as they passed and she nuzzled her face deeper into his neck. He could feel the warmth of her breath on his skin. He dared not look to her, their faces were so close.

They descended the back stairs and entered the dark kitchen, where the butler and handmaid were already placing a recently acquired cushioned chair. Gently, Ainsley slipped Lillian into the chair and took a throw blanket from another maid who stood close by. He nodded to the help in thanks. Cook stood at the hearth fire, silent, a hand perched on her round hip as Ainsley placed the blanket around Lillian.

"You say you know your way around a kitchen, Dr. Ainsley. I will take you at your word," Cook said sternly. "But if I find one kettle out of place..." she raised a fist in the air as warning.

"I promise to be respectful," Ainsley answered with a hint of humility. He bowed slightly.

"Dr. Ainsley?" Lillian asked looking around the room as the faces of the hired help looked on. Mary, somewhat cleaned up from the prior escapade, remained hidden toward the back and looked on with caution. The inner workings of the household were meant to be hidden from the residents of the house.

"Trust me," Ainsley said. He turned to the hired help, "Ladies, if you wouldn't mind." He motioned to the door with his hand asking them to leave. All the undermaids did as he bid but Cook did not move. "I can tolerate a parlour chair in my kitchen, and would even risk the wrath of my mistress but I will not be removed from my post by any man or beast." She huffed. "I ain't about to leave, young sir," she pronounced with respectful vehemence. "This 'ere is my kitchen."

Ainsley looked to Lillian, who was trying not to laugh. The young doctor shrugged and resigned to her presence. "Very well," he answered. "You will not help me then, not even for a moment."

Cook eyed him suspiciously and reluctantly agreed. "The scullery is just around the corner here," she said, pointing to a room off of the kitchen. "I could finish the cleanup from dinner and still remain close to keep a watchful eye." Ainsley saw Cook eye the eager Miss Lillian, who sat in the parlour chair, blanket pulled up to her chin, knees gathered to her chest. There was a smile of delight on her pale lips. "A smile is such a rare thing in this house even in the best of times," Cook said, as she slipped into the scullery slowly.

With Cook in the scullery, Ainsley stood on the other side of the room, the long butcher block table separating him from his patient. He removed his overcoat and draped it over a nearby stool. Tying an apron around his waist, he glanced around the room for something he could make. His plan was simple. He would make Lillian a good dinner right before her eyes so she could see no one had poisoned it. Ainsley knew that with a bit of effort he could convince her that he, of all people, could be trusted.

There was a kettle already at a boil over the cook stove and so at first he made a fresh pot of tea. He was careful to perform each task in full view so that she could not question him. "Now, Miss Lillian, may I ask how you like your tea?"

"Just a bit of honey, please," she answered meekly before biting her lower lip.

Ainsley could feel her watching him as he fumbled slightly with the tea leaves. He wondered if this was her first time out of her bedchamber since she first fell ill. He presented her cup of tea, small specks of leaves floating on the surface, with an apologetic smile.

Steam rose from the liquid as she held it with both hands wrapped around the china cup. Ainsley watched with amazement as Lillian sipped her tea ravenously. He saw her eye it lovingly before raising it to her lips again. "You must be famished," he said as he watched.

Lillian's trance was interrupted and she looked at him over her teacup. She nodded but said nothing.

"Well, I will get to it then." He glanced around the room and saw a bunch of carrots resting on the shelf, and some herbs that were hung to dry above them. With a quick scan he saw parsley, onions, and butter. In a crockery jar, he found a bit of rice and was instantly reminded of a soup his mother made for him once. He began by peeling and chopping the carrots. He became very much aware of two sparkling eyes watching him closely as he worked. With one carrot peeled he offered it to Lillian. She eyed it suspiciously.

"Try it," he offered. He broke off a piece and popped it into his mouth to demonstrate before holding a piece out to her. As a child, it was nothing for him to pluck a carrot from the ground, brush it on his pant legs and munch away. His mother's kitchen garden, her special sanctuary in which no servant was allowed admittance, was abundant with herbs and vegetables. When denied access to the kitchen Ainsley and his sister always found a treat in the garden.

Lillian took the whole carrot and gingerly put it to her lips. Aware of his watchful eye, she nibbled a piece from the whole. "You eat carrots like this? Raw?"

Ainsley laughed. "All the time." A raw carrot plucked from the garden was so commonplace to him as a child. How could it be that Lillian had never had a raw carrot before?

"My mother used to say carrots are good for your eyes," he said as he turned his attention back to the bunch in front of him.

"And are they?" Lillian asked, "Doctor?"

Ainsley smiled. "A healthy diet is the first step to better health. Vegetables are nature's wonder food." His knife hit the chopping board with marked regularity. "Food is our best defense against disease."

"And what if the food is what is making you sick?"

"Then I would say, 'tis not the food, but something else. A way in which it was prepared, or stored—"

"Or if something is added to it?"

His chopping stopped but he didn't take his eyes from the carrots. "Yes." Ainsley let out a breath and looked up, leaning slightly on the table. "What you need is to gain your strength back. If I have to come here every day to make you your meals, I will. And I will sit here and watch you eat until I am satisfied."

"You would do that for me?" Lillian beamed.

"Of course," he answered with a smile. "I'm your doctor."

Lillian's grin slipped away. He turned to the stove and started cooking the chopped carrots and onion in a bit of butter.

Cook slipped in from the scullery and threw another

shuttle of coal into the cook stove. "Fire's nearly out," she said dryly. "Wasn't expecting to do any more cooking today." She glared at Ainsley like he was an intruder she was only barely tolerating. With her hands on her hips, she inspected his concoction with a raised eyebrow. "And where did a man like yourself learn to cook?"

Ainsley smiled. "My mother, ma'am," he answered willingly. "I'm afraid our cook wasn't as well versed as you. My mother often stepped in because she couldn't bear the thought of us eating so poorly."

Cook grinned.

"You wouldn't happen to have a splash of brandy, would you?" Ainsley asked eyeing the vegetables as they cooked.

"What for?" Cook asked her eyes narrowing.

"For the soup, of course."

She pursed her lips and pulled a small bottle of brandy from one of the cupboards. She placed it on the butcher's block behind him. "I can finish if you like," she offered.

"No thank you, ma'am." Ainsley glanced to Lillian. "I'd like to do it, if you don't mind."

"Be sure to clean up now, when you are done. Don't want to come down in the morning with twice as much work to do."

"No, ma'am. I will take care of everything."

Cook lingered for a moment more. She walked slowly to the back of the kitchen, toward the servant stairs. Before heading up she turned, "I will send the butler in intermittent-like... just to make sure you are behaving like a gentleman."

Ainsley tilted his head down. "I would expect nothing less."

Appeased, Cook nodded before turning to leave.

Lillian nursed her tea, cupping the porcelain teacup in both hands. The young woman looked longingly at the food Ainsley was preparing. "What are you making?" she asked, craning her neck to see.

Ainsley smiled. "It's a surprise."

The day had slipped away, conceding its command to the arrival of night. Ainsley lit a few candlesticks and spread them out on the table between him and Lillian to give some light to his preparations. He worked in silence for a long while, his mind giving the task at hand his full attention when Lillian spoke up.

"My mother tells me I should not trust you," she said, placing her now empty teacup on the butcher block and sinking further into the folds of her warm blanket.

"Is that so?"

"Yes, my sister too. They say I am becoming too attached."

Ainsley smiled a crooked smile. "Are you?" he asked while stirring the nearly ready soup.

Even in the dim light, he saw her smile. The pause that followed unnerved him. She was either thinking of a way to politely agree with them or thinking of a way to subdue her regard.

"Perhaps I should be more guarded with you. You don't plan to stay in Picklow forever, do you?"

Ainsley shook his head reluctantly. "My work is best performed in London." He filled two bowls with the warm carrot soup and garnished it with a sprig of parsley.

"You will leave me then." Lillian shifted uncomfortably in her chair as he approached her with the soup bowl.

"Not until I know you are well."

"I wish you could stay." She lifted her gaze as he placed the bowl in front of her. She reached out her hand and touched his before he could pull it away. "I wish I could go with you." Her voice was nearly at a whisper but her eyes were determined.

Ainsley hesitated. He met her gaze squarely and did not move right away. "I wish you could too," he found himself saying before he could stop himself. He pulled away, reluctantly, and fetched his own bowl of soup, which waited for him at the other end of the butcher block.

"It had to be this way," he heard Lillian say as he positioned his soup across from hers. "Otherwise, we would never have met." She smiled sweetly.

She was stunning and he found himself adoring everything about her. Her smile, her whispering voice, her challenging eyes. In essence, she was every beautiful woman he had ever beheld all together in one person. There was a sadness, though, something that veiled her true feelings from him, something that only enticed him to find out more, to discover every inch of her inside and out.

It was ludicrous really, that he should fall so quickly for someone he was employed to assist. If she liked him, it was because her family didn't. His profession represented a certain amount of intrigue, though he doubted that she truly wanted to be a surgeon's wife. Inadvertently, a smile spread over his face as he thought about it.

"What amuses you?" Lillian asked. She had seen his mischievous smile and felt no shame in calling attention to it.

"I was thinking of you in one week's time, fully recovered and playing the piano once more," Ainsley answered. It was only a half lie.

"And you so far away in London, you won't be around to hear it."

Ainsley lowered his gaze to his soup. It wasn't that he wanted to return to London, it was just there was no acceptable reason for him to stay. "Perhaps I will have the pleasure just once before I go."

"Perhaps."

Ainsley watched as Lillian drew the soup to her mouth with the spoon. She licked her lips as she lowered the spoon back to the bowl. "Tastes wonderful," she said, taking up her spoon again. "Your mother must be a delight."

Ainsley smiled nervously. He wasn't prepared to broach the subject of his family with her. His mother, father and their antics were of greater consequence to his reputation than his profession and he wondered if Lillian would be as understanding if she knew the truth.

"She is a beautiful woman," he said, "both inside and out."

"Does she approve of your profession?" Lillian asked, slowly dipping her spoon in her soup to break the surface.

"She's always been supportive of anything I wished to do. My father, on the other hand, is another matter. He would rather I study business or law."

"Why did you choose to be a surgeon?"

Ainsley smiled. "For many reasons. The most important is that I wish to help people. I can offer peace in a terrible situation or I can track an illness before others die." He stared at the opposite wall while he spoke. "I have seen some terrible things in this world," he said in a near whisper. "Things I never thought possible until they were in front of me on the examination table. Sometimes I think if I were a better man I could have saved them. I could save us all from such hardship and pain." He looked up and saw Lillian staring at him.

"You are a good man, Peter. I know you will save me." She smiled sweetly then and lowered her gaze to her soup.

"Do you like your soup?" Ainsley asked, trying to free his mind from the harsh memories of the work that awaited him in London.

"Very much." Lillian smiled. "Can I have some more?" she asked, titling her bowl to reveal it had been emptied of its contents.

☙ ❧

Lillian insisted on another cup of tea while Ainsley washed up the dishes. When he returned from the scullery, Lillian was curled up in the chair beneath her blanket sleeping soundly. He blew out all of the candles but the one closest to her. As he bent to extinguish that one as well, he paused. The gentle curve of her cheek looked smooth and inviting, and it was all he could do to stop himself from reaching out to stroke it. She looked like an angel, innocent and naive. She looked so frail, so vulnerable. All he wanted to do was protect her, save her from whatever was making her ill.

Her body folded into his as he scooped her up from the chair. She hugged her arms around him again and buried her face in his neck. Blowing out the final candle, he left the room, carrying his patient up the stairs to her chamber.

Nestled into her bed, he hesitated to let her go. She

held fast to him, preventing him from moving away. She seemed to wake slightly then, her eyes opening as she whispered, "Stay with me."

Ainsley dared not move. He hadn't the strength to pull away nor did he have the audacity to act upon the undeniable urge to kiss her. He knew if he threw caution to the wind at that moment he would be compromising his position as her doctor. He knew, by the way she clung to him, that he would not be denied. Their faces were mere inches from each other and he could kiss her, wildly, if he had any less resolve.

In a sudden surge of composure, he brushed his lips gently over the curve of her cheek and secretly hoped she would forget about it by morning. "I can't," he whispered, and finally found the strength to pull away.

Chapter 26

But not the dark arch,
Or the black flowing river:

Ainsley reached Dr. Bennett's house just before midnight. The house was silent, not simply audibly silent but everything was gripped by the hush of recent death. The intensity of mourning may not have been as pronounced as it was at the Lloyd residence but it was unmistakably there. As Ainsley walked through the front door he could also sense an emptiness and he knew at once that the body of Dr. Bennett was gone, most likely on its way back to Edinburgh for burial.

Ainsley paused momentarily at the bottom of the stairs, his hand perched on the handrail, his gaze fixated on the closed door at the top of the stairs, the room in which Dr. Bennett slept and then died. Exhaustion taking hold, Ainsley shuffled to the parlour and found Jonas at a side table, a microscope in front of him and medical texts arranged around him. He wore his spectacles, perched on the bridge of his nose, while he looked into the lens of the scientific tool. Jonas took one look at Ainsley, and seeing the fatigue on his face, abandoned his intense study. "Should I ask how the rest of your day went?"

Ainsley shook his head, said nothing, and slipped into the armchair.

Mrs. Crane emerged from the kitchen. She looked to the empty chair beside Ainsley, the chair in which Bennett had sat when she served them sandwiches and tea just days before. Ainsley could see her pushing back tears as she straightened her stance and addressed him directly. "Dr. Bennett's brother came for him this afternoon while you were out," Mrs. Crane explained, evidence of recent weeping lacing the highs and lows of her voice. "He said he was sorry to have missed you."

Ainsley nodded. "Likewise. I am sorry to have missed him."

The room fell silent for a moment, each occupant lost in their own thoughts. Ainsley had been so focused on Lillian that he had nearly forgotten that he lost a new friend. Even the autopsy did not seem real, just an educational exercise like all the others. It was only then, with the body gone and normal life attempting to move forward, hesitation punctuating each action, that Ainsley saw the loss, the real loss he felt for his new friend and colleague.

It was the weary exhale of breath from Mrs. Crane that drew Ainsley's attention back to the business at hand. "He said you can forward the death certificate as soon as you have signed it."

Ainsley nodded, still unsure of how much information he should give the housekeeper. Would she want to know that the man she worked for all these years had been murdered? Or was it better to keep her believing it was the damp chill that did him in? As the examining physician, Ainsley was bound by oath to give an accurate account of his and Jonas's findings, but perhaps he needed to play his cards closer to his chest. A quick glance to Jonas gave him further reason to keep the cause of death to himself for the time being. There was no point in upsetting things, not when he was so desperate to find out who the killer was.

"I will complete it in the morning." His answer was greeted with a nod from Mrs. Crane before she retreated to the kitchen.

"You don't plan on telling her?" Jonas asked, leaning in closer and placing his elbows on his knees. His hands were in front of him clutching his round spectacles in delicate fingers.

Ainsley gave a quick shake of his head and pursed his lips. "Not yet. Can't have her spreading rumours around town, not when I am so close." Ainsley began to bite his knuckles as he stared at the dying fire in front of him in the hearth. "I told the Lloyds about my suspicions, of course." Ainsley heard Jonas give a slight gasp but did not turn to look. If his method of detection was not clear to his friend, then how could he explain himself? "They will not tell a soul. They wouldn't want to be wrapped up in a scandal now, would they?"

Jonas looked skeptical.

"I told them as a way of deciphering more about their character. Would they be shocked, or would they take it easily?"

"Which was it?"

"Mrs. Lloyd and Miss Elizabeth were both dismayed. They seemed to have a professional, yet slightly personal regard for Dr. Bennett; yet when I saw Mrs. Lloyd today it appeared to be business as usual for the Lloyd family."

"What do you make of that?"

"Can't say. Margaret and I have been invited to visit tomorrow."

Jonas raised an eyebrow at this, most likely wondering why he had not been invited as well.

"Cheer up, my friend," Ainsley said with a slight laugh. "I can't say you will be missing much. Margaret will be under strict orders not to eat a morsel. I will not have that on my conscience as well." Ainsley slipped further into his chair, stretching his legs to the ottoman in front of him.

"As well? You can't mean to say you take responsibility for Dr. Bennett's death?"

Ainsley gave his friend a questioning look. "Why is it so outlandish? He and I were partners. For all I know that funeral cake was meant for me. I should have seen it coming, quite frankly. Dr. Bennett himself told me he suspected poisoning. I was simply too analytical to believe it straight away. I feel like I should have listened to him."

Jonas leaned forward and looked intently at Ainsley. "Do not be so hard on yourself. You could not have known."

For a moment, Ainsley remained pensive. His fingers danced over his chin, as if imitating the thoughts swirling in his head. "What if that funeral cake was meant for me?" His eyes were grave when his gaze found his friend. "He ate his and mine, since I haven't much interest in sweets. Mine could have been the poisoned one."

"I suppose it's possible." Jonas reached for the desk and grabbed the two tonic bottles Ainsley had given him earlier. "These were clear," he said. "There was a slight amount of arsenic in this one though completely within standard medicinal amounts."

Ainsley nodded.

Dr. Bennett was killed with arsenic, this they had proven, but there was no evidence that either Mr. Lloyd or Josephine were poisoned, save for some anecdotal evidence of their illnesses. Ainsley needed more proof if he had any hope of diagnosing Lillian.

"I need to see the bodies," Ainsley said suddenly. "With or without Mrs. Lloyd's permission." Ainsley looked over to his friend. "Care to join me?"

"What? Tonight?" Jonas rubbed his hand over his tired eyes.

Ainsley stood up quickly. "It would be like old times." Ainsley flashed his friend a mischievous grin. For doctors in training, grave robbing was a way to make enough money to pay for schooling. Ainsley did it for the thrill, of course, giving all of his earnings to Jonas. They stuck to the cemeteries on the outskirts of London, since harvesting bodies for science had been outlawed and the city's burial sites were more heavily patrolled. With only a pale moon to light their way, they would target the recently buried and cart them, under the cover of darkness, to the university, where they would be paid handsomely. The professors all knew and would even encourage the practice, seeing it as beneficial to both student and school.

Enticing Jonas to come with him, Ainsley was anxious to head out. "I need to see it," he said, grabbing for his jacket, "with my own eyes."

Chapter 27

Mad from life's history,
Glad to death's mystery,

The town was asleep with scarcely enough light to navigate the streets. Once in the graveyard their anxiety rose. They carried no lanterns, lit candles, or any other source of light that may have given their presence away. They did, however, have a shovel each swung over their shoulder and a cache of candles stashed in their jacket pockets.

"Do you think we could come back in summer when it is a bit warmer?" Jonas asked, warily.

"I hardly think it would be as useful to us by then," Ainsley answered. He led the way through the sizable burial grounds, weaving between headstones and grave markers, with only the haphazard light of the moon to guide him.

"Ow!"

Ainsley turned, ready to admonish his friend for calling out so loudly, when he saw that Jonas had walked into a headstone and broken it in half. "For Pete's sake!" Ainsley retraced his steps and helped him lift the stone. They leaned the broken half against the base and quickly moved on.

Ainsley reached into his pocket and pulled out his flask. "Here, this will help keep us warm."

A few moments later, they had found Josephine's grave. The fresh mound of dirt used to cover her coffin had settled somewhat during the recent rainfall. Ainsley stood for a moment looking at the headstone. The clouds thinned partially, allowing the moon's glow to light their work and they began, slicing into the dirt with their shovels. Their pile of overturned gravel grew larger and larger as they worked silently. They soon forgot the cold, as their hard labour warmed their bodies, and eventually they threw their jackets over a nearby gravestone before continuing.

The work was intense, slightly more so than Ainsley remembered. The palms of his hands began to burn as the shovel's wooden handle rubbed his soft, privileged hands. He remembered what had been appealing about grave robbing, and surgery, in the first place. He loved the work, the physical act of completing a task, something that was so rare among his class, whose work revolved predominately around the pushing of paper and pens behind a striking mahogany desk, if they were required to work at all. While Ainsley didn't want to be required to labour like this all the time, he saw value in it, perhaps more so than his peers.

The pile beside the grave grew high and the pair sank deeper and deeper into the ground. Their shovels worked in unison, slicing into the somewhat compact dirt before heaving it over their shoulders in one movement. Neither one dared to stop, though Ainsley was tempted to many times. His arms ached and his hands burned but he knew if he stopped it would be harder to get moving again.

Finally he felt the tip of his shovel hit wood, the top of Josephine's delicately made coffin. Gingerly they scraped the rest of the dirt from the top of the coffin and then threw their shovels up to the grass level.

"I'll give you the honours," Jonas said, making a retreat from the grave. Once on top, he pulled out the candles they had stashed in their jackets and wedged them in the dirt that made the walls of the grave. Ainsley pulled out a box of matches and struck one, and used it to light the hole in which he was required to work. He saw Jonas above him, laying on his stomach in the grass, his head over the edge to watch. He reached out to warm his hands on the tiny candle flames.

"Do you think this will be enough light?"

Ainsley looked up and saw Jonas's breath as he spoke. "Has to be, I have nothing else."

With the wax dripping from the lit candles, Ainsley pulled at the lid of the coffin. It wouldn't move. Using a shovel, he was able to pry it open, the creaking wood sending involuntary shivers through his body. It was loud, which made him cringe at the thought of someone discovering them. The coffin lid came off its hinges. He passed it to Jonas while he straddled the walls of the coffin ensuring he did not disturb the body.

Josephine's skin was a dark blue, her hair was damp and no longer did she resemble the doll-like young girl Ainsley had seen when he first arrived at the manor. Normally, Ainsley would not look to the face, not unless he absolutely had to. In this case, he found himself unable to pull his gaze away. She resembled Lillian to a degree and seeing her in the deep underground pit made his stomach lurch. Lillian did not deserve such a fate, nor did Josephine, but he knew there was nothing left that he could do for the younger sister. Lillian was still alive, and he could keep her that way if only he could find the source of her pain.

There was something else as well. Something about Josephine that made him stare. He grabbed one of the candles from the dirt walls and placed it next to her face. She looked familiar. He knew that he had seen her body before but looking at her then, decomposing and further along in rot, he felt as if he had seen her alive at one point, eyes opened wide, breathing and laughing perhaps. He had seen her at one time, alive and well. But how could that be?

He willed himself to focus on the body, not the person, before him.

Jonas passed Ainsley his tool case and Ainsley laid it out at the side of Josephine's head. His dirty hands and mud-smeared boots tarnished the lavish white of the coffin's satin lining. He could not care for that now. If he did his job properly he could find what he needed quickly, replace the coffin lid and the soil without anyone ever seeing the need to exhume her.

He cut her dress at the middle, pulling it apart and peeling the layers of under clothes to access her stomach. He did not intend to do as thorough an examination as he would in normal circumstances. All he wanted was the stomach. That organ alone would reveal what he needed to know.

With one quick slice, he opened her abdomen and slipped his bare hand into the opening he had created. He searched with precision, and found the stomach within seconds. He pulled back the skin and then the muscle of her stomach and cut the organ out from the body with quick, decisive actions.

"Get the jar!" he called up to Jonas, holding the near black organ in both hands so it did not fall.

Jonas held the jar for him as he placed the stomach inside.

There would be no need to sew her back up, no need to clean the skin or replace her clothing, though the last thing he did out of respect. With slightly bloody hands, he folded up his tool case, and handed it to Jonas. He replaced the coffin lid and then scrambled to ground level.

"You can't just leave her like that," Jonas said when Ainsley climbed out. "It's indecent."

"No one will see. We can fill it in and no one will ever know," Ainsley said. He sealed the jar with Josephine's stomach and turned to the shovels. "It's just a body, nothing more."

Jonas eyed him indignantly for some time, no doubt wondering if what they were doing was as harmless as the grave robbing they performed as students. Ainsley crouched down and began to extinguish the tiny candle flames and collected the remaining candles.

"She cannot be buried in pieces," Jonas said at long last.

Ainsley rounded on him suddenly, his face tense with fury and his eyes wide. "Why not?" he yelled. "I cannot let Lillian die!" His jaw was clenched and he held fists at his side. Was he prepared to fight for her? At this point, he would do anything for her. "All I need is the stomach, now help me or get out of here!"

There was a snap, a twig splitting somewhere in the near darkness around them. Ainsley's desperate fury was forgotten and they both stared into the darkness, trying to decipher its clues. The hairs on Ainsley's neck stood on end and he could feel they were being watched. He wanted to call out, as he had done the other night, demanding whoever it was to identify themselves but he dared not call attention to their misdeeds. Ainsley gripped the shovel's handle tighter, and scanned the darkness. After a few moments, the unease alleviated and he glanced to Jonas.

He had a vise grip on his shovel as well and was ready to pounce should the need have arisen.

"Let's just clean this up and get out of here," Ainsley said.

The first glow of the sun began to seep over the horizon just as they placed the last two shovelfuls of dirt back on to Josephine's grave. Ainsley patted it down with the back of his shovel before using his hands to dust away the impressions the tool had made. If they were lucky it would rain and then no one would notice the disturbance to the grave.

Jonas hoisted the shovels over his shoulders, and Ainsley carried the jar beneath his coat. The blood on his fingernails was hidden among layers of dirt that seeped into the wrinkles of his skin. He wanted to get back to the house quickly, clean himself up, and get back to work but he did not want to risk walking through town in case they were happened upon. There was a way to get to Bennett's house through the woods but it would take longer and they were already spent.

Chapter 28

*Swift to be hurl'd—
Anywhere, anywhere
Out of the world!*

They slept like the dead, Ainsley in the chair, Jonas on the sofa. Neither one stirred when the sunlight began to stream boldly into the windows. Even the smell of Mrs. Crane's baking did not disturb them. Her scream, however, would have woken everyone in a ten-mile radius. Jarred from deep sleep, Ainsley fell from the chair while trying to untangle himself from the quilt. He was still clothed from the night before.

Jonas, still hazy from much needed sleep, tried to pry the sealed organ jar from Mrs. Crane's trembling hands. "I will take care of it," Jonas said, sleepily.

"What is it?" she asked in a near shriek.

"Does it matter?" Jonas asked.

In their haste to get some sleep, they must have left the jar in plain view.

"Mrs. Crane," Ainsley said, approaching the pair slowly, "it is a vital part of my research."

He saw the housekeeper's grip loosen and Jonas slipped it away and hid it in a box near his microscope and other assorted devices.

"Who is it from?" she asked.

"That does not matter," Ainsley explained, hoping she would not press for further information.

Mrs. Crane hesitated, hands on hips and lips pressed together. "My last days in this house and I find that on my table." She clicked her tongue. "What are the both of you wearing?" She looked over their dusty clothing. "You look like the church gravedigger—" She cut her words short as she realized what it all meant.

"I beg you not to tell a single soul," Ainsley

implored. "A young woman's life depends on it."

She eyed the pair of them suspiciously. "Is this about Lillian Lloyd?" she asked.

"Yes," Ainsley confirmed.

"And we'd appreciate your discretion on this rather delicate matter," Jonas added, with a smile.

Mrs. Crane shook her head in disbelief. "Fifteen years working for a doctor and I never saw the like. I will keep your secret but next time do better so I never have to know." She turned from them and walked toward the kitchen. Ainsley secretly wished he could take her back to London, perhaps employ her in his own home once he was able to acquire one. She was a hoot, if not a damn fine cook. Her discretion was necessary especially for his line of work.

Ainsley looked to Jonas, who was running his hands over his face in an apparent effort to wake completely. "I suppose we should get started," he said, rolling up his shirtsleeves.

Jonas nodded slowly.

Ainsley pulled out the jar from the box and prepared the surface of the table while Jonas retrieved the appropriate tools. Both doctors leaned over the stomach and reached for the scalpel at the same time.

"Oh," Ainsley said, "why don't you do the honours?"

Jonas nodded.

Ainsley reasoned his friend was far more experienced in toxicology than he was. Besides, Ainsley was so anxious for the results that he could hardly keep himself from subtly shaking. He retreated to a chair a few paces away and sat to watch as Jonas sliced open the stomach cavity.

"There it is," Jonas said.

Ainsley jerked awake. He must have fallen asleep while waiting because when Ainsley opened his eyes he saw Jonas bent over his microscope, the dissection finished.

"What is it?" Ainsley jumped to his feet to take a look himself. Jonas stepped out of the way so his friend could see. Ainsley peered through the lens.

"Arsenic," Jonas said, "Enough grains to take on a full adult. That child didn't stand a chance."

"Was she poisoned deliberately?" Ainsley asked, without taking his eyes from the microscope.

Jonas twisted his mouth to one side and pulled his spectacles from his face. He looked as if he wanted to say yes but he hesitated. "In my professional opinion, yes. I'd be willing to testify to that, should it come to it."

He knew it to be true and he had hesitated, as Jonas had, not wanting to say the words. Arsenic was everywhere, in cloth dyes, skin creams, and wallpaper. Arsenic could be found in every household in the empire and was a very efficient rat poison and parasite control for sheep.

Ainsley let out a deep growl in frustration. "But who?"

He pulled out his flask and drank half of it down before coming up for air. His head hurt, the millions of possibilities, the who's and why's making a mess of his internal comprehension. His days had been so long, so packed with information he doubted he would remember it all. Soon the realization that he was in over his head hit him, and hit him hard. He thought he was too recently graduated, too inexperienced for such a task. How could he ever decipher all these clues, nuances, and behaviours to come to a firm conclusion?

The young doctor found no solace at the bottom of his flask. His drinking only muddied the waters, made his face burn red and his mind dizzy. He was in no mood for being a doctor anymore. He could be a complete dredge on society, gamble, drink, and whore his way to death. He could live quite comfortably in his own right without the bother of blood, death, and human attachments. It was during times like these, when the work piled up and the stress grew, that Ainsley agreed that ignorance truly was bliss.

"Why do I do this, Jonas? Why do I insist on being a surgeon?" Ainsley stood and walked to Dr. Bennett's mahogany hutch, pulling a glass bottle of scotch from one of the doors. He filled his flask and then poured himself a glass.

"Goodness knows you don't do it for the money," Jonas answered with a laugh. He stepped to a nearby chair and practically fell into it.

Ainsley smiled crookedly. "You do, though." He had not meant the comment to be mean but it came out as such. Jonas winced at the suggestion and Ainsley realized the connotations of what he had said.

Ainsley glanced to the bottle in his hand. "I think I drink too much. Forgive me." He returned to his seat but did not let go of the bottle.

Jonas did not meet Ainsley's eyes, and eventually Ainsley looked away. He stared at the ripples of the flames in the hearth, his heart sinking deeper into his stomach with each passing moment. His face soon turned into a scowl and he began pulling at the loose threads on his trousers, a gesture that reminded him of his last meeting with his father.

"I am just like him, aren't I? My father, I mean." Ainsley finally looked over to his friend, who had turned to him. "The drinking, the arrogance, our attachment to money. He and I are so similar and it vexes me greatly."

"You are not so dissimilar, though I would leave out the attachment to money bit."

"No, it is true," Ainsley disagreed. "Or else why would I say such a thing?" Ainsley curled his hand into a fist and dropped in onto his knee with an intended force. "I hate the man, despise him for his very existence, and I hate him for passing all his faults on to me. I try to dampen it with this." Ainsley tossed his empty silver flask onto the table beside him and watched as the curved metal container rocked back and forth before finally coming to a stop. "I wish I were more like Mother."

Ainsley saw Jonas become suddenly uncomfortable, adjusting his pant leg as he shifted in his chair. "What? What is it?" Ainsley asked.

Jonas shook his head and appeared quite uncomfortable about speaking on the subject. "I promised not to say anything."

"Margaret said you went with her to Tunbridge Wells. Something must have happened. It isn't Father, is it? Has he decided to divorce Mother?" Ainsley turned in his chair to look his friend squarely in the face. The somber look he received only further fuelled his alarm. "Goddamn him."

"Peter, calm down. It is not your father."

"Then tell me. Tell me at once, or do not call me friend."

Jonas let out a deep exhale of breath. "I promised I would not tell. Margaret made me promise."

Ainsley stood up suddenly, and Jonas flinched at the anger he displayed. "I have been your friend far longer than she!" Ainsley raked his hand through his ruffled hair while he paced in front of the hearth. "Go to her then. Go to her now if she is so important to you." Ainsley pointed to the door with an outstretched arm and a clenched jaw.

Jonas gave Ainsley a startled look.

"Don't play coy with me. I have seen more than enough sideways glances between you two these last few days. Let me give you some advice: if you expect to marry into this family you'd better find a way to make a heck of a lot more money, because that is the only way my father would ever approve such a step down."

Jonas rose and began gathering the books in his arms.

"Oh, have I offended you?" Ainsley asked, his anger sending spittle into the air. He tried to look unaffected while Jonas gathered his things.

Ainsley saw him glance to the stomach. "Don't you touch it!" Ainsley demanded, throwing a pointed finger at the specimen. "I am the attending physician here, not you," he bellowed.

"Now that I think of it, 'attachment to money' seems just about right for a drunk snob like you." Jonas began to gather the specimens he was studying before Ainsley had walked in the room.

Jonas's mouth twitched as if suppressing a comparable rage. He slapped Dr. Bennett's medical texts down on the table, creating a thud that echoed through the house, before reaching for his jacket, which had been placed over the back of his chair. "Allow me to leave you to it, Dr. Ainsley. Lord knows you know all the answers or, at the very least, you can buy them!"

Ainsley jumped at the sound of the slamming the door as Jonas left.

Chapter 29

*In she plunged boldly—
No matter how coldly
The rough river ran—*

Margaret realized something was wrong when Jonas charged past her inn room's open door. He was a flash before her and then gone, disappearing into his room next to hers.

"Jonas!" she called after him. She followed him into his room. "What's happened?" she asked, hovering at his door. She saw him drop his valise on the bed, unlatch the clasps and unfold the top. "What are you doing?"

"Heading back to the city." His voice was harsh, and much shorter than he had ever been with her before. His gruff stare lasted a mere moment but it gave quite an impression. Margaret nearly retreated but then decided to linger.

"Have I done something?"

"Your brother can be fed to the wolves," he said, gritting his teeth.

She pulled the door closed, secretly saying to hell with proper convention. "Peter can be difficult sometimes," Margaret said at last. "But there is no need for you to leave."

Jonas finally stopped his fury-driven packing and looked to her. "I will never be accepted by him. You and your family have their ways." He let out a deep exhale of breath. "Socially closed aristocrats. Peter may believe he's better than me, and he probably is, but goddamn it if I am going to stand around and take his abuse." As if he could no longer bear to look at her, he turned away suddenly and focused on gathering his belongings.

"But, Jonas, you've done so much for us here."

"Precisely!"

The tension between them was rising rapidly and Margaret had to try not to let her emotions spill over. She had never before spent so much time with Jonas as she had in the previous days. She'd always seen him with her brother, or at well-attended receptions, gatherings with other people present, but never had she been able to feel such intimacy with him. She didn't want to see him go. It would ruin her fantasy, a fantasy in which she was falling in love with him. A fantasy that had her believing that he could return her affections.

Jonas moved about the room before finally turning and pulling out his metal cigarette case. She watched as he lit his cigarette and inhaled deeply. All his possessions were between them, a valise, a medical bag, and a stack of books with ragged bindings.

"You didn't come back last night," Margaret said, taking a moment to glance over his clothes. He looked like he had been digging a ditch. His pants were dusty from the knees down, and his shirt had a large rip in the front.

Jonas followed her gaze and immediately started unbuttoning his shirt.

Embarrassed, Margaret turned from him, and faced the opposite wall. Unlike most men she knew, he wasn't a gentleman. He was far wilder than Peter but Jonas had not been raised as Peter and she had. He was a rogue. She remembered that about him. She had forgotten how she first found him, so much of him changed when he was with her. "A gentleman does not undress in front of a lady."

"You mistake me, miss," she heard him say behind her. "I never said I was a gentleman."

Margaret glanced to the waistcoat he had thrown over the bedrail and saw another rip in one of the elbows. She reached for it and held it out in front of her.

"I was with your brother," he said before she could ask.

Margaret swallowed, feeling a tight knot in her throat. "What were you doing?" she asked. She turned then, almost involuntarily, in time to see him buttoning up a clean pair of trousers, his shirt still unbuttoned and open at the front. The cigarette was held loosely in his lips.

Jonas looked as if he were preparing to reproach

her for being so curious. He must have thought better of it because he didn't say a word.

"Did you go to the graveyard?" she asked cautiously.

Jonas did not answer.

"Jonas, you didn't!" Margaret took another step toward him and leaned on the foot rail of the bed. "You disturbed that young girl's final resting place!"

"Yes, we did!" he sneered. "And I'd do it again if it meant saving another life. We found arsenic, just like the old man. There is a murderer in that manor Margaret, and Peter is going to need all the help he can get. Too bad he's too arrogant to recognize his own folly!"

Fully dressed in fresh clothing, Jonas grabbed his bags and moved to walk around Margaret.

"Jonas, please stay," Margaret implored. "If what you say is true then I don't know that I can help him like you can." Before she could stop herself, she grabbed his arm, touching him gently to get him to look at her once more.

When he turned to her, she saw fierce eyes and a stern face. Her eyes searched his face for any part of the Jonas she had known during the many hours together on the train. It was not like him to be so short with her, so reproachful.

As if reading her thoughts, his face softened the longer he looked at her. "You are stronger than you realize, Margaret Marshall." He released his bags then, letting them drop to the floor on either side of him. He placed his hand over her hand that still clung to his arm. Raising it to his lips, he brushed the top of her knuckles with his mouth and then, leaned into her and kissed her lips.

Margaret allowed her lips to be parted as he kissed her. She sank into his arms as they encircled her and became entranced by the strength that held her up from the floor. She'd follow him if he asked. She'd walk with him to the ends of the earth if it meant she'd be kissed like that every day. He wouldn't ask, though. He meant to leave her with Peter, and there was nothing she could say to make him stay.

Her eyes were closed when he finally pulled away,

and when she opened them she found him staring at her. She breathed in his warm scent, not knowing if she'd ever have the chance to be so close to him again. She waited for him to say something, anything, but he was silent. He uncoiled his arms from around her waist and released her, stepping back from the intimate embrace.

"Good-bye, Margaret," he said softly.

Margaret felt a lump in her throat, which made it hard for her to breathe. He turned, gathered his bags, and walked from the room without a backward glance. She wanted to call out and bring him back to see the tears he caused, the tears that poured uncontrollably down her cheeks. She sucked in air, struggling for composure, knowing she was rapidly losing all sense of control.

She loved him. The last few days had proven it but her little fantasy had ended and he was gone. She sat on the edge of the bed, using the metal bedrail as a brace. She clung to it like a crutch, and cried until no more tears would come.

Chapter 30

*Over the brink of it,
Picture it—think of it,
Dissolute Man!
Lave in it, drink of it,
Then, if you can!*

Ainsley did not realize how much he had drunk until later that afternoon. The headache from two days prior had returned for an encore performance, leaving him ill and nearly bedridden. He lay on the couch, his feet propped up over the edge of the arm, his arms folded over his chest.

"Get up!"

Ainsley felt his feet collapse to the floor and it took him a minute before he realized they had been kicked off of the couch's arm. He felt a tug on his pillow, just a slight one before it was ripped from underneath his head so fast the back of his head hit the other arm of the couch suddenly and with a sharp pain that shot to the nerves behind his eyes.

"Ah!" Ainsley rolled over, clutching his sore head with his hand. Expecting his sister, Margaret, who was no doubt cross with him for his argument with Jonas, Ainsley opened his eyes to see Mrs. Crane standing over him. He gave out a yelp of embarrassment and rolled off the couch.

"Oh, fiddlesticks. Ye ain't the first half-drunk man I've seen, and I dare say, ye won't be the last." Mrs. Crane returned the pillow to its place on the couch. "Near half the day is already gone."

Ainsley remained on the floor for a moment, aware of Mrs. Crane's attempts to tidy the couch now that she had successfully removed him from it. He was equally aware of the exponentially growing headache throbbing relentlessly in his brain. "Mrs. Crane, have you ever drunk too much?"

he groaned, only half-cognizant of what he said.

"Dr. Ainsley, hold your tongue. I am a Christian woman and I will no longer allow that demon liquor into my life, either by my hand or anyone else's." She rounded the couch and stood over him, hands on hips, as if she were his governess come to scold him for breaking a priceless heirloom. "Get up now," she coaxed.

Ainsley clawed his way onto the couch, where he sat for a moment, head in hands. He squinted against the morning sun, which only made the pain intensify. "I swear I will never have another drink again, if only you could take this blasted headache away."

He heard her *tsk tsk* him with her tongue before speaking. "Now, if only I could do that. What a rich woman I would be."

Ainsley rubbed his temples as Mrs. Crane tidied the room around him. She eyed but dared not touch the microscope, the dissected stomach, and the medical texts haphazardly thrown down when Jonas stormed out. And then Ainsley remembered their argument, word for word, and he let his head drop into his hands. "I am such an ass," Ainsley mumbled into his hands.

"Come now, don't be so hard on ye self. Many a good man has fallen a time or two. You will find your sober feet again. Breakfast will be ready momentarily, though I daresay it is more likely to be lunch if you go by the clock."

A few moments later, he met her in the dining room, clean-shaven and properly dressed, though the haggard look on his face gave away his pain. Mrs. Crane shook her head at him before loading his plate with eggs and fried ham.

"Perhaps you should call on Miss Dawson. She may have a remedy for you?"

Ainsley's shoulders dropped as he shook his head. "What kind of doctor am I to be if I cannot relieve my own headache?"

"I'd say one with a headache."

Ainsley could hardly stomach the thought of food but he ate some anyway for Mrs. Crane's sake. The eggs seemed harmless, even welcome, but the ham was far too heavy for his churning stomach and he soon regretted the three bites he had taken. "Perhaps just tea then," Ainsley said at last.

Mrs. Crane shook her head as she took his plate away.

"Suppose she would not take me, Miss Dawson, I mean. Perhaps she would not have anything for me."

"Come now," Mrs. Crane answered with a laugh. "What single woman do you know, all on her own, would turn down a paying client?"

"I don't know," Ainsley's voice trailed off for a moment. "I seem to run into her all over the place. She is so quiet and reserved. She hardly ever meets my gaze." Mrs. Crane left for a moment, through the kitchen door, and returned with a teapot.

"She is a good woman, kind, sensible," she said and began pouring Ainsley's tea.

"Her daughter too, she won't look at me. She hides or runs off when I come near."

"Did you say Miss Dawson's daughter?"

"Yes, the girl won't look at me and I swear she hides from me." Ainsley hesitated. Was he mistaken?

Mrs. Crane laughed nervously and shook her head. "Miss Dawson doesn't have a daughter."

※ ※

Ainsley banged on Miss Dawson's door with a closed fist, ignoring the rattling the force caused on its hinges. "Miss Dawson!" he banged again before scanning the yard for any children, whomever they belonged to. Standing there for some time, he was beginning to wonder if she was even home. He was surprised when the door opened.

"Dr. Ainsley, what in heaven's name—"

He did not wait. He pushed himself in and quickly surveyed the room. There were no toys or schoolbooks or slates or any such things to indicate a child lived there. No tiny shoes or sweaters. Nothing to say a child had *ever* lived there. The cottage was neat and tidy, as it had been the day when he first visited. He found himself whirling around, moving books and pillows, glass jars and cooking pots, looking for anything to tell him he was not losing his mind.

"Dr. Ainsley, what is the meaning of this intrusion?" Miss Dawson stood at her door, which she had probably only closed to keep the draught out. She crossed her arms over her chest. "I could have been with a patient."

Ainsley marched forward and grabbed Miss Dawson by the shoulders. "Where is she?"

"Who? I don't know who you are talking about. Unhand me." Miss Dawson struggled under his tight grip and he relented.

"The girl. The girl I keep seeing at your side, or in your yard, or following you. She was under the piano when Mrs. Lloyd nearly banished you from the manor."

Miss Dawson peered at him suspiciously. "I don't know who you are talking about. What girl?"

"Your daughter, or at least who I thought was your daughter." Ainsley turned from her, raking his fingers through his damp hair. "I have seen her, clear as day, now where is she?" Ainsley was nearly out of breath but he could hardly contain his aggravation. He felt as if he were going mad.

"My daughter," Miss Dawson began, swallowing hard, "is buried in the Picklow cemetery. You saw her internment yourself"—she hugged her body, pulling her shawl tighter over her shoulders—"beside Walter Lloyd Sr."

Chapter 31

Take her up tenderly,
Lift her with care;

It took a moment for what she told him to sink in, and then like a freak storm rising from the Atlantic, it hit him. Josephine was Miss Dawson's daughter, not Martha Lloyd's.

"I had no idea," Ainsley said.

"No one did. That was the way *she* wanted it."

"Mrs. Lloyd?"

"Yes." Miss Dawson passed Ainsley, hugging her arms close to her. That is when Ainsley noticed she was still wearing black and had the appearance of a woman who was very much in mourning.

"Please sit," Miss Dawson offered, gesturing to a chair between them.

Reluctantly, Ainsley rounded the chair and sat. He watched as Miss Dawson took a seat opposite him.

"I met Walter"—she gave a slight smile—"in Bristol, where I lived with my sister. He was so charming at first." She smiled to herself but her eyes remained fixated on something in the distance. "We did not see each other often but when he was in town he always had time for me. I did not know he was already married, you understand. Had I known..." Her voice trailed off and she was silent for a moment. Then she let out a deep sigh and did not finish her thought. "When I found out I was pregnant I couldn't stand the thought of raising her on my own. I came here and went straight to the mill and begged him to help me. He bought me this cottage and told me to stay here until he figured out what to do." Miss Dawson turned her gaze to Ainsley, who was so transfixed by her story he had not thought to move. "Then one day, she came. She sat there," she said, gesturing to the chair Ainsley sat in, "and told me the baby

I carried would not be mine. The child would be hers and Walter's and they would raise it in the Manor house with Walter, Elizabeth, and Lillian."

"But how did she plan to hide it? She clearly would not be large with child and you are so slight in figure, how could you have hid it?" Ainsley leaned into the back of his chair, and glanced around the room, almost picturing the day in his mind.

"No one knew me and I spent so much time here at the cottage. Walter sent the butler here to run my errands. During my confinement they housed me at the manor, discreetly of course, telling everyone that I was there as her midwife, in case Martha miscarried once again."

"This cannot be true." Ainsley raked his hand through his hair, his headache forgotten, his mind busy trying to accept the plausibility of the tale she was telling him.

"It is true, every word of it. On the night Josephine was born, Martha took her from me." A tear appeared in the corner of one of Miss Dawson's eyes, threatening to spill over onto her cheek before she brushed it away. "Walter begged her to allow me to name the baby. I named her Josephine after my sister."

"A mother cannot be so easily separated from her child," Ainsley offered in disbelief.

"Indeed. It ripped my heart in two pieces, but that is the way she wanted it. She had wanted so many children, had been promised them, and God saw fit to take them away before they took their first breath."

"'Twas not God," Ainsley offered with a shake of his head. "Walter Lloyd was sick. Syphilis."

Miss Dawson nodded. "I know that now. His illness made Josephine all the more special. Martha wanted the child for herself. It was the best way to avoid scandal."

Ainsley knew the story must be true. It painted Mrs. Lloyd exactly how he had pictured her, cunning, methodical, obsessed with society and its influence on her life. It was not a far stretch to see Martha orchestrating such a plan, especially if it prevented an enormous scandal and provided a replacement for all the children she had lost.

"She could not handle the stigma of an illegitimate child," Ainsley said, almost to himself.

"Indeed, she could not. Had Josephine been a boy I doubt he would have survived long, not when her son was sitting comfortably as sole heir. The fact that the child was a girl only pleased her. It gave her another doll to dress in frills and bows before handing her back to the nurse. She did that with all three girls, from what I heard. Pampered them until they all spoiled, except my Josephine, who could sing like a bluebird and kept the heart of gold she was born with."

"And you never thought to return to Bristol?"

"How could I? My child was here. Nothing could keep me from my child, not even a pinch-faced old crone like Mrs. Lloyd. I vowed to stay. The day she was born I told Walter I would never leave, unless I had my daughter with me."

"Did he..." Ainsley hesitated. "Did he continue to visit?" Ainsley asked delicately, unsure how to handle the subject of Mr. Lloyd's lovers. "After Josephine was born?"

"He tried but all I wanted to talk about was Josephine. Was she walking? Was she eating well? What new words had she discovered? I think he found me boring after a time. He still brought me an allowance, though, and paid for the upkeep of this place. His son brings me the money now that Walter is gone."

"I met him, on the road a few days ago. I had wondered why he had come so far from the mill and manor."

Miss Dawson nodded. "He's a good boy. Does what he is told. He may have inherited the estate and the mill but he and I both know who runs the show."

"That is my impression of Mrs. Lloyd as well. I am surprised she allows her son to pay for her husband's mistress—" Ainsley stopped suddenly. "My apologies."

"It is all right. I know what I am. A used woman. Truth be told, Martha does not know. I am in the mill books as nurse to the workers. It's a business expense, something she has no control over."

Ainsley smiled at the devious, yet ingenious plot. "Clearly she does not like you. She practically said as much at Josephine's wake. Why does she feel you killed her?"

"It was a display of power, nothing more. She would do anything to strip me of my business and run me from town, She is very dangerous, that woman. I would be very wary of everyone in that house, Dr. Ainsley."

"I have reason to believe Josephine was poisoned." Ainsley spoke the words as matter of factly as he could, knowing the delivery of such horrid news would disturb the girl's real mother. He could not tell her how he knew, lest he incriminate himself.

Miss Dawson raised her hand to her mouth, an action which did not suppress the tidal wave of tears that streamed from her eyes. Ainsley saw her hand shaking and noticed her entire body was shuddering as well. He expected her to collapse at any moment and went immediately to her side. "Can I get you a tea?" he asked in a feeble attempt to soothe her deepest pain.

She shook her head and buried her face in her hands and cried loudly. Ainsley remained close, crouched beside her chair, but his mind was far away from the cottage in which they sat. In his mind, he was at the manor house with Lillian, no friend in sight and danger lurking in every shadow.

"Forgive me," Miss Dawson said at last, wiping her soggy cheeks dry as she spoke. "I had suspected as much, though it is a far graver matter when you hear it to be true. I should have run away with her, as I dreamed of doing so many times." She dabbed her eyes with her lace handkerchief. "You said you saw her with me. Josephine was beside me, in the graveyard?"

"Yes, she was walking quite close. And I've seen her playing in the yard here when I came a few days ago."

Miss Dawson smiled, bringing some sudden cheeriness to her distressed face. "He would bring her sometimes, when I begged him to. Perhaps she knew then. Perhaps she knew I was her real mother."

"I believe she knew somewhere deep inside." Ainsley placed a soothing hand on top of Miss Dawson's. He squeezed her hand in a comforting gesture. She looked up at him, red and glistening eyes imploring to him. "Be careful," she said, returning his squeeze more tightly than he had done. She met his gaze sternly. "That family will be the ruin of you, just like it was the ruin of me."

Chapter 32

*Fashion'd so slenderly,
Young, and so fair!*

Miss Dawson's words of warning ringing in his ears, Ainsley made his way back to town, very aware of the social call he and Margaret were expected to make to the manor later that day. He had yet to recover from the shock of learning Josephine's true parentage and his mind was awash with possible motives for killing the poor girl. It was possible Mrs. Lloyd, consumed with hatred and anger at her husband's infidelity, killed the child as revenge. Possible, but highly unlikely as someone cunning enough to perpetrate such a crime would not kill the object of the anger first. No, Ainsley thought, Mrs. Lloyd would keep her husband alive so he could live through the pain of losing a child, just as she had with all those pregnancies lost thanks to him and his wandering eye. If Mrs. Lloyd had killed Josephine, why did she kill her husband first? Unless Walter had died of natural causes, pneumonia as Dr. Bennett said, and Mrs. Lloyd was no longer interested in caring for the girl who was not her own.

Ainsley reached the Inn by late afternoon, the sun hidden behind a veiled sky reminding everyone that winter loomed. Margaret was in a sour mood when he went to her room.

"Good, you're here ...finally," she said, her voice laced with indignation.

Ainsley stared after her for a moment, surprised at the tone of her voice and the quick, choppy movements she made as she went around the room. Her trunk took up the end of the bed and her valise was sitting, mouth wide open with a few of her belongings surrounding it. "Are you packing?" he asked, suddenly realizing her intentions. "Margaret, no, we have to call at the manor."

She laughed but did not waver from her work. "You have to call at the manor. I have to try to catch a train." She wiggled her fingers at him and nearly snarled as she spoke.

"Train?"

"Jonas left! Good God, Peter, you treat him like a pebble in your shoe and then you are surprised when he leaves?"

"We had a fight. We always fight. I didn't think he would leave."

Margaret raised her hand to her forehead, covering her eyes as she closed them, and regulating her breathing while she spoke. "I couldn't convince him to stay." There was a depression in her voice, a hopeless resignation that seemed to haunt her still.

Ainsley had been trying to ignore their apparent attachment, perhaps hoping Margaret would grow out of it and move on. No doubt Jonas was the first man to see her as anything but a child. "I don't think Father would approve of this attachment you are forming for Jonas. Quite frankly, I cannot say I approve of it myself."

"He has been your dearest friend for years—"

"Exactly! My friend! I would know if he was not a good match for you."

"This has nothing to do with whether he is a good match. I am angry because you have wronged him just like you wrong me."

He had done wrong by Jonas. He sought his help with Dr. Bennett, but when the stress mounted he lashed out at his friend, who was trying to help him. He would run after Jonas if he could, if he knew his friend was not already halfway to London. As much as he wanted to go to Jonas, he needed to go to Lillian first. He would have to deal with Jonas, apologize later. If Lillian died, Ainsley would never forgive himself.

Ainsley saw his sister, near tears, on the opposite side of the bed. She was looking at him, like she used to when they were children and he'd abandoned her game to chase down their older brother. She was always left behind, either because she was the youngest or because she was a girl. It must be hard, Ainsley thought, chasing after him, even now in their adult life.

His voice softened and he reached out a hand to stop her from packing her things. "How have I wronged you?" She pulled her hand away and did not meet his eyes.

Quietly, she folded one of her dresses into the trunk at the foot of her bed. "You are so focused, Peter." Margaret bit her lower lip and gathered a pair of slippers that had been lying beside the trunk. "Something horrible happened and you have been so focused on Lillian that you never asked what happened to make me leave Tunbridge Wells."

"Margaret, I meant to."

Margaret lifted her head, revealing glistening blue eyes. "But you didn't."

A somber silence hushed the room and the siblings shifted uncomfortably. Ainsley raked his hand through his hair and turned. A cushioned chair sat at the far end of the room and he slid into it. He placed his elbows on his knees and held his head up with his hands while he looked at the floor, studying the grains of the wood that made up the floorboards.

"Jonas told me something happened. He wouldn't say what. Said he was sworn to secrecy but I think I have a right to know."

Margaret swallowed hard. She abandoned her trunk and sat on the edge of the quilt with a look of defeat. "Those women in the hat shop—"

"What women?"

"Delilah Robbins. She was horrible, Peter. She said Mother was having an affair. I had to see for myself." Margaret avoided his gaze then. She glanced around the room without direction. She was distracted, terribly so. "I was worried there was truth to the rumours. I must have known somewhere inside me...I must have thought they were true."

"Margaret."

"The thought never crossed your mind... that the rumours were true and Mother was committing infidelity?" Margaret let out a deep breath. "I know you trust Jonas so I tracked him down and I begged him to take me to the country house. I didn't have the gumption to go on my own."

"I can't believe he agreed. His position at the

university—"

"He was let go. He confessed as much to me."

"Oh, good God...why didn't he say something to me?" That would explain how sensitive he was when the subject of money came up. He must be worried, as Ainsley would be if the roles were reversed. Ainsley stopped his own thoughts, nay worse. Jonas had no family fortune to fall back on as Ainsley did.

"Perhaps he thought you would not understand," Margaret explained.

Ainsley nodded, aware of what an ass he had been that morning and other times regarding Jonas's lack of financial means.

"We took the coach the next day and arrived that evening,"

"And you did not tell Father," Ainsley reminded her.

"I thought to leave a note but I knew he'd be furious."

"No doubt all society is rife with rumours about *your* impropriety. Jonas has a reputation that even I can't rival."

"So now he and I are perfectly matched," she answered defiantly. Suddenly, she lost her resolve and the tone of her voice softened. "I am well aware of the damage I have done to my reputation, but I doubt it will matter very much once word of what I saw reaches London."

"Word of what exactly?"

"I saw them; Mother and her lover..." She hesitated not wanting to say it aloud, "naked in the parlour." Her eyes became glossy as she spoke and finally turned away. Ainsley watched as she wiped away her tears and that is when he knew she was telling the truth. "When Jonas and I arrived, we surprised them. They had the entire house to themselves and were not expecting anyone. You have to believe me. I could not bear it if you did not believe me."

Ainsley nodded, almost against his will. "I believe you." It was no secret their parents' marriage was greatly strained, though it had never occurred to Ainsley that there was any truth to the rumours. He could scarcely see his mother capable of such a thing. She was so sweet, so passive. Since he was a child Ainsley saw her as the gentle one, the one he could always turn to for any emotional need. She held her place in society with scarcely any effort and never lost her temper like their father. If Ainsley had been asked, he would have admitted he loved his mother more than his father, who always seemed vile, cruel, and heartless. "I don't want to but... I believe you."

If their mother were having an affair no doubt she had good reason. The man she married was a brute, a rich one, but a brute nonetheless. She endured his constant criticism and unpredictable temper. She had more kindness and patience in her pinky finger then Lord Marshall had in his entire existence. It was no wonder Ainsley often sided with his mother, and he reasoned, he would side with her once more. If she were having an affair, it was their father who drove her to do it.

"How long?" Ainsley asked, the impact of this truth hitting him slowly. He imagined this would not only impact his family and the future marriage of his parents, but no doubt their position among the other socialites was in peril. He cared little for himself, but Margaret—she would be tarnished for all eternity once this scandal was revealed.

"I don't know how long. At breakfast, she pretended like nothing happened and laughed at me." The pain of the exchange appeared fresh in Margaret's eyes as she spoke. Her chin quivered and she turned from Ainsley to hide her pain. She began packing once more, more furiously than before, her movements accenting her anger. "She was not the mother I remember at all. She's changed. I don't know who she is anymore."

Ainsley leaned forward and ran his hands over his face, as if trying to rub the feeling of sadness that overcame him while Margaret spoke. Once he had wished his parents would separate, become officially estranged as a few ill-matched married couples had done before. Never had he imagined a divorce, and the scandal that would bring. Not only were they facing imminent divorce, their family would be ostracized, shunned, and tainted for many years. The Marshall name would be synonymous with illicit affairs, lustful tendencies, and infidelity. The impact would be far-reaching. The entire family would be marked with a scarlet letter, and according to Ainsley, it was all his father's fault.

"I'll kill him!" Ainsley jumped from his chair, his hands bound in tight fists at his side. He walked the length of the room, his face twisted in rage.

"Mother's lover?"

"No, Father! He drove her to do this. He made our lives miserable. He made *her* life miserable. It is his fault and I will not listen to anyone who says otherwise." Ainsley paused briefly at the fireplace mantel and retrieved his flask from his inside pocket. Without thinking of Margaret's presence, he took a long gulp, which only soothed his temper momentarily.

"Peter, be reasonable! It is not Father's fault. He had no more control over Mother than any of us."

"He made her this way. He brought this upon himself and we are all caught in the middle. Do you have any idea what kind of disaster this means for all of us? Margaret, anyone you wish to marry will not wish to marry you." Ainsley pounded his fist on the mantelshelf, causing the trinkets on display to shutter from the impact. "I cannot blame Mother. She is just as much a victim as you and I."

"You did not see her, not as I did. She is not who she appears to be. She is much changed." Margaret slipped onto the edge of the bed. Clearly, the heated and emotional exchange had drained her. Ainsley watched her crying silently, unaware of her audience.

He knew things had never been good between his parents. He had once suspected his father of harbouring a mistress but never did he dream his mother capable of such an act. The reality of it, the confirmation from Margaret that the rumours were true was almost too much to bear. Ainsley found himself walking to Margaret and embracing her. She cried tears of hopelessness in to his shoulder as he held her.

"Our family is broken. It will never be the same now," she said through muffled sobs.

Ainsley tried to hush her gently, rubbing her back as he held her. "Perhaps it was never whole to begin with."

They held each other for some time, Margaret crying and Ainsley deep in thoughts laced with both anger and distress, not sure which parent deserved which emotion. Eventually, Margaret pulled away and wiped tears that had gathered on her cheeks and eyes.

"The day is getting late," Ainsley said. "We are expected for tea."

"Peter, I cannot go to tea feeling as I do. How could you expect me to sit and be cordial at such a time?"

"There is nothing you or I can do about that. Lillian has been through far worse and I must help her."

Margaret opened her mouth as if to rebuke but she quickly closed it. She began packing again. "I don't care about the Lloyds. Really, Peter, I don't understand why you have dragged me into this. I have a mind to leave this instant, escort or no escort."

"And where will you go? London? Tunbridge Wells?"

Margaret stared at him, unable or unwilling to reply.

Raking his hand through his hair, Ainsley turned from her and walked to the window. He pulled back the curtain and looked to the street below. "They are going to kill her, Margaret. I simply could not live with myself if that happened."

When he turned back he saw Margaret pause mid-motion while folding a chemise. She laid the article of clothing on the top of the bed, unfolded, and closed her eyes for a moment. When she opened them again their eyes met. "Nor could I."

Chapter 33

Ere her limbs frigidly
Stiffen too rigidly,
Decently, kindly,

Margaret took her brother's arm as they walked down the main street that would eventually lead them to the manor. Ainsley had offered to hire a carriage but Margaret refused. She was just as fond of walking as he was; besides, she reasoned, it would give her a better opportunity to assess exactly what they were both up against.

"Where were you this afternoon?" she asked, falling into step beside him.

"I was visiting Miss Dawson, the midwife, and finding out some rather astonishing facts about the Lloyd family." He was looking at his shoes as he walked before lifting his face up into the gray sky. There was a marked chill in the air, and the clouds threatened snow.

"Oh?" Margaret perked up at the idea of small-town gossip. It always seemed more interesting than any scandal that could be found in London. "What could be more scandalous than a convoluted murder plot?"

"Josephine Lloyd was not Mrs. Lloyd's child."

Margaret stopped abruptly and watched her brother take one more step ahead of her before turning. "Josephine belongs to Miss Dawson then?" she asked, knowing the answer already. "By whom? Not Walter Lloyd?"

Ainsley gave a nod and Margaret struggled to keep her composure. There were even less people on this portion of the road but even still Margaret dared not draw any unwanted attention. Ainsley offered his arm once again and Margaret stepped toward him, pulling her fur-lined cape tighter across her shoulders and chest.

"Are you sure?" she asked in a hushed tone.

"Miss Dawson confessed as much."

Margaret bit her lip, trying to suppress her next question without effect. "Was she taken by force?" she asked, not sure she could feel sympathy for the now dead man if Miss Dawson had been raped.

"No, thank goodness," Ainsley breathed. "It is widely known that Walter had many affairs of his own, though I confess I did not know with whom until now."

"I cannot believe Mrs. Lloyd would agree to raise the child as her own."

"It was her idea, or so I have been told."

Margaret could not fathom a cheated spouse willingly agreeing to raise a child born by her husband's mistress, at least not without resenting the child for being a daily reminder of her husband's infidelity. Quickly her mind turned to her own parents, and her mother's lover. Perhaps she was not truly Ainsley's sister? Or worse, perhaps Ainsley was not their father's son and that is why they despised each other so much? Margaret shuttered at the thought and quickly brought her mind back to the mystery at hand. "There's a strong motive for murder then," she said, forcing her thoughts to remain linear.

"My thoughts exactly."

"But why Lillian then?"

"That I cannot tell."

"Perhaps she is from another mother as well, another of Mr. Lloyd's mistresses," Margaret offered. "No doubt she took on the children and continued the charade to save the family from scandal."

"Murder is a greater scandal than any other I can fathom. Why protect the family, then expose it to the deepest ridicule?"

"I imagine it became too much for her. Her husband, the source of her shame, is dead. Why should she pretend?" Margaret felt a chill as they walked and she clung closer to Ainsley's side. "What about Lillian then? Will you confront Mrs. Lloyd?" Margaret looked to Ainsley, who seemed to be avoiding her gaze. He stared straight ahead.

"I intend to take Lillian to London with me," he said softly, barely loud enough for Margaret to hear.

"Peter! You cannot be serious!"

"I am terribly serious. I am expected back in London in two days and I simply cannot leave her to fend for herself." Ainsley glanced to her. "She hasn't a friend in the world."

"She has a family. You can't just take her away. It would be... a declaration." Margaret could feel her face become flush. "You don't mean to take her as a wife, do you?"

Ainsley was silent for a long time and Margaret could scarcely contain her anger at the notion. He had all but disregarded her attachment to Jonas on the basis that he was Ainsley's friend, but he could not see the conflict in marrying one of his patients.

"Not right away," he said.

"She's a patient, a girl," Margaret said at last.

"She is the same age as you."

"And she has been out here in this desolate place her entire life. She would not know what she was getting into. Please, be reasonable. You have not thought this through—" Margaret's words trailed off when she saw a young woman exiting the church that the pair was walking near. She carried a basket with a cloth over it and she was hanging her head so she did not see them. "She's crying," Margaret said.

"That's Mary, a servant at the Lloyds," Ainsley explained in a whisper.

Margaret quickly dropped her brother's arm and hastily walked to the girl, who seemed quite visibly shaken. Ainsley remained at the gate.

"May I help you? What troubles you?"

Mary looked up, startled at the sight of Margaret. The maid wiped her tears with a sense of urgency. "'Tis nothing, ma'am," she said in a mumbled tone. Margaret reached for the basket she carried, wanting to lighten the young woman's burden, but Mary pulled it away.

"I'm Margaret. Let me help you."

Mary pushed past Margaret in the walkway but stopped suddenly when she saw Ainsley standing at the gate. It was then that the maid began crying openly, nearly crumbling to the ground. Instead, she leaned on the short stone wall that separated the churchyard from the road and sobbed into her handkerchief. "I just need a moment," she said softly, barely loud enough for Margaret to hear. The maid's body collapsed in a fit of tears and the girl became an inconsolable heap on the damp churchyard ground.

"Mary!" Margaret rushed to the maid's side. "What has happened?" Margaret looked to Ainsley, fearing the worse. "Is it Lillian? Has she passed away?" Margaret saw her brother raise his hand to his face, a look of terror striking him suddenly.

"No, Miss Lillian was in good spirits when I left. 'Tis not that."

Margaret looked up and saw Ainsley had wandered to the other side of the road, rubbing his face with his hands, no doubt upset that he may have lost his first live patient. "She is all right, Peter." Her brother looked relieved but this still did not explain why the maid was so upset.

"What is it then? Are you still mourning for Josephine?"

The maid nodded slowly and Margaret rubbed her shoulder in an attempt to soothe her.

"The Lord takes people from us and often we do not understand why," Margaret explained.

Mary sniffled loudly, a sound that made Margaret's skin crawl. "I understand why and it has more to do with the devil than the Lord. There is an evil in that house, Miss Margaret."

"What do you mean?" she asked, unsure if she really wanted to know the answer. The maid hesitated, using her soggy handkerchief to wipe her nose. "It's okay, Mary. My brother and I, we're trying to find out what is happening so we can make it stop." Margaret positioned herself in front of Mary so she could look her in the eye. Ainsley had returned, though standing at a distance, watching Margaret. "If you know something you should tell us."

Mary shook her head, almost violently, at the idea.

The girl was either very loyal or truly terrified. Margaret decided a different tactic was in order. "The Lord does not only punish the sinners but also those who were not brave enough to stop them. You should tell me what you know."

The maid burst into another round of tears, covering her face in the soiled handkerchief and blubbering nonsense into the cloth.

"I'm sorry, Mary, I did not hear you. What did you just say?" Margaret asked.

"I killed Dr. Bennett!" she yelled. "It was me. I did it. I gave him the funeral cake and he died. Now I am damned." The girl truly was hysterical. She cried violently and mumbled incoherently. Her face was scrunched up in agony, and she tried to cover it with her hands that trembled so badly Margaret was sure the girl was slipping into hysteria.

Propelled by frustration, Ainsley walked through the gate and, kneeling in the grass beside her, he grabbed the girl's shoulders and shook her sharply. "Mary! Mary! Stop this!"

Margaret watched, too startled to do anything as her brother admonished the girl so harshly.

"Did you poison the cake? Did you?" Ainsley grew frustrated at his inability to get the girl to speak. "Mary!"

At last the girl looked up, and tried to pull her shoulders away from his tight grip. "I didn't poison it but I *am* going to hell. I gave it to him and he died. I came here to confess but I am lost. My soul is lost." She let out another loud cry and slipped out of Ainsley's loosening grip. She crumbled to a heap in Margaret's arms and sobbed.

Margaret looked to her brother over the girl's shuddering shoulder. "Someone gave it to her. Someone must have told her to give the cake to Dr. Bennett."

"She gave me the cake." Mary's hair covered her face as she spoke. "She gave me the cake and told me to make sure the doctor received it. She told me to do it."

"Who?" Ainsley asked. "Who gave you the cake?"

Mary ignored his question and continued her rambling. "I disobeyed a commandment and now my soul is lost."

Margaret pulled the girl from her and tried to force her to look up. "Mary, you must tell us who. Who gave you the cake? Mrs. Lloyd?"

"What is going on here? Mary!" Both Margaret and Ainsley looked to the road and saw Walter on his horse, looking down at them.

Mary looked up and Margaret could feel the waif of a girl trembling.

"It's all right, Mary," Margaret whispered reassuringly. "We won't say anything." Margaret helped the girl rise to her feet, though she was still unsteady. Walter dismounted from his horse and held tightly to the reins as he approached them.

"Mary fell," Ainsley lied, stepping toward the road and reaching out a hand to greet Walter. "We were helping her." Walter looked past Ainsley to Margaret and Mary.

"She looks well enough now," he said, surveying her. "Off with you now Mary. Cook will be needing your help."

Pulling from Margaret's protective shield, Mary curtsied, slipped past Ainsley, and hurried up the lane, almost running toward the Manor.

"Calling on the manor today?" Walter asked.

"Yes. Allow me to introduce my sister, Margaret." Ainsley gestured to Margaret, who was obliged by custom to curtsey. Margaret realized he did not say her last name or else compromise his secret life as a doctor.

"Good day, Miss Margaret." Walter extended a hand in greeting and smiled broadly. Margaret accepted his hand but was glad when he released it again.

"We shall be along shortly," Ainsley said, allowing Margaret to slip her hand into the crook of his arm.

Walter nodded, and remained a moment simply staring at Margaret before turning to his horse. Margaret could not watch as he mounted the saddle, positioning his reins in his gloved hands. "I will receive you shortly." Walter tipped his hat before digging his heels into the horse's side, spurring it to a canter.

"Did you see the way he looked at me?" Margaret asked once Walter was completely out of view.

Ainsley laughed heartily. "You are a very attractive woman. You are simply going to have to accept the fact that men admire you for your beauty."

Margaret sighed heavily and laid her head on her brother's shoulder as they walked. "Oh, what I wouldn't give to be admired for something a little more substantial."

Chapter 34

Smooth and compose them;
And her eyes, close them,
Staring so blindly!

Ainsley would never admit it to Margaret, but he was more than a little fearful heading to the manor house for a social call. He hardly knew what to expect from a hostess that could be killing her children one by one. Whether from jealousy, shame or revenge, the Lloyd family was now paying the price for one man's misdeeds and disloyalty.

"Do not eat anything," he cautioned Margaret. "Pretend you are, for their sake, but do not allow the tea to touch your lips."

"I wish you had told me that before we left the inn. I would have requested a *petit dejeuner*."

"You heard what Mary said, *she* bid her to give Bennett the funeral cake. It is either Mrs. Lloyd or Elizabeth." He saw Margaret nod in agreement. "I wish Walter hadn't interrupted us then."

"Who do you think it is?" Margaret asked, keeping her voice low, knowing they were drawing near.

"Elizabeth," Ainsley said. "She strikes me as the jealous sort but there is something in the way Mrs. Lloyd has been hampering my attempts to find the truth. Neither one of them can be trusted."

Margaret took in a deep breath while her fingernails dug into the flesh of his arm as they climbed the slight hill to the manor. Ainsley willed himself to remain calm, not allowing himself one ounce of fear to betray his calm exterior. He patted her hand in a feeble attempt to reassure her.

"Suppose that poisoned funeral cake had been meant for you," Margaret suggested, careful to keep her tone low as the house came into view.

"The thought had crossed my mind," Ainsley offered.

"What's to say she won't try again?"

"Nothing." Ainsley pressed his lips together and continued to walk, keeping his gaze straight ahead.

As they drew nearer to the front door, the unmistakable sound of a piano could be heard wafting from the walls. The melody was hypnotic, with soothing highs and lows lulling any audience into serenity. The skill was unlike any Ainsley had heard before. The sound was crisp, direct, and exact. It was certainly a far cry from the incessant stops and starts that Margaret produced whenever she sat down to play.

The current song was spectacular, the mark of a true genius at the ivory. All apprehension at their arrival soon disappeared as the pair became entranced by the sound. Ainsley thought he saw a smile on Margaret's face as he leaned in to hit the door knocker. How could one not enjoy such a treat?

The butler arrived instantly and showed the pair into the foyer, where Ainsley relinquished his overcoat and Margaret allowed him to take her wrap. Margaret and Ainsley were shown into the parlour and were greeted with a scene much different than the one they both expected. The room was now completely set to rights. There were even fresh flowers, none of them funeral lilies, arranged in vases throughout the room, a decorating choice that brought colour to the muted decor.

But the atmosphere shift was due to more than just the flowers. The piano played on as Ainsley took in the room. He was delighted to see it was Lillian who was playing it. She was fully dressed in a tightly fitted fanned bodice and a flowing, layered skirt that billowed around her on the piano bench. She looked far better than when he had left her the day before. Her hair had been curled and pinned halfway up with copious blonde curls streaming down her neck and shoulders.

She did not notice Ainsley at first, or at least she made no move to stop playing to greet him. Like any real artist she performed her craft with true dedication. She closed her eyes slightly and Ainsley could see her chest rising and falling ever so slightly beneath her low cut bodice, timed perfectly with the movement of her hands.

Mrs. Lloyd had risen to greet them but Ainsley did not notice. He was focusing on Lillian, hardly comprehending she was the same girl he had been worried would die. A smile tickled the edges of his lips. He had never seen a sight so breathtakingly beautiful.

"She plays beautifully, doesn't she?" Mrs. Lloyd asked, seeing the intense focus Ainsley was giving her daughter. "One of our family's greatest joys is to hear her play."

"Are you sure she is well enough? Just yesterday she was weak as a kitten." Ainsley wanted to smile but the situation perplexed him. How could she recover so completely, so quickly?

"Her recovery is astounding, is it not?" Mrs. Lloyd beamed. "I owe you a great deal, Dr. Ainsley."

It was then that he noticed Elizabeth was seated farthest from the family, at the small writing desk near the window, with paper and a fountain pen perched in her fingers. She showed little interest in the movements of the room. It was as if she were in a world all her own. When his gaze returned to Mrs. Lloyd he found her looking at Margaret with a smile.

"Mrs. Lloyd, please allow me to introduce my sister, Miss Margaret Mar— Ainsley." Ainsley was quick to correct himself but both he and Margaret realized how close he had come to revealing his true name.

Margaret gave a slight curtsey but Mrs. Lloyd simply bowed her head in acknowledgement. "Please forgive the state of our home." Mrs. Lloyd gestured to the rest of the room. She did not see how absolutely perfect the home appeared to the visiting pair. "We have been in deep mourning for some time. Lillian's recovery gives me hope that our sorrows have ended."

The song came to an end, and as Lillian struck the last few keys Mrs. Lloyd turned and clapped her gloved hands, a show of appreciation that everyone else in the room soon joined, except Elizabeth, who did not even raise her head.

"Wonderful, my darling!" Mrs. Lloyd approached the piano, clapping daintily as she went. "Our dinner guests have arrived," she said to Lillian, giving a flourished gesture toward Ainsley and Margaret.

Lillian's face lifted and she saw Ainsley, her wide eyes and budding smile betraying her regard. She rose to her feet at the sight of him. "Peter!" and then, as if realizing her mistake her smile faded and she approached him more slowly. "Dr. Ainsley," she said, offering a slight curtsey. "You must be Miss Margaret. It has been a delight to hear Dr. Ainsley speak of you so warmly. He must truly love you for a sister."

Margaret returned the curtsey and gave a sly glance to her brother, which Ainsley chose to ignore.

"Dr. Ainsley told me you play," Lillian said with a smile. "You must come sit with me." Lillian slipped her hand into Margaret's and pulled her gently toward the shiny dark-stained piano that dominated the parlour room.

"No, I can't. Not after such an impressive treat." Margaret hesitated at the piano bench, stopping short of taking a seat. "Everyone will find my hands too clumsy compared to yours." She glanced around the room nervously.

"Nonsense," Mrs. Lloyd said, giving a diminishing flick of her wrist. "You are among friends here." The self-satisfied look on her face betrayed her true feelings. She was content in her daughter's abilities and assured than none surpassed them. She slipped into the sofa and gestured for Ainsley to take a seat opposite her.

Margaret begrudgingly sat next to Lillian on the bench and Ainsley could see Lillian giving his sister a few pointers on the keys, though the movement of their hands was completely hidden from his view.

"We owe you a great deal, Dr. Ainsley," Mrs. Lloyd said, eyeing the girls as they flipped through the sheet music trying to decide what song to play. "You see she is quite well."

"I can see. She looks..." Ainsley searched for an appropriate word. He wanted to say beautiful but stopped himself. To him, on that day in particular, she was astonishingly beautiful, practically gorgeous behind the piano. "Better," he said at last.

"Better? Why Dr. Ainsley she is completely recovered. She is the Lillian I know and love. I have never seen her so robust."

Ainsley smiled. Content and yet perplexed, he wondered what had brought about such a rapid recovery. "I wonder what her newfound health stems from?" he asked.

"Your care, I am sure. That is the only reasonable explanation I can fathom. You have done us a great service, Dr. Ainsley. You have given me back my daughter and for that I am truly thankful." Her expression gave nothing away. She spoke of gratitude but her gaze was intense, her smile forced.

Margaret's song started then, a perfect excuse for Ainsley to hide his discomfort at Mrs. Lloyd's contradictions. Ainsley shifted nervously in his seat. Was her pleasure genuine, or did she secretly curse him for spoiling her plot?

Instead of replying, Ainsley kept his eyes on the women at the piano. Margaret missed a note, most likely her finger slipping as she played, and both women giggled but kept playing. "See, I told you," Margaret laughed, without taking her eyes from the sheet music in front of her. "I have not played in months—" She dropped another note, but kept playing.

Ainsley could see the girls talking at the piano but he could not hear what they said over the music. Margaret looked uncomfortable. Her smile faded as Lillian spoke and she dropped another clumsy note, which only made Lillian laugh.

The song came to an end with a choppy flourish and Margaret bore a look of relief. Though she smiled, Ainsley knew she was glad it was over. She was even further relieved when Lillian suggested they sit with the others.

"My son tells me you stumbled on our maid today on the laneway," Mrs. Lloyd said, as her eyes followed Lillian and Margaret making their way to the sitting area.

"Oh, you saw Mary?" Lillian asked, slipping into a seat opposite Ainsley, which allowed Margaret to take the only seat beside him.

"Weeping and wailing or some such nonsense, apparently." Mrs. Lloyd raised an eyebrow as she leaned on the armrest of her chair and clasped her hands together delicately. "I am somewhat glad it was you who spotted her and not some others in the village. She does have a way of prattling on so, and can be quite dramatic." A nervous laugh escaped her.

"She appeared to be very upset," Margaret offered, glancing from Mrs. Lloyd to Lillian.

"Oh, Mother, you did not tell me," Lillian said, giving her mother a look of dismay.

"There is nothing to be done for it now," Mrs. Lloyd shrugged. "She is in the kitchen helping Cook prepare our tea" Mrs. Lloyd turned to Ainsley and Margaret then. "I hope she wasn't a bother to either of you. She fancies herself a rather delicate girl."

"What upset her so much?" Lillian implored, clearly concerned for the maid. They were both a similar age and most likely had found companionship whilst in the manor, Ainsley reasoned. If Mrs. Lloyd or Elizabeth found out what the maid had confessed there was no way of knowing the extent to which the murderess would go to in silencing her. Ainsley decided not to tell them what he and Margaret knew.

"We found her near the churchyard, crying," Margaret answered before Ainsley had a chance. "Poor girl was—" Beneath her full hoop skit, Ainsley pressed on her toe with his shoe and rather hoped no one would notice. Margaret looked to him sharply, without finishing her sentence.

Ainsley decided to finish it for her. "She was praying for the soul of Josephine and had become overrun with emotions. It appears she had a soft spot for the girl and is finding it hard to come to terms with her passing."

"Oh, dear," Mrs. Lloyd answered. "Walter did not indicate that to me."

"It was a good thing you were there, Pete— Dr. Ainsley," Lillian offered, "with your experience with grieving families...and you, Margaret," she added as almost an afterthought.

Ainsley watched Mrs. Lloyd closely through the

exchange. If she was worried her help had exposed family secrets, her face did not betray it. Ainsley found his gaze travelling to Elizabeth, who remained as unconcerned about their guests as anyone could be. She must have known he was looking at her but she made no move to stop her activities, whatever they were.

"Please excuse my eldest daughter," Mrs. Lloyd explained, more for Margaret's benefit than Ainsley's. "She is quite tired of late and Lillian's sudden recovery has done little to perk her up."

When Ainsley looked back to Lillian her face had become somewhat downtrodden as the conversation switched to her sister. Seeing Ainsley looking at her, she smiled before her eyes darted to her mother and then the floor.

"Perhaps she is feeling similar to Mary," Margaret said, "still in mourning."

Mrs. Lloyd nodded, and gestured to her black attire. "As am I," she said. "I doubt I shall ever recover from the loss." Her words lacked sincerity. Ainsley imagined her doing away with her widow's robes as soon as the custom allowed, in a year's time. In the meanwhile, she would play the role of devoted widow and the loving mother of a dead child, though he and Miss Dawson knew she was neither.

The butler appeared shortly after, Mary at his heel pushing the tea trolley into the room.

"Thank you Charles, Mary," Mrs. Lloyd said, without bothering to make eye contact. "Please inform Walter that our guests have arrived for tea, should he care to join us."

Charles and Mary left the room quickly but not before Mary gave a glance over her shoulder.

Ainsley followed her hesitant gaze to Lillian, who suddenly looked flush and unwell.

"Are you feeling all right?" Ainsley asked. Without waiting for a reply, he went to her side and placed a hand on her forehead. She stared blankly at the door, her breathing labored. Ainsley reached for her wrist but she collapsed in his arms before he could check her pulse.

"Oh!" Mrs. Lloyd yelled, standing up suddenly. "What is wrong with her, Dr. Ainsley?"

"She's overspent. Too much excitement," Ainsley offered as an explanation. "She needs to rest."

Lillian did not move as Ainsley gathered her, hoop skirt and all, into his arms. She was limp as he stood up and started for the door. He walked around Walter, who had just entered the room, and continued steadily up the stairs to Lillian's room. He used his knee to tap open her door and was relieved when she was finally lying in her bed. The weight of her dress added many more pounds than the day when he carried her to the kitchen.

She stirred then, turning to him as he knelt at her side adjusting the pillows around her head. "I feel so tired," she said softly.

"I believe you pushed yourself too far this day," Ainsley said, holding her head as he placed a pillow behind it.

Lillian smiled. "I agree."

He stared at her lovingly, brushing her cheek with the back of his hand. "You haven't eaten anything, have you?"

"No, doctor's orders."

"Good girl. I will bring you something before long."

Lillian reached for his hand and squeezed it gently.

"There was something I wanted to ask you," he started, glancing to the door to make sure no one had followed them. "I want you to come to London with me."

"What? But how?"

"You are not safe here. I have to go back to the city and I cannot leave you here. I found arsenic in Dr. Bennett and in Josephine." Her face looked panic-stricken as he talked. "You will be all right, just do not eat anything." He squeezed her hand in a gesture of reassurance.

"In Josephine?"

"I cannot say how but know that I would not say such if I was not sure."

Lillian struggled, lifting her head from the bed. "But how could I go back to London with you? I haven't a shilling to call my own."

"I do. I have more than enough for both of us. I will spend every penny I have to know you are safe."

The door to the room creaked open and they both

looked up to see Margaret standing there. "Peter," she said, inching into the room, "How is Lillian?"

Ainsley smiled. "She just needs some rest." he squeezed her hand and stood up, releasing her hand gently so it slipped onto her stomach.

Margaret and Ainsley left Lillian's room, closing the door behind them gently.

"She will be all right?" Margaret asked.

"Yes, just overextended," Ainsley explained. "I knew it was too early for her to be in corsets and hoop skirts." Ainsley raked his hand through his hair.

Elizabeth appeared at the top of the stairs. When Ainsley and Margaret turned to her, she spoke. "Mother has decided you should stay for dinner. Until we know Lillian has not completely relapsed."

Margaret was startled at the suggestion but Ainsley nodded in agreement. "We'd be honoured."

Elizabeth remained muted, barely taking her eyes from Ainsley. "I warned you, Dr. Ainsley, not to be fooled," she said with stinging monotone. "Nothing is what it seems."

"I agree," Ainsley answered. He felt Margaret's hand on his arm, reaching for him from behind. She must be scared. "I know about Josephine and Miss Dawson," Ainsley ventured, unsure how much the older children knew of the parentage of their youngest sibling.

Elizabeth raised an eyebrow. "You think I speak of them and that unfortunate situation?"

"Don't you?" Margaret asked.

"No. I do not."

Ainsley felt Margaret's hand grow tighter at his arm, though her face did not betray her discomfort. "Help me understand then," Ainsley implored. "If I do not understand, tell me what it is I need to know."

"I have told you everything. Everything else is here in front of you, if you wish to see." Elizabeth turned then and disappeared down the hall

Chapter 35

*Dreadfully staring
Thro' muddy impurity,
As when with the daring
Last look of despairing
Fix'd on futurity.*

"Cook was raised in the highlands so her menus are somewhat... rustic," Mrs. Lloyd explained to Margaret as they met in the doorway to the dining hall. "I hope you are an experimental sort."

The dining hall was home to large floor-to-ceiling windows draped in rich red velvet. Just beyond the windowpanes flakes of snow dotted the early evening darkness, creating a maze of swirling precipitation that blanketed the ground with a marked determination. Walking back to the village was out of the question. They would be forced to accept a carriage ride.

The dining table was small given the size of the room, with only eight chairs pulled up to its edges. Two at the ends, and three on each side. Despite the number of seats, only six place settings were to be used, while the two remaining seats were left empty.

Margaret, Mrs. Lloyd, Elizabeth and Walter were already in the dining hall when Ainsley finally entered. Despite Margaret's instance that he should stay with her, Ainsley chose to spend the previous two hours checking on Lillian or stationing himself outside her door. His affections for Lillian unnerved Margaret, who was so used to him lavishing his attention on her. It was slightly disconcerting that he should be so doting and yet neglectful as well.

Walter was seated at the head of the table, farthest from the door, in a grand, hand-carved and gold accented chamber chair fit for a king. "Come in, Dr. Ainsley," Walter called boisterously across the otherwise sober gathering. "Sit." The head of the house gestured to the empty seat at his side, the one opposite Margaret, who was more than a little nervous. She had wanted to leave as soon as she arrived and the more the visit dragged on the more she wished she had left with Jonas, even if it meant facing her father alone with the terrible truth about her mother.

"How is our patient?" Mrs. Lloyd asked, as Ainsley took his place.

"Yes, Doctor," Elizabeth piped up. "How is Lillian? She must be in great danger of relapse for her to be so closely guarded." She unfolded her napkin and glared at him as she placed it over her lap. Margaret noticed a slight, devious smile in the corners of her lips as she spoke.

"She is resting," Ainsley answered diplomatically.

First course was a cold cucumber soup, "fresh from Cook's hothouse," Mrs. Lloyd was quick to point out. "We have been very blessed by her skill with the soil." Mary appeared beside Ainsley then. The bowl she was placing in front of him shook in her grasp before it was finally safe from collapse on the solid table. Ainsley looked to her and saw her face pale, with beads of sweat slipping down from her temples.

"Mary, are you well?" Ainsley asked, turning to her. She returned to the serving cart to bring another bowl. The girl avoided his gaze and continued with her task.

"Do you always address the staff so directly, Dr. Ainsley?" Mrs. Lloyd asked coldly, impervious to the health or well-being of her servants.

Margaret gave Ainsley a look of reprove. "I beg your pardon, Mrs. Lloyd," he said, ignoring his sister's look of caution. "I am a doctor first and foremost," Ainsley explained. "I was just asking after the girl's health."

"The girl is quite well." Mrs. Lloyd pursed her lips tightly. She glanced to her son at the other end of the table. "Don't you agree, Walter?"

Walter smiled. "Perhaps you should allow the doctor to examine her, if it would set his mind at ease." He was teasing, of course. Margaret knew as much.

"I will do no such thing. If the girl is ill, I will summon—" Mrs. Lloyd's words broke off suddenly.

"Who mother?" Elizabeth asked daringly. "Miss Dawson, perhaps?" Mrs. Lloyd gave her daughter a look that might have turned the girl to stone. "You have always summoned Miss Dawson to assist with the help." Like poking a sleeping bear, Elizabeth seemed to be daring her mother to show her true personality, in front of company as well.

Ainsley and Margaret's eyes met across the table. It seemed all movement, utensils or wine glasses, napkins or serving spoons, had ceased and an inaudible warning slipped into the room. The tension rose, wafting like the plumes of smoke drifting from the tapered candles in the candelabras between them.

"That woman is no longer welcome in this home," Mrs. Lloyd commanded, snatching her crystal goblet from the table and taking a sip of the wine. "With my husband gone, she has outworn her welcome."

"Then allow me an opportunity to check on the girl," Ainsley implored. "She seems to have lost all of her colour."

Mrs. Lloyd exhaled deeply, and fiddled with her fork, which lay flat on the tablecloth. "I do not wish to discuss any illness. We are celebrating." She lifted her goblet and paused while she waited for everyone else to follow her lead. "To my beautiful daughter and her full recovery. May we never have to live through such horrors again."

Everyone raised their glasses to the air before taking a sip. Margaret and Ainsley's eyes met over the table as they both put their goblets down. As dinner progressed, it became so much more apparent that both guests were not enjoying the food as much as the host and her family.

"Are you not hungry?" Elizabeth asked. "Do women in London not eat more than a spoonful?" Elizabeth let out a laugh and glanced around the table. Mrs. Lloyd smiled as she brought the napkin to the corners of her mouth.

Margaret was hungry, ever so hungry, but she had been shifting food, raising her fork to her mouth before placing it back down to her plate. The task of eating nothing seemed so simple when her brother first suggested it, when they had been coming just for tea. Hours had passed and she had not realized how much of a trial it would be to watch others eating what could be perfectly benign food.

Margaret raised an eyebrow and looked directly at Elizabeth. "If you were implying that I was one of that sort then I say you are sadly mistaken. I rather enjoy my meals."

"Clearly."

Mrs. Lloyd cleared her throat, in an effort to clear the air, and changed the subject. "How is London these days? It's been many years since I was last there. Is it still filled with dust and smoke?"

Margaret smiled.

"Only when it's not raining," Ainsley answered for her.

"Why would anyone want to live in such a dirty, smelly place?" Elizabeth muttered under her breath. "Murderers and thieves must be your best patients, Dr. Ainsley."

Mrs. Lloyd's spoon slipped out of her hand and crashed into the china. Grabbing her napkin, she dabbed the edges of her mouth. "Elizabeth, you may be excused. Your commentary is not appreciated."

Elizabeth looked at her mother coolly. Her jaw tight and gaze stiff, she relented. She scooped up her napkin from her lap and placed it, crumpled, beside her place setting. Slipping from her chair, she glanced around the table. Walter and Ainsley stood as well until after she walked through the door and they were able to reclaim their seats.

"My apologies," Mrs. Lloyd began, "She is troubled lately. She is not herself."

"Of course," Ainsley said, with a slight bow of his head.

The second course was brought thereafter. Cornish hens, and curry rice. Margaret's mouth salivated at the look of it in front of her. The butler came behind her and poured her some red wine, which also seemed too tempting for the famished woman. She glanced up and saw Ainsley picking at his hen with knife and fork. She waited for him to take a bite but he did not. He glanced up at her, and moved his mouth as if he was chewing but she knew he had not taken a bite.

Mrs. Lloyd looked around the table with false delight. "These were—"

A scream rang out in the hallway, followed by hysteric sobbing. Everyone in the dining room dropped their silverware. Walter and Ainsley jumped from their seats and ran to the hall. Margaret saw Mrs. Lloyd reach for her wine, but her face fell as the screaming hysterics continued. She looked almost faint and braced herself against the edge of the table.

"Are you feeling ill, Mrs. Lloyd?" Margaret asked, getting up from her seat.

"I'm all right, dear. Go to them and tell me what you see. I cannot bear it."

Margaret nodded and hurried away.

Chapter 36

*Perishing gloomily,
Spurr'd by contumely,*

Ainsley followed Walter into the hallway, where they found Cook on her knees at the base of the stairs. She clung to the stair handrail and rested her head on it as she wailed.

"What is it?" Walter asked.

"The scullery." She barely got the words out through gulps of air and sobbing. "She's in the scullery."

Ainsley ran first, bounding down the kitchen stairs and pass the crying servants, who were too traumatized to say or do anything to help. Ainsley found the body of Mary, bloody and lifeless, on the cobblestone floor of the scullery. She lay with a gaping wound on her head, one hand clutching her stomach as if the wound were nothing compared to the pain she felt from her illness. The smell of bile wafted from one of the nearby buckets where the girl must have thrown up moments before her death.

Ainsley was leaning over the corpse just as Walter entered. "Good God!" Walter placed his arm over his mouth and nose seconds after he entered the sour-smelling room. The mix of bile, blood, and recent death had no effect on Ainsley. "What is it?" Walter demanded, hovering at the door.

Ainsley surveyed the scene, lifting Mary's limp arm from her stomach to see if she hid anything. He glanced over the room and saw the implement. A cast iron fire poker lay a foot from the body, sitting in a ring of blood.

Margaret slipped passed Walter, who hadn't the stomach to enter, and met Ainsley in the small, confined room. She lifted her skirts from the pool of blood and crouched down next to her brother. "Something is not right. The girl was sick."

"She wasn't dying quickly enough," Ainsley explained, the only possibility becoming crystal-clear. "The poison was taking too long."

"Who could have done this?" Walter spoke from behind the threshold.

"Anyone," Margaret replied without hesitation.

"Upstairs, everyone!" Ainsley yelled at the group that stood sobbing at the far end of the kitchen. "No one leaves this house," he ordered as he marched past Walter and into the main kitchen. Ainsley removed his jacket swiftly and began to roll up the white sleeves of his dress shirt. "Send one of the servants for the constable and magistrate. Send someone you trust." Ainsley removed his tie and looked at Walter. "Go, now!"

Walter left the kitchen at Ainsley's command, running up the stairs to the main floor.

"Ainsley, what is happening?" Margaret leaned in on the table. She closed her eyes momentarily.

"Someone killed that poor girl because she knew something about who killed Josephine and Walter Sr. Whoever it was tried to poison her first but cornered her there and bludgeoned her to death because it was taking too long. That girl knew something and she almost told us, do you remember? She almost told us what happened before Walter showed up." Ainsley pounded his fist on the worn wood table that was between him and Margaret. "Damn!"

"She told us the murderer is female. She kept saying 'she bid me to do it. She told me to give it to the doctor.'" Margaret rounded the corner of the table. "The murderer is one of the women. It has to be Elizabeth or Mrs. Lloyd."

Ainsley nodded in agreement. "Mrs. Lloyd was with us the entire time. Elizabeth had been excused."

"But how did Elizabeth get past the servants here? They must have been preparing dessert." Margaret and Ainsley glanced over the plates of pudding at the other end of the table, near the base of the kitchen stairs. A crumpled pile of mint leaves was set in among the plates, with a few already garnished with sprigs of the herb.

"They must have all been down there," Ainsley

explained. He turned and opened a door behind him, revealing another set of stairs. "These lead to the servants' rooms. She must have slipped through there. She is often down here making meals for Lillian. No one would have questioned her if they saw her. She was in her element."

"But wouldn't the servants have heard something?" Margaret asked.

"Not if Mary was in there vomiting."

Margaret nodded. "It must have happened very fast. What do we do now?" Margaret grabbed for Ainsley's hands, her fingers trembling.

"Here," he reached for a small black key hanging from a nail above the door. "Take this. No one gets in until the magistrate gets here."

Margaret nodded. She locked the door to the scullery, the body of Mary still inside. Ainsley saw her slip the key into the crevice of her bodice. "No one will think to look there," she explained.

Ainsley led the way to the main floor, suppressing the feeling of rage rising up inside him. He felt Margaret grab his arm. He stopped in the hallway and touched her hand. "I won't let anything bad happen to you," he said. Margaret nodded but her face betrayed her true feelings. He placed a hand on the side of her face. "I promise."

He could hear muffled cries from the parlour, and saw the lamps were lit. He led Margaret down the hall and rounded the threshold.

"Let go of me!" It was the voice of Lillian. "No!"

Ainsley saw Elizabeth holding Lillian by the wrist. She tried to pull her arm away, jerking back and forth, but Elizabeth held fast. "Shut up!" Elizabeth yelled.

Ainsley ran to the pair and pulled Elizabeth from Lillian, who crumpled to the floor. Ignoring Ainsley's attempts to pull her away, Elizabeth lunged for her sister, fury driving her sudden outburst.

"Hands off her!" he yelled as he grabbed for her. He pried Elizabeth's vise-like grip from the slight form of Lillian, who cowered from the strength of her sister. He held to Elizabeth and watched as Margaret ran to help Lillian stand.

"Dr. Ainsley, she—" Elizabeth started.

"She killed her." Lillian pointed to Elizabeth, tears streaming down her panic-stricken face. She hid behind Margaret, who stood between her and her enraged sister.

"You liar!" Elizabeth screamed, struggling in Ainsley's tight grasp.

"You saw her," Lillian said between sobs, "She just tried to kill me."

"I did not! I didn't want you to get away—"

Ainsley pulled Elizabeth back from the scene, using a great deal of his strength to subdue the enraged woman in his grasp. "Elizabeth, stop!" he commanded. "It's over."

"She's lying! I didn't try to kill her." Elizabeth turned her focus from Lillian to Ainsley. He gripped her tightly on the arms, aware of her strength and desperation to get away. "Let go, you are hurting me!" She began to cry then, and Ainsley could feel her strength slipping away as her emotions erupted. "I didn't do it. I swear," she sobbed.

Pushing her from the room, he found an empty chair placed against the wall and forced Elizabeth to take a seat. She buried her face in her hands as she sat.

"You saw her lunge at me. She's always been so jealous of Josephine and me. She hated us because of the affection father showed us," Ainsley heard Lillian explain from behind him. "She killed Mary. Look at the blood on her dress."

Ainsley looked to the skirt of Elizabeth's dress and saw a long smear of cherry red blood down the one side. Elizabeth followed his gaze and did not hide her shock. "Dr. Ainsley, please," she implored, "I only just heard of Mary's death."

"Quiet!" he bellowed. "The magistrate will be here soon enough."

Mrs. Lloyd exited the dining room. "What is the meaning of this?" she asked. "What are you about, Dr. Ainsley?"

"We were just witness to Elizabeth's attack on Lillian," Ainsley explained, "Margaret and I."

"Attack?"

Lillian ran to her mother. "Mother, you believe me, don't you?" she said, slipping easily into Mrs. Lloyd's arms.

Martha tried to soothe her sobbing daughter but

her movements were awkward, detached, something that stood out to Ainsley as he watched the pair. Was it possible Mrs. Lloyd was part of the plot as well? Could the events have been a team effort from both the Lloyd women? The look on Margaret's face echoed his sentiments, though neither one acted upon it immediately.

"I trust you will see to the body in my scullery?" Mrs. Lloyd asked Ainsley coolly.

"Once the magistrate and constable have had a chance to collect evidence."

"Evidence? What possible evidence could there be?"

"A great deal, I would imagine," Ainsley answered without pause. "For now, nothing will be tampered with."

"No one did as much for my daughter when she lay dead!"

"Mother, please," Lillian begged. "Dr. Ainsley is a good man. You were singing his praises not an hour ago."

Mrs. Lloyd swallowed hard. "A good doctor he may be, but he has forgotten his station. The girl was just a servant. There is no need to make such a fuss."

"Even if the death is at the hand of the same person who killed your husband and daughter?" Margaret dared to ask.

Mrs. Lloyd rounded to Margaret, pushing Lillian away, and walked toward her. "How can you know such a thing?" she asked. "So soon?"

"Mother, please." Lillian reached out a hand to pull her mother back but the woman ignored her. Mrs. Lloyd turned again to Ainsley. "What do you plan to do with Elizabeth?"

"She will have to answer for her crimes," Ainsley explained. "There will be an inquest, no doubt, into the deaths of Mr. Lloyd, Josephine, and now Mary. She will be forced to stand trial."

Mrs. Lloyd's chest filled with air as she inhaled deeply. Her face remained stoic and unmoved. Her hands, clasped in front of her, did not move from their poised state. "We are finished then," she said in a near whisper. "The Lloyd family will be marked with the greatest shame."

"Mother," Elizabeth reached for her mother but Ainsley kept her back. "Please, I beg you. Look at me." Mrs.

Lloyd walked past both her daughters, staring straight ahead and betraying no emotion other than forced calm, and left the room.

The encounter sent a chill up Ainsley's spine that only abated when Walter came in a few minutes later. "It is done," he said. "Constable has been sent for."

"Walter!" Elizabeth stood this time. "Don't let them take me. I didn't do it."

"What do you mean?"

"It was her, Walter," Lillian said with greater force than Elizabeth showed. "She killed Father and Josie. She killed Mary!"

"How can you say that?" Elizabeth looked as if she could cry but her strength held. "I have been taking care of you all these weeks."

"You were the one making me sick."

"That's preposterous!" Elizabeth turned to Walter. "Mother has deserted me. You are the only one left to believe me."

Walter remained silent, scratching his temple while staring at the floor. Perhaps he was too drunk to realize what was taking place, or better he knew as well what Elizabeth was capable of.

"Do you have a room with a locking door?" Ainsley asked him. "Not the scullery, of course."

"My study," he suggested.

ಊ ಆ

Ainsley led Elizabeth into the room and forced her into a chair opposite the desk. Everything seemed darker in the house now, even though the relatively small fire blazed energetically, casting long shadows over the room and the occupants. Elizabeth glared up at Ainsley defiantly, her hands clenched into fists, as if she could strike him at any moment.

Ainsley turned to Walter, purposely avoiding her gaze, though he knew she was still staring at him. He could feel it on the back of his neck. He didn't want to look. Despite her anger, she had the feminine touch and it bothered him greatly that she could be possible of the atrocities that had taken place at the manor. A child of twelve, innocent of any purposely sinful act, had been struck down by Elizabeth's jealousy and sinful nature.

"How long before the constable will arrive?" Ainsley asked, raking his hand through his hair. He looked to the window and saw how the snow accumulated rapidly, covering everything in view with a thick blanket of dazzling, white snow.

"Not long, though it is late." Walter seemed to be struggling as much as Ainsley, though he seemed far less in control of his unease. Touched by the many drinks he had imbibed earlier, Walter was flush, and struggling to remain sober in the midst of the evening's events. "Is Mary truly dead? Can nothing be done for her?"

Ainsley shook his head. "No. She's gone."

Walter paced the room, his hand shoved deeply in his pockets, though his eyes wandered to the half-full whiskey decanter that remained on his desk. "How was it done?" he asked, staring at the decanter, his hand poised to snatch it. It was as if he were readying himself for the worst, knowing anything Ainsley told him would drive him to drink.

"A single blow to the head. There was an iron poker near the body with blood on it."

As expected, Walter filled his glass and drank away the horror. "Lord have mercy on her soul," he breathed after downing an entire glass. "She was good to the family, through it all."

"I agree," Elizabeth said in a tiny voice, her face turned to the floor as she spoke.

Both men looked to Elizabeth, her anger gone and worry now dominating her expression. Ainsley did not know how to address her words. He stared at her for some time, trying to decipher if she truly felt the loss of the servant girl or if this was another act in her long performance. Her fingers were clenched around the ends of the chair, holding all of her evident anger in her white knuckles and fingertips.

"I didn't kill Mary. I would never do such a thing."

Ainsley shook his head and turned from her. How long could the woman keep up the charade? A day? Two perhaps. She was caught with her hands on Lillian. There were red stains on her dress. She had regular access to the kitchen and even personally presented Lillian with her food. She was the slighted sister, neither as talented nor as praised, always overlooked and regularly forgotten. How much evidence did a person need to prove her capable and willing?

"I didn't! I swear." She began to cry then, making no move to push away the tears that slipped down the mounds of her cheeks, spilling on her pale-coloured bodice. "Josephine was not my full sister but I loved her more than I loved Lillian."

Ainsley was startled at the suggestion.

"It's true. Lillian has never been kind to me. Josephine was my real sister, even if she was born from my father's whore." Elizabeth's words became desperate.

"Do not listen to her, Ainsley." Walter slipped into his chair, glass in hand. "Drink. I think it's going to be a long night."

Ainsley eyed his glass, the decanter next to it, and marveled at its alluring nature. A drink would certainly take the edge off the evening. The constable was on the way, the killer caught. He snatched up the glass and finished the nearly full contents in a series of long gulps. Walter poured himself another glass but Ainsley refrained and repositioned himself near the window.

Beyond the front steps of the manor, he could see two faint lights swaying slightly as if adorning a moving carriage. "The constable has arrived." He turned back to Walter and Elizabeth. Walter held his glass close to him, unable to focus beyond his own miserable state. Elizabeth stared at Ainsley, her eyes burning into him as if they had special powers.

"It's over, Elizabeth." In a few strides, he was at the desk and reaching for the lantern that was lit on top of it.

Her hand grasped his wrist suddenly, slapping his skin with a quick jolt. "Eventually, she is going to kill you." She stared into his eyes, pulling him down close to her as she spoke. He could see a single vein in her neck pulsing rapidly. "Do you hear me? I warned you. Many times. She is not done. They will hang me and she will have killed me without bothering to poison my food."

Ainsley did not move, a decision that surprised even him. Elizabeth's eyes searched his face. A look of weakness came over her face, revealing another trait he had not seen in her until then. Sincerity.

The door opened and the butler sent to fetch the constable stumbled in, in a much more disheveled state than Ainsley was used to seeing from an upper servant. The butler was out of breath. "Constable Smith is...unavailable until morning," he swallowed hard, "sir." His breathing was unmistakably laboured.

"Blast!" Ainsley turned to Walter, who was loosening his tie and rolling up his sleeves as Ainsley had done.

"What are we to do with her until then?" Walter screamed at the butler, who took great pains to remain staring straight ahead.

"We will have to keep a vigil. One of us must stay with her all night until the constable arrives."

Walter did not like the proposal. He pressed his lips together and threw his tie to his desk in a defeated gesture. "We could just lock the door. No need for all of us to do without sleep."

Ainsley shook his head. He knew any murderer, desperate to avoid the gallows, would escape at the soonest possible opportunity. If they left Elizabeth unattended, she surely would find a way to slip through their fingers. "No. It's too risky. I will stay, if it suits you better."

A look of resignation came to Walter's face. "I will assist. My man here as well." He gestured to the butler, who had recovered his breath and waited for further instruction.

"Very well."

Ainsley turned to Elizabeth, still carrying the face of an innocent, yet desperate girl. He looked at her like he were accusing her of witchcraft. A single tear slipped from her cheek. She would have to be an excellent actress to maintain such a look and forced tears to accompany it.

"Desperate words from a desperate woman," Ainsley said, looking at Elizabeth. He adjusted his shirt, pulling it squarely on his shoulders as he walked away from her.

Chapter 37

*Cold inhumanity,
Burning insanity,*

Margaret sat on the settee while Lillian played a soft, mournful song at the piano. Neither woman had said much since discovering Mary's body in the scullery. Margaret seemed more struck with grief than Lillian. Not grief, Margaret corrected herself, there was no grieving for those who went on to a better place. It was the shock of it all, the shock of seeing the body, the life, by way of blood, pouring from her wound. How could her brother handle such scenes each day? He seemed so calm and collected, far more detached than she could ever hope to be. She had consoled the maid not hours before and now the girl was dead, never to be consoled again.

Margaret was so deep in thought she had not realized Lillian's song had come to an end and Lillian was now standing in front of her.

"Miss Margaret?"

Margaret jumped, startled from her morbid thinking.

"May I see Mary now?" Lillian asked. Margaret hesitated, wondering if she was obliged to grant such a request. The scene was not a pleasant one. She could not banish the images from her own mind and she could hardly see why Lillian would volunteer to partake in such a scene. Lillian must have seen her hesitation because she was quick to give an explanation. "She was a good servant to me during my illness. I would like to say good-bye before Mother forbids me. She did not allow me as much with Josephine."

Margaret saw a look of sincerity and knew Mrs. Lloyd was capable of such strict limitations. She nodded and agreed to lead Lillian to the body of the most recent murder victim.

At the scullery door, Margaret pulled the key from her bodice and unlocked the door, hearing iron scraping iron as she did so. The door creaked as they opened it to reveal the now cold body of Mary. The scullery was as they left it. Mary's head was closest to the door, her feet pointed to the wall. She had been struck from behind, Margaret concluded, and the girl struggled for a step before falling close to the door. The blood that had spilled from the wound had congealed on the floor in a smooth pool, undisturbed and reflective.

Lillian stepped inside the room, apparently not as concerned as Margaret was with tampering with the evidence. "We must be careful," Margaret reminded her. "Peter will want to have a better look."

Lillian nodded but that did not stop her from stepping close to Mary's body and leaning over it with more curiosity than grief. Lillian began to stare at Mary's face, the wound on the side of her head gaping and shimmering with sticky, coagulated blood. "She almost doesn't look real," Lillian said. She raised her hand to touch the maid's face.

"Don't!"

Lillian ignored her and tucked a tendril of hair behind the girl's one intact ear. "She was a good servant to me," Lillian explained. She looked to Margaret from her crouched position. "She always did what she was told." Her gaze went back to Mary. "Never questioned me. Not once."

There was something about the way Lillian spoke that made Margaret uneasy.

"She looks at peace," Lillian continued. "Does she not?"

Margaret had seen dead bodies before. She had touched them, cut them, and rooted around in their insides, but never had she done so with a person she knew in life. It was so much easier to view them as less than human, and more animal. But Mary's body was different. As much as she wanted to comfort the girl, as she had done in the cemetery, she knew she could not. Mary was dead, and no amount of comfort could be derived from being held or rocked. Even still, Margaret stepped in the room and, crouching on the opposite side, she picked up the girl's hand and held it, cold as it was.

"She was so young," Margaret said after a while. "How could someone hurt another human being in such a way?"

Lillian said nothing. She stared at the body, using her finger to outline Mary's pale cheek. When she finally looked up, her gaze met Margaret's and they stared at each other for a long moment.

This was not the face of a dying girl, weakened by endless days of illness and tainted food. Lillian looked cold, heartless, and unaffected by the bludgeoned body in front of her. It was calculated, all of it. Lillian had faked her illness to remove herself from suspicion.

"You did this," Margaret said. "You poisoned Josephine. You killed Dr. Bennett."

Lillian's face remained blank. She stood up and moved toward the door. It took a moment for Margaret to realize what was happening and when she stood up she saw Lillian pulling on the heavy wooden scullery door. "You are too smart, Miss Margaret. Fortunately, Peter does not see things as you do."

The door caught the latch with a loud slam, and in that instant Margaret remembered she had left the key in the lock when she opened the door. "I don't share the applause," Margaret heard her yell from the other side. "And I will not share Peter's affection."

Hearing the key turn, Margaret ran to the door but it was too late. She was locked in the scullery with a corpse.

Chapter 38

*Into her rest—
Cross her hands humbly*

Ainsley walked into the parlour expecting to see Margaret and Lillian but was surprised to find no one. It was extremely late and he wondered if Lillian had offered Margaret one of the guest rooms so that she could sleep. The rest of the house was dark and quiet, exhibiting no evidence of the drama from earlier.

Knowing he could not possibly sleep Ainsley stood in front of the fire for a long while, watching the ribbons of flames clinging to the logs, licking the dry wood and consuming every square inch. The words Elizabeth spoke, the confession she refused to give, was her final act of defiance. He could scarcely believe her last-ditch attempt at naming Lillian, one of the victims, as the perpetrator as well. How could a person poison themselves and, moreover, why? Bargaining, he reasoned, anything to save herself from the gallows. Elizabeth was right about one thing—she would hang once the jury found out she was the murderess who snuffed the life from little Josephine Lloyd. Her half-sister, no less.

Ainsley rubbed his mouth and chin, the stubble freshly grown during that day scratching his hand. He let out a long breath he had not realized he was holding, and then held his eyelids closed with his fingertips, rubbing his temples. Besides, he could scarcely believe Lillian capable.

He stopped himself suddenly. He could no more discount Lillian as the murderer than he could himself without looking at the facts. Walter and Josephine died so suddenly, and yet Lillian languished for so long. Her illness was drawn out. If Elizabeth wanted her dead, why would she not increase her doses? By all rights, Lillian should have died months ago, and yet she lingered. Her symptoms were weak. She felt strong that first day he met her. He was unsure what to make of it since she appeared to be in near-perfect health.

But Lillian? What was her motive?

Jealousy.

Suddenly aware of another presence in the room, Ainsley turned and saw Lillian standing at the door. "I didn't want to disturb you," she said softly. She stood almost completely in darkness, though the light colour of her nightgown gave form to her otherwise darkened figure.

"Not at all," he said, shaking his head, trying to shake the rebellious thoughts that had just occurred to him. How could he believe her capable of such atrocities?

Lillian came into the room. "Where is she?"

"Your brother's study. Do not worry. She is well-guarded."

Lillian nodded. "I knew it all this time. I must have not wanted to believe it." She walked past Ainsley and headed for the window seat. The falling snow could be seen on the opposite side of the glass but nothing could be seen beyond.

"Murderers are often not what they seem," Ainsley said, in an attempt to comfort her.

"That is the truth of it, is it not?" Lillian glanced to Ainsley and quickly turned away. She took a seat at the window, her nightgown falling over the ledge. She pulled her knees up and hugged her body, wrapping her arms around herself tightly. "Perhaps she did not mean to kill Josephine. I should like to think that it was an accident."

"How so?" Ainsley asked, inching closer.

"Father was a brute. We all feared him but..." her voiced became a sudden whisper. "She must have just meant to make her ill, never intending to kill our sister." Lillian turned to Ainsley, revealing tears that spilled from her eyes. "She must feel positively awful."

Ainsley reached out a trembling hand to comfort her. He knew without a doubt she spoke of her own remorse, and not Elizabeth's. Her words were practically a confession, though he was hardly in a position to act upon his knowledge. All he had by way of evidence was Elizabeth's desperate attempt to shift blame, and now

Lillian's subtle acknowledgement of her own guilty conscience.

"Dr. Ainsley, come quick!" Cook was at the door, out of breath.

"What is it?"

"It's the Mistress, she's—" Cook looked as if she could cry and Ainsley quickly agreed to follow. She led him out into the front lawn, the rapidly falling snow covering his shoes and slipping into his socks as he ran alongside the servant. She pointed above them toward the house. At first Ainsley had a hard time seeing what she was pointing toward. The large flakes of snow rushed at him wildly, almost blinding him.

"Mrs. Lloyd intends to take her life!"

And then, Ainsley saw Mrs. Lloyd perched on the second-floor balcony, her skirts on the wrong side of the stone barrier, her hands grasping the railing, the only thing that prevented her from falling.

"Mrs. Lloyd, don't!" he yelled through cupped hands. "Mrs. Lloyd!" She gave no indication that she had heard him. Ainsley looked to Lillian beside him. She was looking up at her mother. "It's not high enough," he said to her. "She'll be maimed but it is not high enough to kill her." Though it was dark, he could see a smile spreading over her face, a smile of glee.

Ainsley tried to run past her to the house, but Lillian stopped him. She grabbed his arm and made him turn to her. "Let her do it," she said. "And then you and I can go to London."

Ainsley searched her face, not believing the words she spoke to him.

"She won't let me go otherwise. This is our only chance."

He tried to pull away but she kept her grip tight. Her nails began to scratch his skin below his rolled-up sleeve.

"Don't you love me?!" she yelled after him when he broke free.

Ainsley ran for the front door, and slipped on the sleek marble tiles in the foyer, the snow from his shoes melting into his socks as he ran up the flight of stairs. He headed toward the west wing, guessing the balcony was off of her own suite of rooms.

After fumbling his way through various rooms, he found her on the snow-covered balcony, her hands almost slipping from the ice-encrusted stone. Her fingers were red from the cold, her face looking equally as pained by the searing sub-zero temperatures. "I am finished," she said, as if sensing his close presence. "She has shamed us all."

Ainsley inched closer but Mrs. Lloyd cringed, so he stepped back again. "If your intention is to die," he began in a soft tone, "You will fail. The drop you face is a mere twenty feet. You will be maimed and languish in agony for days, weeks even."

"I am already in agony!" she yelled over the wind. "She may not have been my child, Dr. Ainsley, but I loved her. More than any woman could love a child born of her husband's sin."

"It is evident, Mrs. Lloyd. All around me I see the evidence to that love."

"She is gone and everyone will think I did it because she wasn't born from my body." Mrs. Lloyd cried openly but never loosened her grip on the railing that anchored her. "I did not cry when my husband died. He was a monster and it was all I could do to not dance on his grave." She turned to Ainsley, her face streaked with tears and melting snowflakes. "I knew it was Lillian even then, but I did not stop her. I was grateful to her for having the strength I did not possess."

"You knew it was Lillian all this time?"

"Yes," Mrs. Lloyd confessed. "By the time Josephine died, I knew it was too late. I'd be accused of assisting in a murder."

"So you didn't say anything."

Mrs. Lloyd nodded. "I locked her in her room, for our safety. I saw her in the house at all hours of the night, walking and waiting. She'd leave the house and roam the grounds at night. I had to lock her in her room. I was afraid for my own life. But then you arrived and she seemed to be better. I was so hopeful that you had changed her. But I was wrong." Mrs. Lloyd hung her head and glanced to the ground in front of her. "I bear a shame greater than you will ever know. I cannot be forgiven. I was damned to hell the day my husband died." She leaned forward then, her eyes clenched tightly as she readied herself to jump.

"And what of Elizabeth? What of her fate? She will be sent to the gallows if you do not speak out. She will hang for Lillian's murders." Ainsley dared to take a step forward.

Mrs. Lloyd looked to him. "Can you not help her?"

"I need you to help me."

After a moment of palpable silence, Mrs. Lloyd nodded. "Maybe I can save one daughter."

Ainsley stepped closer, helping her over the railing with great care. Her body was practically a block of ice in his arms as he guided her back to the warmth of her room. He knew the fire was ablaze, just the thing to warm her quickly. They walked gingerly toward the door, aware of the growing ice on the balcony ledge.

Lillian appeared at the balcony door preventing them from going any further, her hands hidden behind her back. "Peter!" she yelled, "You should have let her jump."

Chapter 39

*As if praying dumbly,
Over her breast!*

Margaret perched herself on the edge of the washbasin, careful not to drag her skirts in the pool of blood accumulated on the stone floor. Her hands ached from pounding on the scullery door, and her voice was croaking by the time she silenced her cries.

That conniving wench! It was her all that time. And Margaret had felt sorry for the leech. But now it made sense. She was ill for far longer than her father or Josephine was. She was faking her illness, perhaps giving herself castor oil or some other elixir to induce vomiting. She released herself from suspicion by posing as a victim. Peter needed to know.

Margaret had already tried the latch, the hinges and everything else she could think of to break free. The one window to the room was a small sliver at the very top of the wall, and there was scarcely enough furniture within the room to stack. She became resigned. She was stuck.

Then she heard a faint sound, the lock unlatching with the unmistakable sound of iron on iron. For a moment, Margaret thought she was hearing things. When the door began to creak open she braced herself. At best, it was Ainsley who had come to rescue her, at worst it was Lillian returned to do far worse than lock her in the scullery.

Margaret grasped for the closest item she could use to defend herself and grabbed a laundry plunger and held it at her side while she stood up. She kept her eyes on the door, watching it slowly pry open. Unsure who to expect to see on the other side of it, Margaret carefully craned her neck to look. No one was there.

Slowly she inched toward the door, plunger at her

side, and widened the opening. There was no one in the kitchen at all. There were no footsteps of retreat or any sign at all that anyone had been in the room. She dropped the plunger on the kitchen floor and slowly made her way up the kitchen stairs to the main floor. The manor was completely silent with very little illumination to light her way. She paused at the bottom of the stairwell and glanced around the foyer.

There was a line of water, melting snow it looked like, leading from the front door and up the stairs. Her gaze tracked the glistening footsteps up the wood of the stairs and then she saw her. A small girl, standing in a loose-fitting nightgown, at the very top of the stairs. Her blonde curls fell over her shoulders and she stared at Margaret without blinking.

"Josephine?" Margaret whispered.

The girl said nothing. She waited and finally Margaret began her ascent. Halfway up, the girl began to walk away toward the west wing. Margaret followed but soon lost sight of her. A strong gust of artic wind engulfed Margaret and she looked to an open chamber door.

She could hear Ainsley's voice faintly and followed it inside the room, which was clearly a bedroom, perhaps Mrs. Lloyd's, judging by the oversized four-poster bed. From her spot just inside the door, she could clearly hear Ainsley talking. He was calm enough to anyone else, but to Margaret she realized his words were interrupted with his hastening breath.

Peering around the edge of the door, she could see her brother on the balcony, huddled, almost protecting Mrs. Lloyd, who clung to him with abject terror. Lillian was at the door to the balcony, an iron fire poker in her grasp behind her as she blocked the way into the house.

"Peter," she said into the wind, "you should have let her jump."

Margaret watched helplessly from the shadows as Ainsley raised his hand in a protective stance. He positioned himself between Lillian and Mrs. Lloyd, who hid her body behind the obvious strength of her protector.

"No one else dies today," he said calmly.

Margaret could not see Lillian's face but she

imagined the girl was smiling before she spoke. "Everyone dies today."

A slight squeal of terror escaped Mrs. Lloyd as she clutched Ainsley tighter.

"Lillian—" Ainsley began, keeping a hand in front of him, as if the gesture would keep the mad murderess at bay.

"They paraded me like a circus mouse, playing second fiddle to that bastard child. She couldn't even sing!"

"It was your father's idea, not mine," Mrs. Lloyd yelled over Ainsley's shoulder. "He wanted to save the mills."

"I know. That's why I poisoned him first."

Margaret began taking steps closer, tempted to snatch the weapon away from Lillian while her attention was elsewhere. With her third step, the floorboard moaned under her weight. Lillian's head turned toward the room and Margaret slipped back into the shadows. She wanted to inch closer but dared not move, not yet.

"I know Josephine was an accident," Ainsley said. Margaret could see his eyes looking around him, searching for a way out, an escape for both him and Mrs. Lloyd. "I know you didn't want to kill her."

"You were supposed to send her back to that witch doctor," Lillian said to her mother, taking a step closer to them.

"How could I?" Mrs. Lloyd asked.

"She was not your daughter. I am!" Lillian's anger returned, harsher than before. Margaret watched her grip tighten on the handle of the iron poker, her knuckles turning white.

"Why Dr. Bennett?" Ainsley ventured to ask. He was stalling her, Margaret realized, postponing the violence long enough to devise a plan of escape.

Lillian swallowed. "That was supposed to be for you. I thought you were smart enough to figure me out but I overestimated you." Lillian laughed but her grip did not lessen on her weapon. "Mary would do anything I asked. But I had to kill her too. She was too weak in the end. Elizabeth will be hanged for my deeds and all I needed was my mother to do her own self in, so I could rest assured that my secret died with her." Lillian paused, and moved her poker from behind her back, revealing it to her hostages.

Margaret quickly crossed the room as Lillian raised the fire poker in the air.

"You ruined it!" Lillian lunged for Ainsley, who pushed Mrs. Lloyd into the snow behind him.

Margaret pushed Lillian, sending the slight woman into railing. She almost flipped over the side but Lillian clutched manically to Margaret, who tried desperately to unhinge the deranged murderer from her. Face to face the women struggled, teetering over the edge of the icy balcony. Within seconds Ainsley was beside them but not before a smiling Lillian threw herself over the edge, clinging to Margaret as she went.

Ainsley grabbed Margaret with one hand, Lillian with the other and used his body weight to anchor them both to the balcony. His face twisted with the strain.

Mrs. Lloyd appeared beside him, pulling on Lillian's arm but she was little help.

"Peter, let go!" Margaret yelled.

He answered her with a visceral growl, squeezing her wrist with more force.

"Peter, don't!" Lillian pleaded, "Save us, Peter! Save us!"

Ainsley's face contorted as he pulled on them, attempting to save them both.

Margaret tried to ease the strain by holding her weight on the wall of the house, searching with her feet for a ledge to stand on or a foothold to cling to, but the ice made her slip. "You have to let go!" she yelled. "You can't save us all!"

Ainsley gave Lillian an apologetic glance before opening his hand and letting her arm slip from his grasp. Mrs. Lloyd could not hold her weight alone and she too was forced to let go.

In desperation, Lillian clung to Margaret's skirt but couldn't get a proper grip. Her hands slid down Margaret's legs before locking onto her boot. Margaret kicked frantically, aiming for any part of Lillian she could come in contact with. With one swift kick she hit Lillian's upturned face. Lillian let go instantly and fell twenty feet to the snow-covered patio.

Heaving her over the railing, Ainsley pulled Margaret to safety. They both collapsed on the balcony floor, the last ounces of adrenalin draining from their bodies. Beside her, Margaret found the poker Lillian had attempted to use. She held it up and stared at it. She struggled to bring her breathing back to normal and her hand shook as she held it out. Eventually she tossed the poker aside and watched it slip into the undisturbed snow beside them.

For a long while the only sounds they could hear were their own rhythmic yet rapid breathing and Mrs. Lloyd's sobs. Margaret drew her body closer to her brother, nestling herself under the warmth of his arm.

"For a moment, I thought you wanted me to let go of you," Ainsley said, slipping an ice-cold hand into his sister's.

"You'd be dead if you had," Margaret said with a laugh.

"You'd kill me?"

"No, Father."

Ainsley smiled, as Margaret leaned further into him. She could hear his rapid heartbeat beneath his shirt and she could feel his strong muscles holding her close.

Chapter 40

Owning her weakness,
Her evil behaviour,
And leaving, with meekness,
Her sins to her Saviour!

Ainsley smiled as Margaret leaned into him. The walk to the train station was breathtaking with the snow clinging to the naked tree branches above them. The air was crisp and still without the slightest breeze. Within hours, they would be on the outskirts of London, the memory of the last week feeling like little more than a dream.

They had stayed in Picklow for two days after Lillian fell. She was horribly scarred from her fall. Her legs bore the brunt of the impact and she broke her pelvis. There was some suspected head trauma, which made her stare vacantly despite activity all around her. Ainsley had offered to operate, to minimize the damage but Mrs. Lloyd declined. Lillian was expected to expire within days; her internal organs would fail soon enough and little could be done to halt the internal bleeding.

The magistrate called an inquest in which both Ainsley and Margaret gave testimony. No further action was pursued. It would seem Lillian's injuries were enough of a punishment, and no one was willing to incarcerate the girl when she was already a prisoner of her own mind. The proceedings made Ainsley's return to work a day late but he doubted Crawford would mind, considering.

"Do you think Father will be cross with me?" Margaret asked, breaking into Ainsley's thoughts.

"He'd be more angry with me than you."

Margaret shrugged. "I doubt that." She walked silently for a few steps before speaking again, "Do you think I should tell him what I saw in Tunbridge Wells?"

Ainsley let out a deep breath. "I imagine he already knows."

Margaret nodded and said nothing more.

Further down the road, Miss Dawson appeared. She clutched her basket. "Greetings," Ainsley said, as she drew closer. "Lovely day for a walk."

Miss Dawson smiled as she came to a stop in front of them. "How is Miss Lillian?" she asked.

"As well as could be expected," Margaret explained.

Miss Dawson nodded with an air of understanding. If anyone had an interest in the outcome of Lillian's fall, it was Miss Dawson. She seemed pleased enough that the person who murdered her daughter would soon perish. Miss Dawson gave the pair a quick glance up and down. "You are leaving us," she said.

"There is no further reason to stay," Ainsley explained.

"And many more reasons to go," Miss Dawson ventured to guess.

Margaret and Ainsley nodded.

"I should let you know I have decided to accept Walter's offer and sell my cottage. I am returning to Bristol to live with my sister. The climate is milder on the coast and I can find work there." Her face lit up slightly as she spoke. "My mind is made up. I am pleased to have found my freedom again," she explained.

"An ingenious plan," Ainsley said. "Godspeed to you."

Miss Dawson nodded and gave a slight curtsey. "And to you."

❧ ☙

At the train station, their trunks waited, having been previously taxied from the Inn. "Perhaps I should become a doctor," Margaret said suddenly. She pulled away from her brother to look at his reaction.

"You? A doctor?"

"And what is wrong with it?" Margaret asked, expecting him to tease her relentlessly.

"Well, you are a woman," Ainsley answered with a

cocky laugh. "Unless you want to deliver babies exclusively."

"For Pete's sake, no. A real doctor, a surgeon perhaps."

Ainsley laughed wholeheartedly then. Imagine his own sister attending the male-dominated schools from which he had barely made it out alive. "Margaret, please."

"What?" Margaret's face became stern then, her gaze piercing.

"You can not be serious."

"I am."

Ainsley found it hard to look her in the eyes. She hardly had the stomach for such work. She was stronger than most women, that was a given, but strong enough to stomach the daily intake of death, the most terrible things man perpetrated on he each other? He doubted that very much.

It took him a moment to decide how to let her down without being too harsh. "I don't feel medical school is the place for you," he explained.

"Of course. Can't have two doctors in the family. That would create too much competition." Her voice was laced with annoyance. She turned from him, and spied the ticket office to the side.

"Margaret, that's not fair."

She began to walk away from him. "Father would never allow it," he called out to her over the mechanical churning of the locomotive engine. She did not answer and proceeded to purchase their tickets.

Ainsley nodded toward a nearby porter and indicated which pieces of luggage belonged to them. The porter nodded and began installing the trunks onto a flat cart with wheels.

Their luggage safely stowed, Ainsley turned to see Margaret walking toward them, a telegraph paper held in front of her in a gloved hand. Her other hand clasped over her mouth.

"What is it, Margaret?" Ainsley asked.

Margaret hesitated, unable to formulate her astonishment into words.

"Margaret?"

She looked at Ainsley, suddenly glancing up, and offered him the telegram. "It's about Mother." Margaret had a look of abject fear on her face. "She's gone missing."

The Bridge of Sighs
By Thomas Hood (1798-1845)

One more Unfortunate,
Weary of breath
Rashly importunate,
Gone to her death!

Take her up tenderly,
Lift her with care;
Fashion'd so slenderly
Young, and so fair!

Look at her garments
Clinging like cerements;
Whilst the wave constantly
Drips from her clothing;
Take her up instantly,
Loving, not loathing.

Touch her not scornfully,
Think of her mournfully,
Gently and humanly;
Not the stains of her,
All that remains of her
Now is pure womanly.

Make no deep scrutiny
Into her mutiny
Rash and undutiful;
Past all dishonour,
Death has left on her
Only the beautiful.

Still, for all slips of hers,
One of Eve's family—
Wipe those poor lips of hers
Oozing so clammily.

Loop up her tresses
Escaped from the comb,
Her fair auburn tresses;
Whilst wonderment guesses
Where was her home?

Who was her father?
Who was her mother?
Had she a sister?
Had she a brother?
Or was there a dearer one
Still, and a nearer one
Yet, than all other?
Alas! For the rarity
Of Christian charity
Under the sun!
O, it was pitiful!
Near a whole city full,
Home had she none.

Sisterly, brotherly,
Fatherly, motherly
Feelings had changed;
Love, by harsh evidence,
Thrown from its eminence;
Even God's providence
Seeming estranged.

Where the lamps quiver
So far in the river,
With many a light
From window and casement,
From garret to basement,
She stood, with amazement,
Houseless by night.

The bleak wind of March
Made her tramble and shiver;
But not the dark arch,
Or the black flowing river;
Mad from life's history,
Glad to death's mystery,
Swift to be hurl'd—
Anywhere, anywhere
Out of the world!

In she plunged boldly—
No matter how coldly
Over the brink of it,
Picture it—think of it,

Dissolute Man!
Lave in it, drink of it,
Then if you can!

Take her up tenderly,
Lift her with care;
Fashion'd so slenderly;
Young, and so fair!

Ere her limbs frigidly
Stiffen too rigidly,
Decently, kindly,
Smooth and compose them;
And her eyes, close them,
Staring so blindly!

Dreadfully staring
Thro muddy impurity,
As when with the daring
Last look of despairing
Fix'd on futurity.

Perishing gloomily,
Spurr'd by contumely,
Cold inhumanity,
Burning insanity,
Into her rest—
Cross her hands humbly
As if praying dumbly,
Over her breast!

Owning her weakness,
Her evil behaviour,
And leaving, with meekness,
Her sins to her Saviour!

About the author

A former journalist and graduate from Humber College's School for Writers, **Tracy L. Ward** spent five years developing her favourite protagonist, Dr. Peter Ainsley, completing six books in the Marshall House Mystery series before starting work on a new mystery series set in 19th century Toronto. Tracy currently lives on a farm near Barrie, Ontario, with her husband and two kids.

Her website can be found at www.gothicmysterywriter.blogspot.com